THE WEIGHT OF CHANGE

JENNIFER WALTERS

To Sue

—signature—

D1600090

BARBRA JUNE PUBLISHING

* * * * * * * * * * * * * *

The Weight of Change

Jennifer Walters

* * * * * * * * * * * * * * *

For my husband, partner, and the love of my life,
Owen Walters.

CHAPTER 1

I would be lying if I said this day was like any other day. I cooked a big dinner, cleaned the house, and picked up my daughter from swim practice. But today was July 5th. Twenty-one years had come and gone, but we would never forget the day my father was killed.

"Are you sure I can't help you with something, Val?"

Maria was sitting at the table with a cup of coffee in hand. She was always giving and kind, that once in a lifetime kind of friend.

"Can I cut up something for you? Or stir the butterscotch?"

"No, it's my great-grandmother's butterscotch pie recipe, and if it isn't stirred continuously, it will burn. Only a few people can get this recipe right. Plus, I'm out of vanilla extract, so if it burns, I have to run to the store, and I'm not feeling like going anywhere today."

Maria nodded and boosted herself up on my cupboard. "What time is Eric coming home? Are the two of you taking the boat out, then?"

Every year on July 5th, my husband and I took the boat

on the chain of lakes where we lived in the town of Side Lake, Minnesota. We turned off the motor once we reached Sixberry's landing, and every year I stared at the water and talked to my father because I knew he could hear me, and Eric would sit beside me, holding my hand. Well, it had been a couple years since he technically held my hand and since I talked out loud to my father in front of him, to be honest. As the years went on, the ritual only made Eric feel more uncomfortable. He thought time should erase the pain of that day, including my heavy heart. He even asked if returning to the scene of the boating accident every year was healthy. How dare he? Did he not know me at all? Time had helped a little. I no longer thought about the accident every minute of every day, but I still had nightmares, which was hard for Eric to understand.

This was the first year my husband had gone to work instead of spending the entire day with me, to support me, and just be there for me. We usually went boating in the morning, and then we always had a picnic in the grass by the water in our front yard.

"I'm not sure. I haven't heard from him yet. I'm sure he's busy."

I always caught myself defending him, but how could I not? Wasn't that what a marriage was all about?

"Did you remind him what today is?"

I looked up at her, trying to hide my sadness. "He knows what day it is, trust me. He wouldn't forget, we have been doing this for many years."

Maria shrugged. "Okay. You just never know with him. He's quite selfish."

Maria was always negative toward Eric. She had not known him that long, but from the first day she pegged him as a lazy jerk, and she was not afraid to vocalize her thoughts

2

and feelings. It never offended me. I loved her honesty. It was refreshing.

Maria was a new friend of mine. We met a couple months back when my mom hired her on at our family bookstore. It was love at first sight. We just clicked. When we met, she told me she was the mother of five and was looking for part-time work so she could get away and do something for herself. As soon as she told me reading was her favorite hobby, I knew I needed her in my life. Sure, my mom already hired her, but I'd like to say I had the final say.

I could not imagine working anywhere but in the bookstore. Since my daughter, Alexandra, was older now, I could cook and clean after work and still have plenty of time to relax and read a good book before bed.

"I'm just saying, call him, ask him when he is coming home. It's already two o'clock."

My phone dinged in my pocket.

"Is it Eric? Is he on his way home because I should probably take off before he gets here?"

The message from Eric took my breath away.

Maria moved closer. "What is it? What did he say?"

"He said he's going out for drinks with the guys from work, and that I shouldn't wait up for him."

Maria was right. He had forgotten. Or maybe he didn't want me to put a damper on his night. He would not do this on purpose, would he?

Maria gave me a soft tap on the arm. "How about if you and I bring the boat over to the landing instead? This isn't about Eric, it's about you and your dad."

There was no 'I told you so' from Maria, and I knew she wished she were wrong about Eric avoiding me today as much as I did.

My eyes watered, but I couldn't help let out a chuckle. Neither of us knew how to drive Eric's boat. We preferred to sit in the front and let the wind blow our hair back and the sun warm our skin while we relaxed with a glass of Pinot in hand. "Cheers," we would say. Sure, we went tubing and skiing with the kids, but neither one of us had an interest in driving the boat. We left that for the boys.

"You know we would probably crash the thing if we took it out," I said with a laugh.

"Yeah, I wouldn't even know how to start the thing. Okay, how about we drive over to the landing then?"

I raised my eyebrow at her.

She smiled. "With the car."

Maybe it would be good to stand on the shore instead of in the boat when I went back to where the accident took place so long ago. Although Maria never got a chance to meet my father, she still cared enough to come with me for support. How could I turn her down? I really needed to do this, and Eric was not planning on coming home any time soon.

"What do you say?"

I looked up and smiled at her, brushing away the wetness under my eyes. "I say, how did I ever survive for so many years without a friend like you in my life?"

Maria grabbed her keys and purse off the table. "That's what I keep telling you."

I stared out the window at the bright green grass and the familiar twists and turns of the road ahead. Growing up, my family struggled a lot financially. More than they let on, I realized later in life. We never went on vacations, and we definitely did not have a cabin on the lake like most of my friends.

I still spent the weekends in the summer with my parents boating, fishing, and just getting away from the busyness of life, but I never forgot to bring a book for those down moments. I would rather bring a book and not have time to read than not bring a book and have a minute to read.

My family could not afford a cabin, especially not in Side Lake. The city of Side Lake had a chain of five lakes connected by rivers. It was a popular area, and though there were too many boats on the water the water was clean, the sky blue, and the people, genuine.

My parents invested in an old 1980 Glastron SSV-176 boat instead. I loved that ugly red and white boat when I was a little girl. I didn't see the old and ugliness in it. I saw memories and happiness that my family created on our adventures in the boat. My father hauled that boat up to the lake on the back of his truck, and we took it out on the chain almost every weekend in the summer. The best time was when my dad drove the boat to McCarthy's Beach for a picnic. The lake was so overloaded with people we had to get there early to pick a good spot, but it was a clean, sandy beach.

My mother would lay a large comforter on the sand, and my sister and I would sit and eat peanut butter and jelly sandwiches while watching the waves from boats roll into shore. Mom always packed nacho cheese Doritos and a package of Oreos, along with a variety of pop.

My mom and I always had a book in hand as we lay on the blanket in the sun.

The trees protected us from the sun in the morning, but once it moved over to the west, there was no hiding from the rays except in the water. That's when my mom brought out the sunscreen and slathered it on us.

The water was so shallow; we swam way out where our parents could hardly see us, and we could still touch the bottom. My sister, Sabrina, and I would race out to the buoys to other kids who would join in and play games in the water with us. It was the most popular beach on the Iron Range, and I believe that is still true.

We pulled up at the landing and suddenly all my happy memories vanished, and all I could think about was the darkness of that terrible day. As my eyes landed right on the spot in the water where it all happened, I remembered that day as clearly as if it was yesterday.

My dad and I dropped off my mom and Sabrina at the beach so they could get a spot ready at McCarthy's while we took the boat for a ride to warm it up and make sure everything was working right. It was an old boat, so there were days the boat wasn't running right, and my dad would end up spending most of the day trying to fix it.

We were coming through the channel and into the lake when a boat hit us. My dad tried to dodge the boat, but all I remember was the force of my body flying through the air in slow motion, and then the world went black. Later on, I found out the man driving the boat had been drinking and said he did not see us.

I woke up lying on a dock next to my dad and the driver of the boat, like dead bodies carefully laid out to rest. My lungs were burning from a sharp pain with every breath I took, but I could not move. At first, I thought I was paralyzed. I turned to look at my dad again, but this time I noticed he was not moving, and I knew right away he was no longer alive. The man driving the other boat was covered in blood and screaming at the paramedics about not being able to feel his legs. I don't think he knew how lucky he was to be alive, and how much I wished it were him instead of my father.

The paramedics placed a brace around my neck and a stiff board under me. My face was sticky with blood, but at the time I thought I was imagining it. Later, in the hospital, the nurse told me a mystery man pulled us all from the water. He was a hero. But even a hero couldn't save my father.

My mother and Sabrina were a mess of tears, and I was in shock. At first, they were glad I was okay, but when they found out my father died, nothing was the same between us again. How could they be? I always felt like they blamed me because I had begged my father to take me for a ride in the boat that morning. I had a fight with my sister over who was going to ski first, and like always, my sister won. I begged my father for a boat ride instead, insisting it was only fair. I was glad to be rid of my sister for a few minutes. I had no idea those few minutes would affect me for the rest of my life.

Maria held my hand as we climbed over the rocks and down the bank next to the bridge. I sat on a large rock, and she sat down next to me.

"Tell me about your father," she said as she stared into the water with me.

I smiled. The memories were always there, in my mind, and I could replay them whenever I wanted.

"He was tall and thin with a mustache, but not a creepy mustache, more like a well-kept dad mustache. My father loved to fish and hunt, and pretty much anything outdoors. He loved people, and he had this natural way with them. They would come to the bookstore because he was a book guru. He knew all the customers by name, and he talked about books as if he was talking about vacation getaways. My mom was uptight, but my dad was easygoing and always had a welcoming smile. I will never forget the way he made my mom laugh. Oh, it's been so long since I heard her laugh the way dad always got her to."

Maria squeezed my hand again, bringing me back from the memories of what life was like before.

"He sounds amazing. I wish I could have met him."

"He would've loved you. After he died, my family fell apart. My mom had a hard time getting out of bed, she was so depressed. I was a teenager when I started managing the store for her. Then my sister Sabrina left. A part of us died with him. He was the glue that held our family together. We grieved separately and in our own ways, you know?"

Maria nodded. "What about the man who caused the accident? What happened to him?"

"He went to jail for a while, but not as long as he should have. Sometimes I have dreams where I'm filled with rage, running through the woods trying to stab him with a knife. Then I wake up screaming because quicksand is pulling me down. I don't want to hurt him, but I don't understand how he could have been so reckless. A part of me wants him to know what he did to our family."

"That's understandable." Maria reached into her pocket and pulled out a couple of tissues and handed one to me. "I was prepared. For both of us."

The cool breeze of the lake blew my hair around, cooling off my neck and face and leaving me with goosebumps. "I love you, Dad," I whispered.

"Goodbye, Valarie's dad," Maria said.

"Are you sure you don't want me to come in? I'd love to just hang out with you."

"No, no. You have your own family. Go home. I'm going to clean up before Eric gets home. Maybe he will remember what today is and come home feeling terrible."

Maria frowned. "Maybe. Just promise you'll call me if you need me, okay?"

I cleaned up the house, did two loads of laundry, the dishes, and put away the dinner I spent the day preparing for Eric and myself. I had made Atlantic salmon in apricot sauce, mashed potatoes, and a Caesar salad. For dessert, Eric's favorite, homemade butterscotch pie. It hurt more than I expected that he was not here with me today. I guess I should be grateful, because keeping busy was distracting me from the pain of both Eric's absence and the loss of my father.

I made Alexandra and Eric tomorrow's lunches out of the dinner.

Once the lunches were packed, I sat down on the couch in my reading room and grabbed the new Elin Hilderbrand book off the table. My happy place that never let me down. My reading room had shelves of books on two sides and French doors that opened into the living room and let the sun shine in during the day. The bay window had a bench and cushion below it so I could read in the window and have a beautiful view of the lake down the hill.

Our house was built on Big Sturgeon, which was the biggest lake in the chain of lakes. Our grass was bright green, and my flowerbeds of marigolds and lilies bordered the stairs that led to the dock and open water. Some days I would just stare at the beauty of the place I was so grateful to call home.

Alexandra came home from her friend's house around nine and went straight to her room. I read until my heavy lids caused them to close involuntarily. I gave up trying to keep them open and made my way to bed. Where was he?

I looked at my phone again. It was eleven o'clock, and he had not even sent a text about the day. I crawled beneath my cotton sheets and cried myself to sleep. How could he forget what this day meant to me? My heart was broken, and I couldn't help but wonder if he even cared about me anymore.

CHAPTER 2

The floor creaked beneath his feet as he tip-toed into the empty spot in bed next to me. Did he really think I would sleep? I turned toward him and put my head on his chest. He came home to me. That was all that mattered now. "How was your night?"

He groaned. "Not tonight, Val."

To be honest, my heart broke right there.

"I'm not trying to be rude. I'm just asking because you have been working really hard, and I genuinely hope you had a great night. You deserve it, and I missed you."

This was no lie. I missed him and would not bring it up and make him feel bad. I was just glad he was here now. I slid my hand up his shirt and touched his bare chest. He tensed at my touch, but I was overthinking like always. He was very good at reminding me when I was overreacting, so I ignored my concern and instead slid my hand down to his belly button where my finger traced the circle then changed route and made its way down to his waist and under his draw-string pajama pants. I was spontaneous and showed him I was ready to get frisky.

He forcefully grabbed my hand and set it down by my side. "I said not tonight. I'm tired. It's been a long day, and I just want to get some sleep." He rolled away from me and tucked the sheets beneath his body.

"I'm sorry, it's just been so long," I whispered.

When was the last time we had sex? I could not be sure, but it had definitely been months. I was always the one fighting him off and telling him I was tired, but something had changed between us. He always used to be in the mood, and he would remind me when it had been too long. Was the stress of his job getting to him? There were a lot of late nights and drinks with his work staff or his buddies lately. He said he was stressed about running his business, and I knew it was a lot, but his company was doing so well now. Our finances had never been better, and we had paid off all our debts. But the more I thought about it, the more I realized he had become distant.

Maybe I should plan a vacation for the two of us so he could de-stress, and we could relax with no distractions. Maybe Paris or London? For now, I would get up early in the morning and make him a ham and cheese omelet and toast. He loved when I made him breakfast.

I woke up thirty minutes early, careful not to wake him. I lifted the sheets and looked at my fully clothed husband with so many regrets that I hadn't seen his unhappiness before now. There used to be a time he would come to bed in just his underwear. How did my marriage change so much without me even noticing? What was happening to us? I needed to be a better wife starting today.

I showered and brushed my hair, dabbing on just a bit of lipstick and a bit of perfume. He could never resist the way it smelled. I was already downstairs beating eggs when his alarm went off. By the time I finished the first omelet,

Alexandra was sitting at the breakfast bar with gigantic eyes and a hungry smile.

"That smells so good, Mom. I don't care if I have to swim in an hour, I'm having breakfast today."

My daughter was the spitting image of me. She had long, dark hair and brown eyes that peeked out from beneath her bangs. She loved to swim, and I was so grateful because it gave her something to do in the summer other than sit on her phone or hang out with boys. My sweet girl had not turned into a boy-crazy teen yet, and I hoped that was years away.

I was only a couple of years older than Alex was right now when I got pregnant. It wasn't easy being pregnant before I figured out who I was. I was a child having a child. Lucky for me, Eric stayed with me after we found out. He wasn't a father of the year, but he loved her. He was more like a fun uncle, letting me make all the hard decisions by myself while he was to spoil her and do his own thing. I told him so many times he needed to discipline her, too, but he just told me he wasn't good at it. Like parenting was easy for me. Ha!

We were so madly in love back then. We went parking in the woods and had a lot of fun steaming up the car windows. My mother did not even notice that we could not keep our hands off each other.

It devastated me when I found out I was pregnant at eighteen, but my mother just shrugged her shoulders and never said a word about it. If it disappointed her that I got pregnant and decided not to go to college, she never said so. I loved working at the bookstore and did not want student loan debt. Even with the settlement from the accident, my mother was struggling financially and could not afford to send me to college. She blew all the money right away, paying for Sabrina's law school, and she bought me my house on the lake.

Money doesn't buy happiness, and I'm pretty sure Sabrina never even thanked her. Then again, I'm pretty sure my mother never even noticed. She was a zombie after my father died. Little mattered to her, and she became distant, even after the worst of her depression.

Just as I took his omelet out of the pan and set it on the counter in front of the empty stool at the bar, Eric came running into the kitchen. I smiled at him and watched him walk right past his plate, put his blazer over the chair, and grab his leather dress shoes.

I tried to make eye contact with him before cracking an egg for myself in the mixing bowl. "Hungry?"

He put on his shoes. "I'm running late. It's going to be another long night if I don't get there early."

"What about your breakfast?" I lowered my head. "At least take it for the road."

He didn't even look back at me as he made his way to Alex and placed a kiss on the top of her head.

"Grab your lunch."

I took the bag out of the fridge and handed it to him. I puckered my lips and leaned in. He kissed me on the forehead instead.

"See you guys," he said, slamming the door behind him.

Alex was focused on her phone and likely never noticed her father left.

I threw his omelet in the garbage and the pan in the sink. I went into the bathroom, shut the door and stared at my blotchy face in the mirror. He didn't even look at me. He never even said a word about the house or his favorite pie on the counter. I took a deep breath, splashed some water on my face, and went back into the kitchen. I could fix this.

"Ready, Alex?"

She gasped, her eyes widened and one hand covered her mouth.

"What's wrong?"

Her mouth was wide open in horror. "Dad left his phone."

I shook my head. "It's fine. No one important is going to be calling him this early, anyway. I'll drop it off at the office after I drop you off at swim practice. Get your swim bag, okay?"

I grabbed Eric's phone from her and raised my eyes as I read what had obviously startled her.

I'm wearing a short skirt and no underwear. Don't keep me waiting!

I'm not sure how long I stood there with my mouth open. The message was from Cinnamon, his secretary at work.

Eric would not stray, would he? No, this woman was obviously obsessed with him. He was at least ten years older than her, and he was her boss. I knew Eric, and he would never cheat on me. Would he? I sat down on the chair before my wobbly legs gave out beneath me. It wasn't true. He loved us too much to have an affair and ruin our family. Cinnamon had only been working for him for what? A few months at most. It was probably just a crush. He would fire her the minute he saw her text.

Alex interrupted my thoughts and brought me back to reality. "Are you okay?"

I stood up and forced a wide smile. "Yeah, I'm fine. Did you read your dad's phone?"

Alex looked uncomfortable. "I'm sorry, Mom. I can't believe he would do this to you."

I placed my hand on her shoulder. "Oh, no. Your dad would never have an affair. I'm sure he is going to be furious when he finds out how inappropriate his new secretary is. I feel sorry for her because she is probably going to get fired when he sees this."

Alex rolled her eyes. "Sure Mom, Dad's the victim." She studied my face for a moment and then did a once over. "I think you should go shopping. Those clothes are so huge on you, it's almost like you're lost in them. Buy something pretty and show him the joke is on him."

I looked down at my large t-shirt and sweatpants. "Hey, I love my sweats, they're so comfy."

She looked at me again, with pity in her eyes this time.

"What?"

"Nothing. Let's go. I don't want to be late."

There were two vehicles in the parking lot when I pulled in. One was Eric's and the other I didn't recognize. The door was locked, so I used my key to get in. The secretary's desk was empty, and Eric's office door was shut. I wanted to be careful not to startle him, but as I opened the door, I saw he wasn't at his desk. I took a couple of steps in, following the squeak of what sounded like his desk chair. The blonde head of hair leaned back and all I could see was her bare shoulders, then her boney back bobbing up and down. It may seem strange, but at that moment, I really didn't think it was my husband underneath her. I really don't know what I was thinking or if I was even thinking at all. It wasn't obvious to me until I saw the 'oh shit' look on my husband's face as he threw her off him.

She turned around, and they both stood up, naked.

My heart thumped in my chest and left me gasping for air.

"It's not what it looks like," Eric said. "Oh shit, oh shit, oh shit."

I knew he was talking, but I had a hard time putting his words together in my head. I was too busy staring at the perfect woman beside him. She was model-like thin, and her body was perky and perfect. Did she have an ounce of fat on her body? She bent over to grab her shirt. I shielded my eyes, embarrassed at the sight. How long had this been going on? How was I so naïve?

"How could you?" Was all I could muster.

My words came out shaky, and my legs stuck to the floor. The floor that I picked out just a few years back. I turned around and ran out the door and into the office.

"Wait, wait, I can explain," he said as I opened up the door.

I turned around to face him, tears running down my face. "You can, really? Go ahead," I said, crossing my arms.

He stared at me, at a loss for words. He looked behind him, then at me again. His face had turned beet red. His body language suddenly changed, and he laughed, defeated almost. "I have no explanation. Look at her," he said, as if that explained it all. "I mean, there really is no reason to lie to you. I was going to leave you anyway, we haven't been happy in a long time. Can you blame me? Look at you, you let yourself go after you had Alexandra. I'm just not attracted to you anymore."

Talk about kicking me while I was down. "Really? I had a baby, Eric, our baby."

"Sixteen years ago! You wear clothes ten sizes too big, and you don't even care enough to put on makeup anymore. I've been living a lie for too long when I lay beside you at night. This is your fault as much as it is mine. What did you expect?"

I could not believe my ears. "What?" That was his defense? That I'm fat? That it was my fault he was cheating on me?

"Come on, you didn't really think I was going to stay with you forever, did you?"

Cinnamon giggled and ran up behind him and put her arm around his chest.

I wanted nothing more than to wrap my hands around

that skinny, dumb blonde's neck, but I didn't because I'm an adult and adults needed to have self-control.

"Eric, what happened to you? How could you?"

He took a step toward me, and I took a step back. He held out his hand. "Give me the key to my office and then move your stuff out of the house. It's time for you to find a new place to live because I'm done."

I pulled the key off my key chain with my shaky hands and placed it in the palm of his hand. "Take it then! Good luck with her." I looked her in the eye. "You should really eat a sandwich," I said, but in my mind, I was crying.

I knew there was only one thing that would make me feel better. I drove to the nearest fast-food restaurant and stuffed my face until I could no longer feel the pain. My family was broken, and I needed to be strong for Alex.

CHAPTER 3

O CTOBER

"ARE you sure you are okay, dear?"

That's all I had heard from my mother for the past three months if I happened to not be smiling. I'm glad she cared enough to ask, but it was getting old.

"I'm fine, Mom."

I was far from fine after walking in on my husband with a decade younger woman with long blonde hair and legs that went on for days. How could anyone be fine after that? I was overweight and unattractive in my baggy sweatshirt and black leggings, which Eric was kind enough to point out. My jeans no longer fit over my thick thighs. I thought if I didn't look in the mirror, no one would notice, but my obesity chased my husband into another woman's arms and bed.

"Okay then, the new shipment came in late last night. I put away most of the books, but there are still a few boxes in the corner. I'm going home for a nap. You can handle this, right?"

The bookstore wasn't due to open for another hour. Being surrounded by hundreds of books was just what I needed right now to soothe my soul and lift my spirits. I peeled the shipping tape and opened the box with a deep inhale of the fresh book smell that took me back to my childhood. Back when everything was so much simpler.

Back then, I saved my allowance each week to spend on the one thing I loved more than anything. When all my friends were going roller-skating or to the movies, I roamed my family's bookstore in search of the perfect read. There were just so many to choose from. I read Goosebumps and Fear Street books by R.L. Stine, and when I got older, my true love was Mary Higgins Clark's mysteries with lottery winners and who-done-its.

As a newly divorced woman in my thirties, I now loved romance novels the most. I dreamed of the days when we were all a family, and life was much simpler. I picked up a Susan Mallery book and turned it over to read about *The Stepsisters*. I placed the book on the floor, away from the rest. I had waited for this book for weeks, and I was so excited to go home and escape the reality of my messed-up life, to escape to California where my heart couldn't be broken and there was always a happy ending waiting for me.

I knew what I was getting with charismatic characters, a well thought out plot, and California sunshine in each of her novels. Sometimes I could even smell tanning oil when I was reading. No chances were taken when I was engrossed in books, and my heart wasn't in jeopardy with each turn of the page. There was no worry about risking everything. Giving everything to a man without knowing if he would reciprocate the love and trust would always be a factor for me now. Romance novels were predictable, and I always felt happy and fulfilled when I closed the book after hours of being lost in another world so far away from my own.

Once every book was organized and put away, I closed my eyes and took a moment to enjoy the energy that surrounded me in the place where I felt the most comfort in this entire world. I then unlocked the door and flipped the sign to open before heading back to set up the small cafe.

The bell rang, followed by loud footsteps on the creaky old floorboards.

"One coffee with a shot of espresso, please," a familiar voice said. "Ooh, are those donut holes I see?"

I turned around and handed her a coffee. Maria was right on time. She came in every morning before work for a quick chat like clockwork, even if she didn't have to work. We liked to chat before our workday officially began. She was like a sister to me, even though we had only known each other for a year, and I wondered how I ever survived without her.

"Yes, help yourself."

"Don't mind if I do."

She chose two and took a big bite. Her eyes rolled back, and she groaned in appreciation with each bite. "How does your mom find the time to bake so early in the morning? She has been in and gone before I even get here most mornings."

"I don't know. To be honest, I'm pretty sure that's why she hired you. So she could have more help in the store and only have to bake. She's never really been an avid reader. That was my dad and me."

I spread out the rest of the donuts on the rectangular plate and sprinkled some sugar around the edges. "Can you grab the hot fudge out of the microwave, please?"

Maria handed it over. "I can't image owning a bookstore and not liking to read. Heck, I couldn't imagine my life without you now, without this store, and the energy it gives off. It may put a dent in the checkbook, having a book addiction, but it's worth it."

"I know, right? I've always wondered what my mom does in her spare time. She is all alone, but somehow seems to keep busy. She's so secretive about everything. It drives me insane."

"What could she be hiding?"

"She wasn't like this before my dad died. She's just not her old self anymore."

Maria jumped up on the counter and took another donut. "What about you? It's not like you didn't lose your father, too, not to mention your douche-bag husband."

"I don't mention Eric to my mom. Do you know what she says about that whole situation? That it was my choice to leave him when he kicked me out. That I should have fought harder when he asked for a divorce. I'm like, really, Mom? He moved his secretary into our home."

"The nerve." Maria shook her head. "Like you just forced him on slutty spice, who is obviously just after his money. Ha! Jokes on him."

The mention of Cinnamon was painful. Eric and I were together two decades and had a family together, and he threw it all away because his secretary wore short skirts and low tops to work. The eyelash extensions and dark makeup were, for some reason, more appealing than the natural look of the mother of his child. I was the woman who cooked and cleaned for him, even scheduled all his appointments. The joke was on him because I knew he was going to be lost without me.

But I was sick of fighting with him. I was awarded the house in the divorce, but he begged me to let him stay there a couple more weeks, and those weeks turned to a couple of months. I didn't want to push it and make him angry, not until I knew for sure that it was over between us. I just hoped to change his mind, but I wasn't sure how yet.

"I'm sorry, I know you don't want to talk about it, but what a puke. One day he is going to come crawling back to you on his hands and his knees, begging for your forgiveness, and you're going to tell him where to go, right?"

I shrugged my shoulders and popped a donut hole in my mouth to buy me time so I would not have to answer. If Maria knew I stalked his and Cinnamon's social media accounts every day, hoping for their status to be changed to single, I would never hear the end of it. The number of times I wrote him text messages asking him to please give our marriage another shot, only to erase them and cry into my pillow instead, would devastate my friend. I was not ready to throw in the towel yet. I wanted my old life back.

I dreamed of those days Eric and I would lie in bed, snuggling at night in my dream house on the lake, but instead I was alone in a rundown old house in what Maria and I called the 'ghetto of Hibbing.' The mattress was lumpy and the air stale. Sure, Maria and I joked about it, but I loathed the house I was living in, and I wanted our family to be back together. I hated worrying about how it was affecting Alex. It was not her fault that her dad struggled with keeping his pants zipped. It was always Val and Eric, Eric and Val. Now it was just me. Alone, desperate, and depressed.

My lawyer was angry I was not in my house. My mom paid for it and it was technically mine.

"Please don't tell me you want him back. Val? Valarie?" Maria snapped her fingers in front of my face and then jumped off the counter and turned me by the shoulders. "Earth to Val? Wake up and smell the coffee. You don't want him back, you don't. He will never be that person for you. Do you get that?"

"I don't know. He is Alexandra's father. I mean, maybe he is just going through a midlife crisis or something."

She sighed heavily. "I can't believe you just said that. You need to move on. Why would you even want him back? He sucks, and he doesn't deserve you. I really hate that I have to work right now, or I'd slap some sense into you." She pressed her fist to her mouth, then placed them on my cheeks. "You're being really stupid right now, but I love you, and that is why I am telling you to get your damn house back. It's yours."

I nodded.

Maria disappeared into the back room to put her stuff away. She came back with her contagious smile and positive attitude, as if the conversation never happened. That's what I loved about her. She was not stubborn. And she never held a grudge, but she told it how it was.

The day Maria showed up for her interview at the bookstore before I even knew who she was, I asked her the most important question right off the bat. "Why would you want to work in a bookstore for minimum wage?"

Maria had laughed at the question. "It's definitely not about the money. I love books, and to be honest I've been a stay-at-home mom for so many years, it's nice to get out of the house and spend my time surrounded by books. They are my therapy, medicine, meditation, and happy drug."

I laughed because that was true for me, too. "What books do you like to read?"

Maria's cheeks flushed. "Mainly romance. I told you, I have five children, right? Did I tell you there is usually at least one that crawls into bed with us every night? My books are really the only romance I get anymore, but I don't blame my husband. He works double shifts to support our family, and I get to stay home with the kids. From vomit and food stuck to my shirt most days, I'm not exactly as put together as I used to be, but he still loves me, anyway."

"Sounds like you have your hands full. I like you already. Welcome to The Rangers Bookshop. I have to ask, who is your favorite author?"

Maria was deep in thought for a moment. "I really don't know. I love Nicholas Sparks and Susan Elizabeth Phillips, Kristy Woodson Harvey, Susan Mallery, oh I could go on and on. I love Mary Higgins Clark and Mary Kay Andrews, of course. Just being around books makes me excited to come to work every day. It's probably my one true addiction."

"I think we're going to work very well together, and we definitely have a lot to talk about," I said, unable to hide my excitement at the immediate connection between us. "Why don't you start off by looking around and getting a feel for the place?"

Maria rolled up her sleeves and went right to the new release section, and that was when I knew deep down, she was the real thing. I was getting a friend and a co-worker to work by my side. Someone to talk to about my latest read without feeling like I was boring her like I always bored Eric.

"This is the best job ever. Thank you so much for this opportunity," she had said.

The first customer, a little five-year-old girl named Lily, came in with her father trailing behind her. They were regulars, so Lily knew right where to go. Maria followed them to the children's section.

"Hello, Lily, what can I help you find today? We have a new Disney book I think you will love."

They disappeared with Maria into the children's section. The bell rang, and a man came in with a clipboard in his hand. I met him as he entered. "Hello, welcome to The Rangers Bookstore. What can I help you find today?"

The man had a somber expression.

"Are you Carol Heinz?"

I shot him a curious look. I had never seen this man before.

"No, but I'm her daughter. What can I help you with today, sir?"

He hesitated, his eyes studying his clipboard. "I really can't talk to you about this if you aren't Carol. It's private information. Do you know when she will be back? She doesn't seem to return my calls, and it's very important I speak with her right away."

Was my mother in some kind of trouble? This man looked angry with the world. "She should be back around five. Can I tell her you were looking for her?"

He handed me his card. "Make sure she calls." He turned around and left.

His card read, Tom Broncow Loan Officer at Merchant and Miners State Bank. I took a picture of his card with my phone and sent it to my mother and wrote him off as a terrible solicitor. My mother was so secretive, she would never tell me what this was all about, anyway.

As Lily and her father left, I glanced at the bag she carried out that looked to have at least three or four books in it. Maria was so great at helping customers find exactly what they needed and then some.

Maria walked over to me. I scanned the shelf to make sure the authors' names were in order by last name.

"What was that all about? That guy looked furious."

"I'm not sure. I think that was just the way his face looked," I said. We both laughed. "He was looking for my mom."

"That's weird." Maria took a book off the shelf and scanned the back. "Lily bought four books today, so that's a great start to the morning."

"I saw that. Great job." It wasn't easy to make a big profit in a small bookstore. Books were much more convenient to find online.

"I'm glad I could butter you up a little before I ask you for a favor. I need to leave a little before five today, if that is okay. I have a Calorie Counter meeting at five-thirty at my brother's new gym. I'm cleaning there two days a week, and for that I get three meetings for free."

"That's right, I forgot you said your brother opened that new gym in town. Calorie Counters, huh?"

Maria patted her stomach. "Yeah, I need to learn how to get rid of some of this baby weight."

"That's great that your brother moved here," I said. "You must be so excited. I can't wait to meet him."

Maria had not mentioned her brother until he opened a gym in town. We talked about everything, but she never said much about him. I never knew she even had a sibling.

"You should come with me. I can get you a discount. It'll be fun."

I looked down at my oversized sweatshirt and leggings. I knew I should say yes. When was the last time I could wear a pair of jeans and zip them up? I was too afraid to even try them on anymore, but the thought of being vulnerable and talking about my weight in front of a bunch of people did not sound like an exciting way to spend my evening. That would be something I would need to mentally prepare for.

"No thank you, maybe another time. I have to take Alex to swimming tonight."

I would rather eat junk food and watch television than focus on how overweight and unhealthy I was.

"Ok, but I'm going to hold you to it. Today is the introduction, but tomorrow it starts officially. Will you think about coming then?"

Maria never took no for an answer.

"You know I want to be there to support your brother's gym, it's just ... to be honest, I'm a little exhausted and over-whelmed from the divorce and all. Living in the ghetto isn't exactly what I thought it would be. The idea of counting calories just seems so depressing. Food is all I have right now. It's comforting on the bad days."

Maria laughed and touched my shoulder. "I get it, my friend. How about I come over tomorrow and see your place? We're always meeting out in public to get away and have girl time. I can't believe I haven't made it to your new place yet. I'm a terrible friend."

I had a hard time just getting out of bed and making it to work most mornings after tossing and turning all night. Leaving my beautiful home to live in a run-down old house wasn't exactly uplifting. There were nights I woke up crying as thoughts of Eric and Cinnamon twisted up in bed circled in my mind. Sometimes I'd even roll over to reach for him on the other side of the bed before I remembered he no longer slept beside me at night. Why did I keep torturing myself with these thoughts? I longed to sleep all day and cry, never having to get up. It hurt so badly that someone else was keeping my side of the bed warm next to my husband. There had to be a way to win Eric back and everything would go back to the way it was. I needed a plan to make it happen.

I was counting the till at quarter to five when the bell rang. It surprised me to see my mother walk into the store.

"Hello, dear, how was the day? Hello Maria."

She was grinning from ear to ear, which was out of char-acter for her. I couldn't remember the last time I saw her smile.

"Did you get my message?"

I watched my mother suspiciously as she danced around the room. She grabbed a book off the shelf and hummed softly.

"Mom, did you hear me? I texted you about a bank guy coming here looking for you."

"Oh, yes dear, I talked to him. Thank you."

She did not look up as she hummed, then said, "Why don't the two of you take off a little early? I'm going to close up here soon. It's a beautiful day. Go enjoy it."

Her chipper mood was confusing and out of character for her. When my father was still alive, this would have been a normal day for my mother at the bookstore with my father. The way they looked into each other's eyes and always found a way to touch one another because they were so in love. She was always dancing around and humming a tune back then. Funny how it all changed so much since then.

"Thanks," I said. "We will definitely take you up on that."

CHAPTER 4

I had just enough time to run and get groceries before picking up Alex from swim practice. Spaghetti was the routine dinner the night before a swim meet for carb loading. I rounded the corner to grab the sauce and noodles when I passed the bakery and the cream puffs called out my name. I knew better than to go grocery shopping on an empty stomach. The Bavarian cream puffs looked fresh and delicious.

I grabbed not one, but two boxes and made my way to the register. I passed the chips aisle and stopped in my tracks. Doritos went so well with Top the Tater, my favourite Minnesota-made dip. I deserved to be able to eat what I wanted. In my defense, I was almost out of snacks in my pantry, except for the snacks hidden in my underwear drawer and the ones under my bed, although those were for emergencies only. Like when I needed to get through some big emotional drama, like every time I saw my husband with Cinnamon. As long as no one saw me eating them, it wouldn't really matter, right? A few extra pounds hidden under my baggy clothes? Who would know?

Food made me happy. I didn't need any judgment from others. I also had no self-control and stopped fighting it long ago. I was proud of myself for stopping at just buying two snacks and made my way to the register before something else caught my eye.

The lady behind the register said, "Hello."

"Hi."

Minnesota nice. There was almost always a smile and a little chit-chat when you checked out at a register or passed someone while walking on the road, or washing your hands in the restroom.

"So, when are you due?"

I looked into her eyes. They were eyes of happiness and excitement for my food, baby? I looked down at the bump in my shirt.

I stood there, frozen, as the blood drained from my head. "I'm not pregnant." I did everything I could to hold back the tears. I wanted to pay for my stuff and get the hell out of there. The nerve of this woman. Was I so fat that people looked at me and thought I must have a child in my womb?

The woman looked like she just felt horrible, which made the whole situation worse. I'd rather she was just trying to be mean. She was apologetic and almost looked like she was going to cry, which I prayed wouldn't happen because I would lose it.

It was the pity in her eyes that hurt the most.

"I'm not pregnant," I said again. I looked around to make sure no one could hear our conversation. I tried not to make eye contact and blinked away the tears.

"I'm so sorry, I just thought ..."

"It's fine," I said, pushing a smile to make her feel better.

"Did you just have a baby?"

"No!" I shouted. "Sorry, no," I whispered this time.

"I'm so sorry. I'm making this so much worse, aren't I?"

Was it the oversized sweatshirt I was wearing? Did this woman have any idea what it was like to be too busy to focus on eating healthy or exercising? It wasn't on the top of my list. I may have been overweight, but no way did I look pregnant. Did I? Sure, I knew I let myself go a bit, but pregnant? This was a new low.

I paid my bill and grabbed my bags without another word. I struggled not to cry. I transferred the bags into my trunk in record time, not even checking which bag had the eggs, as I threw them in as fast as I could.

Once safely in my car, I punched the steering wheel with all the anger behind my fist, which made my horn go off. I thought the little old lady putting her groceries away was going to pee her pants or have a heart attack. Instead, she stared right at me with her elbows held out wide from her body and her chest thrust out. I gave her an apologetic wave and covered my face with my hands. I peeked through my fingers as she got into her car and began backing out slowly. Once her car was sideways, she looked at me with her fist in the air and raised her middle finger. I could not believe it. The lady frowned and pulled away in slow motion. I sure pissed her off.

I got out of the car and grabbed the Doritos and cream puffs from the trunk, and began shoving food into my mouth without chewing. Flicked off by an old lady in a parking lot was not at all how I expected my day to go when I woke up this morning. I also didn't expect to get mistaken for a pregnant woman. I continued shoving the food in my mouth and I felt better, like a druggie getting her dose of heroin. For those few moments I ate, I felt so good. The way it tasted was so delicious. How did people not live to eat?

The heavy tears stung my eyes, but did not stop me from

stuffing more food into my mouth. Five chips, one bite of the cream puff until my mouth was so full, I could not swallow. The food was so thick in my throat I had to find some water to wash it down. I remembered I had a bottle of water in the trunk. Without looking, my car door swung open and right into a truck, pulling into the spot next to me.

I inhaled in response, causing the food to get lodged in my throat. I bent over to cough, but I could not cough or even breathe. I bent over and spit out the food right in front of his shoes. I couldn't take in a breath at all. I tried to cough, but that just made it worse.

"Are you okay? Are you okay?"

This was the worst day of my life. I could not breathe. I was choking. My mother's words ran through my mind in those quick seconds. Junk food was going to kill me, and this might as well be the day. What they would write in my obituary? Fat girl chokes on food and dies after stuffing her face? Oh please God, no.

Someone pushed on my back and wrapped their hands around me, then jerked on my stomach with a fist until, to my surprise, the chunk of cream puff came flying out of my mouth. By then, a crowd of people gawked at us.

The entire time his arms were wrapped around my torso, all I could think about was if I gained any more weight, he wouldn't be able to put his arms around me and I would die. I coughed and coughed, and my eyes watered as I gasped for air. The man held me upright so I wouldn't fall over.

He slapped my back like he was burping a small child.

"I'm so sorry about your truck," I said when I could finally speak, still a little winded.

He laughed. "There's hardly a dent. I'm more worried about you. Are you okay?"

Although I was pretty sure I was going to die thirty

seconds ago, when I looked into his eyes, I felt nervous and shy all at once. Not to mention deeply embarrassed. Those eyes, that smile, and he was in great shape. Why couldn't it have been an ugly old man who saved my life instead of him?

He pulled a water bottle out of his car and opened it. "Drink, it'll help."

I did not hesitate as I gulped the whole bottle down, coughing once again. It didn't bother me he had been drinking out of this water bottle. The thought of his lips and my lips both on it made me smile. My nose was running, along with my eyes. I wiped them with the back of my hand. "Thank you so much for saving my life. About your truck ..."

"No worries, I'm just glad you're okay. By the way, I'm Nicholas." He held out his hand, and I was immediately lost in his eyes.

I glanced at my orange fingers and put them behind my back. I nodded at him instead. "I'm pretty sure you don't want to shake my hand right now. They are full of cheese dust, but I'm Valarie."

He laughed and glanced in the car at the open bag of Doritos. My clothes were covered in whip cream and crumbs. I needed to escape before this got even more awkward.

He glanced at my cheese-stained fingers when I brought them forward and started fidgeting. For a moment, I forgot I was hiding them behind my back for a reason. I dropped them to my sides.

"I'm weird about licking my fingers, okay? It's a germ thing." It's a germ thing? I was a complete dork, and I could tell he was trying to hide his amusement at what I would say or do next. He must think I was a complete train wreck.

He shook his head. "Here I thought I was the only one who would rather walk around with cheesy fingers until I found a sink instead of licking them. There are very few of us non-hand licking people in this world, you know."

"Exactly, it's disgusting."

"I am a bag tipper, though."

I laughed. He was obviously trying to make me feel better, and it was working. "Not me, too much salt and cheese at the bottom. It bothers me."

We both stood there in awkward silence until I had to say something to get him to stop staring at me. "Are you sure I didn't dent your truck?"

"Don't you worry about it. I'm just glad you're okay."

Who was this guy? Almost straight out of a Disney movie, coming in to swoop me up and change my life forever. Except the minor fact that princesses didn't stuff their face to the point of choking. Too bad this was reality, and he probably felt sorry for me.

"Okay then, if, you're sure. I have to go. Thanks again."

I didn't wait for a reply. I dove into my car without another glance in his direction. I didn't even remember to buckle up. I wanted to go home, hide out in my room, and stress-eat more carefully this time. My mouth salivated at the thought of the sweet chocolate and whipped cream on my tongue, but first I had to pick up my daughter before she thought I forgot about her.

A row of cars lined the front of the school to pick up their swimmers, which meant I wasn't running as late as the swimmers.. I glanced in the mirror and sure enough, my mascara was smeared in streaks down my face and even on my forehead. The mascara wiped off easily enough with a little spit and my giant sunglasses covered up half my face and any sign of my embarrassing near death experience.

The swimmers swarmed out of the school with wet hair

and big backpacks on their shoulders. Alex walked out with a girl I had never seen before. She waved goodbye to her friend, and her friend waved and yelled something back. Alexandra climbed into my car without a word.

"Who was that girl you were talking to? I've never seen her before."

"That's Regan, she moved here from Grand Rapids."

"Michigan?"

"No, Mom, Minnesota. Don't you think if she was from Michigan, I would have said Michigan and not just Grand Rapids?"

Grand Rapids was just thirty-four miles west of Hibbing. It probably should have been my first guess, but I was a little distracted by the events of my day to think straight. Teenagers were so rude sometimes, but I just shook it off.

"Well, you should have her over sometime. I'd like to meet her. How was swimming?"

Her face was glued to her phone after being unable to check her texts for two hours. How horrible that must be for her.

"Alex, I'm talking to you. Put your phone down, please."

The minute we walked in the door, Alex would go right to her room and sit on her phone until dinner. Was it so much to ask that I got a moment of her attention? I missed when she was younger, and we had family game nights and days spent boating on our lake. When her father and I split up, everything changed, including Alex.

"Tiring. Coach wants me to swim the five hundred at the next meet. I don't think he realizes I'm going to die."

I chuckled. The stress of being a teen.

"Mom, I'm serious. Do you know how far that is? It's twenty lengths. I'm seriously going to die."

"Me," I said, mocking my daughter's teen vocabulary.

"Wow, Mom, you even used that correctly. I'm impressed. Do it again and I'll snap you so I can show all my friends."

Videotaping me was where I drew the line. I shook my head and put my hand in front of her phone that was held up in my face. "No videos, Alex. I'm driving. Can't we just have a conversation without your phone?"

"Fine. How was your day at the bookstore? Did you get any new books?"

She shared my passion for reading even though her phone got in the way compared to how much she used to read. Of course, she was busy with swim practice, basketball in the winter, and track in the spring. I hated that she was growing up so fast. I missed when she was little and I was her entire world. I could tell the divorce was influencing her attitude lately, and I couldn't help but feel responsible.

"Actually, we got a new shipment of books today, and I'm making a whole new section for sci-fi readers, and--"

"That's nice," she said, her phone in front of her face again. Sci-fi was Alex's favorite genre.

I wanted to take the phone from her hands and throw it out the window. What was wrong with these teenagers today? How was this normal? I thought about Cinnamon, who was practically my daughter's age. If I took her phone, Cinnamon would probably just go out and buy a new one for her, just to spite me. I know it sounds ridiculous, but I was worried Cinnamon was going to turn my girl against me. She had already taken my husband. No way would I let her enable my daughter behind my back, too. She had not done anything yet, and Alex didn't even like Cinnamon, but it was bound to happen. She spent every other weekend with them, and I was anxious the whole time.

As a loving mother, I would have to let Alex know it was okay to like Cinnamon, even if it was a lie. But I wanted to win Eric back before it got to that point.

Once we got home, I changed my mind and was now happy Alex was distracted by her phone. I wanted to go to my room and cry without her hearing me. She would have no clue because she was too wrapped up in social media and, well, herself.

I made it through dinner, which consisted of grilled cheese and salad. As soon as Alex went to shower, I ran to my room and slid open my underwear drawer and uncovered my treasures. Eating junk food was justified after the day I had, including almost dying. The words of the cashier at the grocery store replayed in my mind and made me angry that I was no longer skinny. I hated being heavy, but I could never survive without food.

There were so many good snacks, it was hard to decide which to eat first. I needed sugar and salt. I felt happy as soon as I opened the bag of cookies and shoved three in my mouth. To truly appreciate the sweet taste on my tongue, I leaned back on the bed. I opened up the can of pop and chugged it down to make more room for the delicious sweets. If no one saw me, the calories didn't really count, or that is what I liked to think to justify my love for treats, anyway.

I kept thinking about that handsome man in the parking lot. The situation was so stressful I had forgotten his name already. Nathan? Nicholas? I knew it started with an N. No; I think it was Nathaniel. He was so patient and sweet. The odds that he didn't have a young, beautiful wife waiting for him at home weren't exactly in my favor. Men like him were a catch, someone to hold on t,. His wife probably asked him how it went at the grocery store, and he would tell her he had to give some oversized woman the Heimlich maneuver when she stuffed her face until she choked. Ugh, how embarrassing. Although he did not seem like the type of man who would say such a thing, would he? He seemed so kind and sincere, and I needed to stop thinking about him.

I calmed my nervous stomach as I reached for a candy bar and shoved it into my mouth. I had to purse my lips tight to keep from drooling on my shirt.

In the end, I took off my shirt and ran downstairs in the short-sleeve shirt I had on underneath, searching for my scissors. I impulsively cut up the shirt that made me look pregnant. I could never look at the shirt again without thinking about what was said. I cut it into pieces the size of baseballs, but that was not enough.

The leaves scattered beneath my feet as I hurried across the lawn and threw the pieces in the fire pit. I picked up a dry leaf, lit it, and dropped it onto the logs stacked like a tipi, but the wood did not catch. I saw the newspaper from the recycling bin on my deck. The deck's wood was chipping away, and the stairs wobbled beneath my feet as I reached for the paper. The wooden step tipped and threw me flat on my back. My head hit the ground, and I I cried out in pain. That was going to hurt tomorrow. I lit the newspapers and finally the fire was underway. The shirt caught fire rather quickly, and a sense of release fell over me.

My bellybutton indent showed through the yellow fabric of my tank top and a roll of fat hung over the sides of my yoga pants. I grabbed the fat between my fingertips and squeezed until it hurt, silently wishing it all away.

Alex came out on the deck. "Mom, what are you doing out here? I'm going to my room to watch TV and do some homework."

She didn't seem to notice my tears or lack of clothing on the chilly fall night. I felt more alone than ever. Even though Alex lived with me, she was never really with me. I pulled up my pants and sucked in my stomach. If I continued to let myself go, I would never win Eric back. It was time to fight for me and what I wanted.

I scattered the junk food across my bed. I gathered up all the junk food from my hiding places and threw it in the fire, too. I'm not going to lie. It was one of the hardest things I ever had to do. I loved eating, but I needed my family back and nothing was going to get in my way.

CHAPTER 5

Alex was spending the next five days with her dad and Cinnamon, and although I was all smiles and positivity about her going, it was killing me inside. I worried she would end up liking Cinnamon more than she liked me because I had the obligation as a mother to discipline her. I was sure Cinnamon was doing everything she could to get her to like her. Alex told me she hated going there, but I suspected she was just trying not to hurt my feelings. My daughter was maturing, and I was so proud of the young adult she was becoming, but I worried she would become spoiled and ungrateful, ruined by her parents splitting up. I knew I couldn't give up. I needed to fight for our family to become one again. I just needed to figure out how to get it all back. To get him to fall back in love with me.

I spent my morning at the bookstore, decorating for Halloween with pumpkins, spiders, and webs across the ceiling and down the walls. The three-foot scarecrow added so much character to the children's section. Holiday season was always a steady time at the bookstore.

I placed a black stuffed cat in the scarecrow's arms. Children loved the shop's Halloween decorations, but every year a child always stole the cat and ran around the shop.

One year, a mother chased a little girl around the store to get it back. She was so angry and embarrassed, cussing and threatening her daughter, that I was afraid I would have to call social services. At first, it was funny and my mother and I held back the laughter, but then it got a little too serious and aggressive. Another year, a little boy's parents did not seem to care at all. He would have walked out with it if I had not kneeled down and told him he had to put it back or the scarecrow would cry.

Then there was last year. The boy must have been six-years-old, and he refused to put the cat back. His dad ripped the cat in half when he yanked it out of his son's hands. The floor was covered in white stuffing. My mother was in tears from the mess, and I ended up spending half the night hand-sewing the cat back together. It wasn't just a cat to my mother; it was the cat my father had given to her the first Halloween they shared at the bookstore. My mother used to love Halloween more than any other holiday until he passed away.

I patted the cat's head and rubbed my finger along the incision across its torso to make sure it was still stitched tight. Flashes of my father's smiling face on the boat as he drank his pop, the wind blowing the stray hairs from his face, were vivid in my mind. He loved the city of Side Lake and the chain of lakes we spent most of our summers cruising as a family. Out of nowhere, the pain in the pit of my gut brought me to my knees. My chest was heavy, and the air was sucked out of my lungs. My father died twenty-one years ago, but it felt like yesterday.

I took a deep breath and got to my feet, still a little dizzy ,when Maria swung the door open and scared the crap out of me. She pointed at her watch and tapped her foot with no acknowledgment of how startled I was.

"Where's my coffee?" she said with a laugh. She wrapped her arms around me, and I didn't want to let her go. I really needed this hug more than Maria realized.

I led the way to the counter to make my friend an espresso.

"So, what's new?"

I was distracted from my own thoughts by the sound of the bell jingling. My mother entered, humming a song I did not recognize with a gigantic smile spread across her tan face.

"Hello again, it's Marlene, right?"

I handed Maria her coffee and shot her an apologetic look because she could never remember Maria's name and she hired her months ago.

"Actually, it's Maria," Maria said, taking a drink of the coffee.

"You still liking it here? My daughter isn't being too bossy?"

"Not at all."

"We have literally become best friends. I'm pretty sure Maria likes books almost as much as I do," I said.

My mother raised her eyebrows and poured herself a cup of coffee. "I don't think anyone could even come close to loving books as much as you do."

I couldn't argue. That was probably true.

"What can I say, it's the best way to travel wherever you want without having to take a plane," I said.

"True that," Maria said. "I have five kids at home, so I don't think I'll be doing much traveling in the next eighteen or so years."

We all laughed.

"Val acts like she has five kids and weights on her legs. I

keep telling her she needs to go out and do something. She's too young to wear baggy shirts and give up sex." She turned to meet Maria's gaze. "Five kids, huh? How old are they?"

"My Bella is the oldest, she's fourteen, Lizzy is twelve, Tim is eight, Jessica is six, and Mikey is two."

"How are you still sane? Please tell me that your husband helps?"

"Well, it depends on what you mean by helps. After all, isn't it the woman's job to cook and clean and do laundry?" She paused. "My husband comes home after a long day of working at the mines and sits down in his recliner, saying he just needs a minute to relax. I let it go for a while because I was a stay-at-home mom, but soon enough was enough. I told him he needed to help me raise the kids and clean around the house. He didn't take me seriously until I dumped a cold bucket of water over his head when he fell asleep on that damn lazy boy."

We gasped. She never told me she did that. I was impressed.

"I like this girl. I did a really great job hiring you," my mother said.

"Right?" I had to agree. It surprised me as much as it did her, I guess.

The image of throwing a cold bucket of ice on Eric and Cinnamon while they were all cozy, snuggling in my bed, made me perk up. Of course, I would never do something like that, but the thought of it was appealing.

"Anyway, my brother owns the new gym in town. I was just telling Val about it yesterday."

"I'm not sure this town needs another gym, but that's great," my mother said in a dismissive tone.

Maria didn't seem to notice.

"Opening day was such a hit, and I have to tell you guys, Calorie Counters went over better than expected. I really feel like maybe I can lose some weight and feel more like a woman and less like a mother of five, you know. You are more than welcome to come sometime, Carol."

"Thanks, but gyms aren't really for me. So, about that bucket of ice water," she said.

"Oh yeah. So anyway, I poured a bucket of ice water on that recliner. That got his attention. I told him I wanted to work again part time and have a life outside the house, but it didn't happen right away, of course. I was just testing him until I saw the opening here. This was exactly what I was looking for. He understood, and he respected me for it. Best decision I ever made, but I felt a little guilty about the way I went about it."

"I think it's funny," my mother said.

This was the most talkative I'd seen her in a long time. Maria had that way about her. She somehow brought out the best in people.

"Some people choose to get divorced when they are mad, but not me. I taught Mark a lesson he will never forget," Maria said with a laugh. "He still isn't father of the year, but he's getting a lot better."

I envied that kind of confidence. I thought of myself as more of a pushover, which made people more eager to walk all over me.

"You need to teach our girl here a lesson about how to handle men. She gave up on her marriage and let some skinny little twenty-something play house with him."

"Mom!" And she was back to her old self. Ugh.

How could my mother say that about me? She had no filter. First the sex comment from her, now this? She did not know when to stop.

"Oh, come on, Val," she said. She turned to Maria. "She never does a thing for herself and she needs to get laid."

"Mom! I'm serious. That is enough."

She was so embarrassing.

She turned her attention to Maria, then back to me. "She's so defensive. Anyway, a gym membership is just what you need, my dear. Go with her, it'll be a nice stress reliever. Tell Eric to eat his heart out. He will be so jealous when you get all skinny and hot. Trust me, it'll work."

Maria put her hand on my arm. "She's right. Show him he made a mistake, but do it for you and don't take him back."

Although I hated to admit it, they had a point. I intended to work out these last few years, but I always had an excuse and never took the time. Would people stare at me or laugh when they saw me in a gym, so overweight, and with my fat flopping around in all directions? I was glad I could go with someone closer to my size, like Maria. She understood how I felt.

"Fine, I'll try it, but I'm not making any promises."

My mother gave me a tight squeeze. "I'm so proud of you. You won't regret it. I may have to get a gym membership myself so I can keep you on track."

"So does this mean you will go to the meeting with me tonight, then?"

Maria seemed so comfortable in her own skin. I could take a lesson or two from her.

I avoided mirrors and scales, and went for treats after stressful days or when I was lonely and depressed. Ben and Jerry's never let me down and always made me feel so much better, at least for a little while. Ok, so I was nowhere near picky, and I loved almost all junk food. Sure, later on I would feel like I had a brick in my gut, but it was well worth it.

"I'll try it, okay?"

"Yes! I hate going there alone. I'm so excited you're coming with me. You'll love it, I promise."

I immediately regretted making the promise. I wanted to

go home after work and eat chips and chocolate chip cookies while binge watching Netflix. Now it would have to wait.

Maria adjusted her glasses and smiled my way when my mother disappeared without a goodbye.

"I'm sure this isn't easy for you, what you are going through. I want to let you know it means a lot that you are coming with me. I am by far the heaviest woman in Calorie Counters, and it means so much to have a friend by my side."

"I'm excited to try it, but I can't promise you this will be my new routine or anything."

"I get it. I feel the same way. If it wasn't for my brother, I probably wouldn't be going at all," Maria said. "But it was so much better than I thought. You really will love it."

I doubted it. "Well, let's move the children's books to the new area over there," I said. "I set up the table and puzzles so they can have more room to run around. I think the parents will be grateful they are no longer by the bakery when we have free donuts and cookies. Talk about a sugar high."

Maria laughed. "My kids go crazy when they have sugar. I was thinking, and if you don't want to, I understand, but what do you think about maybe having a coloring contest to get more kids to come in?"

"That's a great idea. You can be in charge of it, if you'd like. Just let me know the rules. We can make posters and take them to the elementary schools to spread the word to more kids and parents. We can have prizes. Libraries are always working with us to help get children reading more. Hanging their pictures around the store would be a sure way to get them in here with their parents."

"My mother doesn't always make the best decisions," I said, grabbing a notebook out of the drawer and handing it to her. "But hiring you was the best decision she ever made. What would I do without you?"

She grabbed the notebook to write her ideas. "You'd probably drink a lot less coffee and eat more cookies."

Maria spent the day reorganizing the kids' section. She was a good worker and did not need a constant pat on the back, which left time for me to get lost in my work.

Before closing, I went to see the final masterpiece of Maria's hard work. I was impressed with her creativity. "You did such a good job. What a productive day. The kids are going to love the new section with toys and games, and I can't wait to see their pictures up on the walls."

She printed off pictures of Disney characters and a list of prizes, such as Barbies, board games, and Legos. She even drew out the paper to put in the cubbies to explain the rules to their parents and teachers.

Maria winked. "Not as much as their parents will love to see them all excited about buying their kids' books in this gorgeous bookstore. You about ready to go?" She said, putting her purse over her shoulder and searching for her keys.

I hesitated, then came out with it. "I have to admit, I'm a little nervous about going to the meeting and stepping foot in a gym for the first time in a very long time."

Maria sat up straight in her chair. "You don't have to be nervous. Trust me, no one cares, and they are all so nice, you'll see."

I stared at my coffee cup and ran my finger across the ridges. My mother gave me the cup when I was about ten, back when my father was alive. In my mind, I referred to it as the before. When he died, my mother pretty much died with him. Every time I tried to bring him up, she would give me an angry look and change the subject. Like, how dare you?

My mother used to hum around the kitchen while she cooked dinner, and my father would slap her lightly on the bottom with a towel when he thought no one was looking.

She would squeal until he eventually caught her and kissed her. I don't think they knew I was watching, but I was. It was so cute. I missed the way my mother beamed when she was around him. After all the years they had been married, how did they still have that spark until the day he died? I wanted that. I wanted that with Eric.

"I've kind of let myself go, you know? It sounds dumb, but it makes me feel ..."

"Makes you feel?"

"Exposed. Like everyone is going to see right through me." I looked down at my oversized body and pinched my stomach. "This is hard for me to say, but I don't know when this happened."

Maria's face fell. "You want to know something? You aren't alone. I feel the same way. The women in this group are just like us. Sure, some are actually pretty normal-sized, but in their heads they feel fat. They are fat for them. No one is going to judge you, I promise. I'd kick their butt if they did."

I wiped my eyes, feeling a little over-dramatic.

"Okay, but if I feel uncomfortable, you won't ask me to go back, right?"

Maria nodded and took my hand. "You just say the word, and I will never mention it again."

"Okay, but I'm holding you to that."

CHAPTER 6

I slid behind Maria as we walked through the main doors to the gym. I'm not really sure why I hesitated to be seen. Everyone was there for the same reason, but still I was embarrassed to step into the gym at my weight. I felt like a fraud and I worried everyone would see me for who I was.

The minute I walked in that door, I regretted coming. My heart was throbbing and my fight-or-flight response kicked in.

A few women in their sixties or seventies chatted at tables in the open room. Maria stopped to say hello to them, but I slipped past them to a table at the back. I took a seat and put my phone in front of my face so I did not accidentally make eye contact and feel forced to engage in small talk.

"Hey, don't you work at that bookstore downtown?"

Now I had to look up, or that would just be plain rude. My cover had been blown by a skinny twenty-something woman who was tall and beautiful. Why was she even here? To make the rest of us feel bad about ourselves?

I crossed my arms over my mid-section so she hopefully

could not see the extra pounds I carried as Maria joined us at the table. But I always lit up when asked about the bookstore.

"Yes, I do."

"I love that place. I read little myself, but I always pick out books for my friends for Christmas or their birthdays. I'm Saffron, by the way." She extended her hand, and I shook it.

I forced a smile. "Val." I never saw her at the bookstore, but it was always possible she went there once when I wasn't there, or maybe she was just trying to make conversation.

"Saffron," Maria said with a nod. It was more of a statement than a hello. I got the vibe she knew who Saffron was, but was not really a fan of hers.

Saffron dropped her sweatshirt to save a chair and excused herself to use the restroom. As if it was going to be tough to fend off all the people who wanted to join us.

I leaned close to Maria. "Why is she in Calorie Counters? She doesn't have any weight to lose. Do you know her?"

"Who knows? I've known Saffron for quite some time, and she seems to do everything for attention. She says when she looks in the mirror, she doesn't see a thin girl staring back at her. I wish I had the same problem and didn't see a heavy girl staring back at me."

"Right? Me too."

A woman came in and the room quieted with her presence.

"Hello everyone. My name is Linda Jones, for those of you who don't know me, and welcome to those of you who are joining us here for the first time."

Linda had white-blonde hair and a pixie cut, and weighed about one hundred and twenty pounds. Energy buzzed off her.

"I am so glad you are all here. Today happens to be my sixtieth birthday. Many people ask me, Linda, how do you have so much energy? You may be thinking, why would this woman tell us her age? Realistically, you may think, why is this skinny woman teaching a Calorie Counter class? She doesn't understand what it is like to be unhappy in her skin. Well people, there is a lot about me you don't know. We all tend to cast judgment upon each other. The truth is, I wasn't always thin. Counting calories and practicing techniques you will learn here really do work. The secret is you have to learn to love your body and love yourself. That's it."

It was as if Linda could read my mind.

Linda smiled at the group, turned to the side, and did a roundoff into a handspring. Everyone gasped and applauded her gymnast skills. We all got out of our chairs, and she responded with a curtsey.

Once we sat down, Linda did a back flip, and the room's response was even louder.

I was no longer holding my stomach. All eyes were on the entertainer, and my hand covered my mouth in shock. I glanced at Maria, but she did not seem surprised at all. Like it was normal for her to see an older woman doing handsprings and backflips.

"How many of you would have bet I couldn't do that? I'm sixty, right? Well, now that I have your attention, how about if I told you I used to weigh one hundred and eighty pounds until five years ago? It's true. I practiced good health, but I indulged too much in unhealthy food, too. It's a balance that I had to learn the hard way."

Maria turned toward me and smiled. I gave her an incredulous raise of my eyebrow in response.

"How did I get so big when I was just five foot three, you ask? I was a binge eater. I had social anxiety, and I wore baggy clothes thinking that no one would notice how huge my ass was."

Everyone laughed, some taken aback by her choice of words.

"Look around this room. Every person here has a story you can't see. Look at the person next to you. They might have lost their husband, mother, or a child. Maybe they have financial problems, are going through a divorce, are in chronic pain, or maybe they have just been diagnosed with cancer or are recovering from a diagnosis. Some may have PTSD, maybe they were abused as a child, or maybe they are a victim of abuse now. The point is, we don't know what the person next to us is going through, no matter how big their smile or how perfect their body.. How many people walked in this door today and wanted to run right out because they felt like they didn't belong?"

A few people raised their hands, but I slouched into my chair, feeling my face flush hot. I felt exposed, like she could read all my thoughts. I felt alone on my binge eating. I never thought a skinny person could have had a binge-eating addiction. The thought made my head spin with questions.

"The first step to being happy isn't posting all over social media, pretending to be happy. It's not about being the perfect mother or the perfect wife. It is loving you for you. Don't compare yourself to others, that's a dead-end street, ladies. Don't do what other people expect you to do. No, that is the key to having a terrible life. Losing weight is as much internal as external. You need to believe in yourself and feed your body with healthy foods it needs, one small bite at a time. Many of us are so busy taking care of everyone else, we forget to take care of ourselves. Your family and friends will be so much happier if you take care of you first. I compare it to the flight attendant who tells you if the air pressure is low on a plane to secure your mask before helping someone next to you, including a child. It seems selfish when someone else so dependent and vulnerable needs to breathe, too, but what good are you if you're passed out next to them? Cue in on the visuals, meditate, take time for yourself before you give everything to someone else."

I leaned over to Maria. "I love this lady. Did she do the same speech yesterday?"

"No, it was just a meet and greet day. She talked about the program and answered questions."

"I really have to use the restroom. Would it be terrible if I got up right now? I hate to miss a minute of her speech, but I don't think I can wait. Too much coffee."

"Not at all. Bathrooms are out the door to the right, down the hall."

I shut the door as quietly as I could, careful not to draw too much attention to myself. I walked at a fast pace to the bathroom, looking behind me to make sure I closed the door all the way and when I turned around, I crashed right into someone.

"I'm so sorry, are you okay?"

I looked up from the ground and into his familiar eyes.

"It's you," I said. How was this even possible?

A smile spread across his face, showing his perfect white teeth. He patted the sweat off his forehead with a towel. "And it's you. I'm so glad I ran into you again."

"Um... yeah. Thanks again for saving my life. I'm in the middle of a class so I really must be going."

I did not want to stay for another minute and relive the embarrassment. If Linda was not so inspiring and entertaining, I would have run right out the door.

The rest of the class was just as inspirational. Linda had everyone expressing their struggles and why they were at the meeting. My face grew hot and my palms sweaty when the spotlight shone on me. My hands shook, and I had to sit on them to keep them still.

"Hi, I'm Valarie Renyalds and I really didn't want to come here today, to be honest. My friend, Maria, convinced me to tag along, and although I came kicking and screaming, I'm very glad I came."

My voice shook with each word and I was running out of breath, but I pushed myself to put it all out there like Linda directed, and it felt good. I didn't feel the judgment in this group like I normally did. I felt only support.

Everyone laughed at my honest introduction, which made my nerves calm down.

"Tell us about why you are here," Linda said.

"I rarely put myself out there like this, but for some reason, I really want to share. I married and had my daughter when I was quite young. My husband decided he didn't love me anymore one day, out of the blue, because I let myself get this way." I would not tell them I caught him with his secretary.

"He told me he wasn't attracted to me anymore. I was devastated. I moved out of our home and into an old house in a scary neighborhood while he continues to live at the house on the lake that is technically mine, but I just can't seem to kick him out. I've been broken and depressed for quite a while, and I needed this push to work on me for once, so thank you Maria for not taking no for an answer."

Everyone applauded, and the laughter put me at ease.

Linda smiled sweetly, which made my confidence rise.

"So, tell us what your struggle is. When did you start criticizing your body?"

I took a deep breath. Where to begin. "I'm really not sure. I never thought about it. I guess I always did. The first time I remember was when I was a teenager. I had big legs and thighs, and I never thought I was as pretty as the other girls. I look back and think about how thin I was then, and I didn't even know it. I started to feel more comfortable with my body when I was fifteen or sixteen, but then ... well, it's hard to talk about."

"You don't have to share what happened, but it'll probably inspire everyone here. This is a safe place," Maria said. She put her hand on my forearm.

My vision blurred. I looked up at the ceiling to stop my tears from watering.

"I was in a boating accident with my father when I was sixteen. It wasn't just any accident, he died that day." I paused. I knew I should stop talking, but it felt so good to let it out. I didn't want to hold it in any longer. "I started overeating and hating myself. I'd lay in bed at night and wonder why him? Why not me?"

"Oh sweetheart, I know that wasn't easy. Sharing that with us is a huge start to your healing, and we are all so proud of you, aren't we group?"

Everyone started cheering and stood up to applaud me with sympathetic expressions on their faces. It touched my heart. It was my first meeting, and I had already grown leaps and bounds.

"Holding on to something like this is why we have a hard time losing those extra pounds. It's completely normal after what you've been through," Linda said.

After everyone sat down, I realized Nicholas was sitting against the wall, and he had stood to clap, too. He heard everything I said, and he must have thought I was just a hot mess. My stomach was sick at the thought. When did he sneak in here, and why do I keep running into him?

"That isn't easy to follow, but I'm Nicholas and I started this gym because I wanted to move closer to my family. When my mother approached me about having Calorie Counters at my new gym, I wasn't sure it was a good idea," Nicholas said.

Mother? Was Linda Nicholas's mother? Was this his gym? I looked at Nicholas, Linda, and back to Nicholas, trying to find some similarity between the two.

"But he listened to me," Linda said.

"I did, and I'm so glad I did. To show our appreciation for giving us a chance, we would like to offer two free personal training classes at my gym. Just sign this book on your way out, and we will set you up. You won't regret it, I promise. It's another way to help you on your journey to getting your health back."

He continued to talk, but I could not focus on a thing he was saying because I kept getting lost in his eyes. Every time he locked eyes with me, I would look away, but I'm sure it was obvious I couldn't stop staring at him. He saved my life, and it was understandable that I felt a connection to him, right? He watched me shove food into my mouth until I choked, and now he heard my story. I felt exposed, sitting there naked in front of him as he spoke.

Memories of the incident made me want to run to McDonald's and get a double cheeseburger and fries. Maybe an apple pie and some chicken nuggets. That would make me feel so much better. Sure, it wouldn't erase the events of these last few days, but it would make me happy. Food was the cure all, even if I regretted it when my stomach swelled up, and I was sick for the rest of the day.

He was shaking everyone's hands and saying hello as we exited the room.

I tried to slide past him and avoid another embarrassing moment by going out the other door, but Maria pulled me in. "Nicholas, this is my friend, Val, from the bookstore. Val, this is my brother, Nicholas."

Brother? How could I forget her brother owned the gym? It was all making sense now. Linda was her mother, too?

"We've met," Nicholas said.

Crap. I looked away.

"Really?" Maria looked confused.

"Yeah, I ran into him in the hallway on my way to the

restroom," I said, trying to clarify that I didn't want him to say another word.

Nicholas locked eyes with me and grinned.

"Yeah, I wasn't watching where I was going," he said.

The all too familiar flush crept across my cheeks and warmed my face.

He shook my hand. "But it is great to meet you officially. Val, is it?" He pushed the bridge of my glasses back on my nose, catching me off-guard.

His touch was electric and made my heart flutter.

"You, too, I really should be going. Nice to meet you," I said.

"The pleasure is mine. I really hope you come back again soon."

I turned to Maria once we were on the highway. "So, Linda is your mom?"

"Yes, did I forget to mention that? And Nicholas is technically my cousin, but my mom adopted him when he was a teenager. It's a long story, but he sure seems friendly with you."

"Oh, stop. I'm not interested, but they both seem really nice. Especially your mom. I love her energy."

I parked next to Maria's car in front of the bookstore on Howard Street.

"You would think she's putting on a show, but she really has a lot of positive energy. She has a nasty side though, it doesn't come out often, but watch out when it does."

Nicholas adopted? Linda had a mean side? It was too much for me to wrap my mind around.

CHAPTER 7

After his speech at Calorie Counters, Nicholas had a hard time focusing on anything other than Valarie's beautiful brown eyes and the way her glasses were placed a little too far down her nose. He never expected to have instant chemistry with a woman he just met. Then again, he never expected to give a woman the Heimlich maneuver in the middle of a parking lot, either. Thank goodness he went grocery shopping when he did. What if he had not been there to save her? He shook away the horrible thought. The way she blushed so innocently when she ran into him at his gym. He wanted to get to know her better, because there was something about her innocence that left him curious.

"Hi, I'm home."

Regan walked in the door, a huge grin spread across her face. "Guess what?"

He flashed a close-lipped smile at her. What was going on? His daughter usually came home miserable after transferring to the Hibbing high school. She had a hard time fitting in and was always sulking around, probably thinking if she were sad enough, she could get him to move back to Grand Rapids.

She was popular and confident in Grand Rapids, but here she had to work for it because no one knew her yet. He knew it was only a matter of time before everyone loved her here, too. She was outgoing and beautiful, and she was a natural leader.

"What?"

She set her backpack on the table. "Coach is letting me swim the five hundred in the meet tomorrow night."

"That's great, honey. I knew you'd get there. Did you eat?"

"Yeah, I had half of Alex's sandwich on my way home."

"Alex?"

She shot her dad an annoyed look. "Alex is a girl, Dad. She's on the swim team with me."

"I knew it wouldn't take you long to fit in here."

She rolled her eyes and slammed her bedroom door, but not before saying, "I'm not trying to fit in. You don't get me at all."

He shook his head. Now that was the attitude he was used to. He did not know how to understand 'teen.'

He made a cup of coffee and sat on the couch, clicking through the channels. He found a good movie on HBO.

He heard someone at the door and got up, knowing exactly who it was. He smiled and looked down as his father came rolling in. He had the ramp installed outside to give his father some independence. The move was a big change, but it was great to be closer to him now. And his father was happy they finally made the move to Hibbing. He came over almost daily.

His father never asked for help, even when he needed it. He spoiled Nicholas a lot growing up and even now, always put him first. He insisted it made him happy to feel needed, and he needed him a lot after his biological mother died from cancer when Nicholas was just a child.

His father never wanted to talk about it, and he gave Nicholas his blessing to call Linda "mom" when she adopted him years ago. After his father got into some criminal trouble, he told Nicholas it would be best for him to let Linda adopt him. His father carried a lot of guilt for going to jail and wanted the best for him, and Linda was the perfect choice.

"Where's my granddaughter?"

Nicholas smiled. "In her dungeon."

"Dungeon, huh? Does she know her grandfather is here?"

"I can tell her if you'd like, but if you aren't a teenage boy or have a new cell phone to give her, I don't think she'll come out. Nothing against you."

His father took his hand, making Nicholas turn around.

"Don't let her get to you. She's a teen, and it's a teen's job to make their parents crazy."

He washed a pepper and tomato. "How can this be my little girl? Want an omelet?"

His father nodded and rolled around to the other side of the breakfast bar.

"Nicky, Regan is a young girl growing up without a mother, and she's at a new school and trying to fit in all over again. Just give her some time."

He stopped cutting and took in what his father was saying. "Do you think it was too much? Moving here, I mean?"

"No. No. No. Your family is here. I am here. Why? Are you having regrets?"

"We came here to open up a gym and to be closer to family, but it hasn't been easy on Regan or me. It brings back a lot of terrible memories, you know?"

"That is in the past. We don't need to dig up what is long behind us," his father said.

"I know, but it isn't exactly something I can forget."

"I know. I just never want to talk about that day again. I've done everything to forget it myself."

"Me too," Nicholas said.

"How's the gym going?" his father said, in a deliberate attempt to change the subject.

Nicholas grabbed the eggs and whisked them. "It's coming along. You should check it out. It is your investment, you know. It's everything I dreamed it would be, with thanks to you."

"I think the gym is a great opportunity for you and Regan. Has she been helping out?"

He brought the bowl over to the oven and set it down while he turned on the stovetop. "She plans on working there after swimming is over. Between swimming and homework, it's a little tough, but it'll be over in November."

His dad rolled himself over to the table and watched him as he cooked.

"You ever think about going on a date again?"

He put the omelets on a plate and sat down next to his father at the table. "I'm not sure. How would Regan feel about that?"

"Son, look at me."

He looked up as he put a bite of his omelet in his mouth. "What?"

"Life can change in an instant, don't end up like me before you find a woman to become your partner."

"Mom loved you just as you were. You aren't that old, Dad. You have time to find someone else, you know. Although you probably should have dated a long time ago." As soon as he mentioned her, he wanted to take the words back. It always upset his father when he mentioned her. It was almost as if the thought of her was still too much for him.

His father took a big bite and moaned loudly, swallowing and staring at the ceiling in pleasure before he finally answered him. "There is only one true love for me, and it won't be long before we are together again."

"I guess."

"Linda helped fill in as your mother when you needed a parent because I couldn't be there for you when you needed me. I don't know what I would have done if she hadn't swooped in and taken you in as her own. Your mother would have wanted it that way. She always loved Linda." He sighed. "Regan didn't have the same luxury of a backup mom after her mother left. What a devil she was. But you did well, son."

Nicholas had struggled a lot when Regan's mom left them. Regan was only a toddler at the time, and it was devastating for both of them. He had to be the mother and the father. He worried she would grow up blaming herself for her mother's absence, and he was doing everything he could to make sure that did not happen.

He did the dishes after his father left. He stared out the window above his sink and thought about Valarie and her silky, long brown hair. She seemed so broken deep down. He wanted to know everything about her. She was such a mystery to him.

They held the swim meet at the Hibbing pool the next day. Nicholas got there early because Regan's swim cap broke at practice, and she was practically in tears when she called to ask him to bring one. Her other team swim cap was at home, and she was too nervous to ask the other girls if they had an extra one.

"Dad, please don't go," she had said when he brought it to her.

How could he not stay and watch warm-ups when his teen daughter begged him to stay Even though he needed to get back and clean the gym since the cleaner he hired only showed up when it was convenient for her? He would fire her, but she had two little kids, and he felt bad. Every time he tried to talk to her about doing her job and showing up on time, she would start crying and he chickened out. That was why he never dated. He had a weakness when women cried.

Other parents began making their way to seats on the bleachers within the next hour. A few chairs were set up behind the railing. It might be easier to see the complete pool from there. He got up to move, but saw Valarie walk in with her dark hair in a messy bun. He stopped in his tracks and stared at her. She adjusted her glasses and made her way to one of the metal chairs he was eyeing up. She would think he was following her, and it might even creep her out if he sat there now.

She was looking around the bleachers behind her. Something caught her eye and her face fell. Were there tears in her eyes? He could not tell from so far away, but her expression was definitely an unhappy one.

He turned his head to see who she was looking at, but there were several people sitting in that general direction. He moved down two bleachers and looked around before zoning in on her again. She was leaning against the railing and set her purse down next to her chair. She pushed her glasses back on her nose and stared straight ahead.

He loved the natural bronze color of her skin. Who was she here to watch swim? Could she have a daughter on the swim team? She did not look old enough to have a teenager.

Val turned to a teenage girl running up the stairs in her parka and swim cap. They were deep in conversation when the girl leaned over and waved at someone in the stands, but it looked like a forced wave and a fake smile.

He turned to look. A man and woman were standing up and making their way toward them. They talked for just a minute. The man and woman sat closer to Val, just two rows behind her, and she did not seem happy about it.

Val went to sit on the chair after the swimmer left and missed. She landed on the floor beside it. The metal chair folded up and made a loud echo throughout the pool area as it bounced off the floor. She had the attention of everyone in the room.

He had to do something. It would break his heart to just sit there and watch the scene unfold. He ran down as fast as he could and put his hand out in front of her. He heard the man and woman laughing and snorting behind him. She surprised him when she did not take his hand and instead just sat there with tears in her eyes.

He kneeled down. "Are you okay, Val?"

She started laughing at herself. "What are you doing here? This is so embarrassing. Is everyone looking at me?"

He glanced at the audience. They were all staring in their direction. Mostly with looks of worry on their faces.

"No. Not at all."

She sat up, holding her head. "Liar."

"Don't worry about them. Are you okay?"

"Yeah, I'm fine, my ego is a little bruised though."

She put her hands back to get up and struggled. She tried again and failed.

"Let me help you," he said.

"Give me your sweatshirt." She held out her hand.

He took it off and handed it to her, unsure of why she wanted it.

She tied it around her waist and this time she held out her hand for him to help her up. Once on her feet, she ran out of the pool area, and he followed close behind.

People behind them were laughing again. "She's so fat,"

the woman said. "Did you see she couldn't even get up? I can't believe you married that woman. What were you thinking?"

It took everything he had not to scream at the woman and tell her to grow up, but he didn't want to embarrass Val any more by calling this woman out for her unacceptable behavior in front of all the other parents. Instead, he followed Val and hoped she did not hear the nasty woman. Val hid behind a wall in the mezzanine outside the doors. He made his way up a ramp. Her back was against the wall, her head in her hands.

"We have to quit meeting this way," she said, half-laughing and half-crying as she lifted her head.

"I know. We should really go on a proper date," he said.

She shook her head. "That was so embarrassing. But if I don't go back in there, my daughter is going to be so mad at me."

He sat down next to her on the floor. "It wasn't that bad, really."

"How is it I've never seen you before, and now I see you everywhere? And you always seem to run into me when I'm doing the most embarrassing things."

He wiped away the tear under her eye with his thumb. "I'd like to say you are really entertaining."

She did not seem shocked by his action.

"My ex-husband," she whispered.

"What?"

She crossed her arms. "That guy and woman behind me in there saying the cruel things about me were my ex-husband and the woman he left me for."

"Oh, wow."

She caught him off guard, and he wasn't sure what to say to that. He was not good with woman or knowing how to comfort them. But it was different with Val. He could not seem to stay away from her in her time of need.

"That woman he's with is pretty horrible to me, and I don't understand because he left me for her. Shouldn't I be the one who is mean to her and not the other way around?"

He put his arm around her. "She's just jealous."

She laughed and moved over enough so his arm would no longer be around her. "She's jealous of me? Oh, please. He chose her over me. She loves rubbing it in my face. I can't help it, it bothers me so much. I love him. Is that sad?"

His heart hurt just a little at the thought. "How about this? Let's go out there together and forget this ever happened. Let's cheer on our girls and not think about them, okay? Maybe we can shut her up and make him jealous."

She seemed to be intrigued by his words. "Okay?"

She stood up and turned toward him. She extended her hand out to his. He looked at her curiously.

"It's my turn to help you up. Oh, and I'm going to have to keep this sweatshirt because I ripped my pants when I fell."

He loved her honesty, and it left him laughing under his breath at her comment. She was just so real. He took her hand and jumped to his feet.

"The sweatshirt is all yours, under one condition."

"What's that?"

"That you come back to my gym again and sign up for a personal training session with me."

"I don't know about that. I'm not exactly the exercising type."

"What is the exercising type exactly? Come on. Please?"

"Okay, fine. Now lets go in there and get this over with."

She led the way into the muggy air of the upper deck, and they took a seat as far away from her ex as they could.

CHAPTER 8

"My brother the hero! I'm so glad he gave you his sweatshirt or that could have been an even bigger disaster," Maria said after she heard the whole story. "What a horrible woman. I can't believe she made those remarks to you. I would love to give that mistress of his a piece of my mind."

I told her about the incident at the swim meet, but left out the part about binge eating in my car and that her brother saved my life.

"He really was the hero. Do you know what he did? During intermission, Cinnamon walked past us to go to the concession stand, and she asked me if I wanted something to eat. I thought that was a friendly gesture and maybe it was her way of calling a truce, but when I told her no thank you, she came back with a handful of candy bars. She said Eric told her about my eating disorder. Can you believe the nerve?"

Maria's jaw dropped. "What a horrible woman. I hope you threw them at her."

"Of course not. I don't want her to think I care. Anyway,

your brother was pissed. After the meet, we were standing in the hallway, waiting for our girls and as soon as Eric and Cinnamon turned the corner, Nicholas kissed me all hot and heavy to make Eric jealous. I have to admit your brother is one heck of a good kisser."

Maria pursed her lips. "He what?"

I waved her away. "No, it wasn't like that. It was sweet, and it sure pissed off Eric. You should have seen his face." I left out the part about how I had a hard time thinking about anything other than the kiss since, but most likely just because it had been so long since I kissed anyone else. The kiss was so passionate and firm, electrifying and, well, perfect. He made the kiss look so believable, he even had me fooled, but I wasn't about to tell Maria that.

"Are you sure?"

"Maria, your brother and I are just friends, trust me. It was all part of my plan to get Eric back."

"Why do you want him back? I just don't understand. After everything he did to you."

"Don't judge. Just be supportive, okay? I know he screwed up, but he really loves me. He's having a mid-life crisis."

"I'll tell you what, if Mark went through this so-called mid-life crisis and was screwing another woman, I would kick him to the curb so fast. Eric doesn't deserve you. You could do so much better. I just don't want to see you get hurt again, that's all."

I was not about to get into this argument with Maria. She would learn to love Eric, eventually. It was only a matter of time before we were back together. "So, have you heard from my mother?"

"She should be in any minute. She called when you were with a customer earlier. She mentioned something about a flat tire. She's fine, but she was waiting for Triple A to get there."

"Is she okay? Did she say where she was coming from?"

Maria put a hand up. "Nope, not a word."

"You didn't ask?"

"Don't shoot the messenger, I just answered the phone."

I didn't mean to come off angry, but my mother was being so mysterious right now, and I was worried about her. "I'm sorry."

"I think a little workout and a Calorie Counter meeting will do you some good. It's been a rough couple of days. What do you think?"

"Couple of days? Try months, years even."

The gym was packed with people. I sat at the back table with Maria and Saffron again.

Nicholas was nowhere to be seen, and I should have been happy about that, but his kiss lingered on my lips.

"So, did you guys hear about the motivational speaker coming to The Cities next weekend?" Up in Northern Minnesota, we referred to the Twin Cities of Minneapolis and St. Paul as The Cities.

"It's a huge Calorie Counters event, and we all get in free. Live music, a workshop, and everything. You guys better go."

Saffron was staring at her phone as she talked, not glancing at Maria or me. More evidence of her self-centered behavior, I suspected.

"Yeah, I heard all about it. There's going to be free food and samples. You are going, aren't you Val?"

I almost made an excuse and lied, saying I could not go because of Alex, but she was with her father that weekend. I thought about telling them I was busy, but they would ask what I was doing, and I would have to say sitting at home reading or cleaning my house.

Instead, I said, "Yes, sounds like fun."

Maria jumped up in her chair. "Well, now there's no

excuse for me not to go. I'll tell Mark he better not be working overtime or getting his deer stand ready because this is my weekend. November is like a blackout month in my house, so I'm not backing down in October."

Saffron finally looked up and acknowledged us. "It's going to be so much fun. I can't wait. What will I wear?"

I exchanged an annoyed glance with Maria. Her sentences always started with I. She had to be perfect. She told us she never left home without heels on. We were sick and tired of hearing her talk about how hard it was not to buy another pair of shoes. She was in her mid-twenties and thin. Yet, she constantly complained about being overweight in class. It was sickening for the rest of us that easily had fifty pounds, if not more, on her.

"I'm sure you'll find something. You have the best clothes," I said, just to be nice.

"I do have great clothes, but I need to lose another five pounds or I won't look good in any of them." Saffron leaned in and we followed. "I weighed in at one hundred and thirty-five pounds today," she whispered as she looked around to make sure no one was listening.

As if anyone cared.

"Wow, that's about as much as one of my thighs weighs," Maria said.

"Yeah, we weigh way more than that, and you're making us feel self-conscious," I said.

"I said nothing about you two. Stop acting like you are the only ones who hurt." Saffron turned away from us, like we were attacking her. What a joke. Should we feel so sorry for her when here we weighed close to sixty-five more pounds than her?

"I'm sorry, I didn't mean to come off so rude," I said. Had I seriously hurt Saffron's feelings? The issue was not how much we weighed, but how we felt inside, according to

Linda. I had a hard time understanding this, because I felt great until I looked in the mirror or stepped on the scale. It wasn't until Eric told me he was not attracted to me anymore that I really looked at myself for who I'd become. The thought made me want to stop at Sunrise Bakery on my way home and indulge in some delicious cinnamon rolls or donuts, just not cream puffs again. They were no longer my comfort food after the flashbacks of what I imagined I looked like in the parking lot with Cool Whip all over my shirt, choking on my drug of choice.

"Girls, I may have to sneak out of here early. That trainer keeps looking at me, and I just can't help myself," Saffron said, as if the conflict between us never happened.

We watched as she made her way out of the meeting and into the weight room.

"Who do you think she's talking about?"

Maria shook her head. "There are a lot of trainers here. I'm sure Saffron will find a way into their pants and maybe she will lose a pound, chasing them around." We both laughed, but went quiet as Linda came in.

"It's so great to see you all back here today. Let's share how our eating and exercise went yesterday. How about you, Val?"

"Well, I had to work and then my daughter had a swim meet, so I didn't really eat the best, I guess. I tried to, but it was quite a struggle. Also, I ran into my ex and his new girlfriend."

Saffron came back in and sat down. "What did I miss? He left. Can you believe it? I'm sure he's just playing hard to get."

Linda walked closer to our table. "Valarie was just sharing with us her frustrations with healthy eating. How are you doing, Saffron? Would you like to share with us today?"

"I think I'm going to ask out one trainer here. He kept looking at me earlier."

Everyone looked away with annoyed glances and eye rolling.

"I started coming to this group because I have struggled with an eating disorder my whole life, like Val here."

Why was she copying me? Saffron was nothing like me, and she had never been fat a day in her life. She was just trying to get attention again.

"I wrote down all my calories yesterday, worked out for an hour at the gym here, but I still don't see any results. I'm not sure if it's because I hate to sweat so maybe I don't work as hard as I should, but it wasn't a good day."

I caught Maria glaring at Saffron while she talked.

"Okay, thanks for sharing," Linda said, cutting her off.

Was Linda as annoyed with Saffron as every overweight person in the room?

"It's so much easier for everyone else to lose weight in this room than it is for me because you guys have so much extra weight to lose. When I lose weight, no one even notices. It isn't fair."

Maria placed her hand on Saffron's. "Poor you."

Everyone laughed. Saffron stared at Maria in shock and ran out the door, crying.

Linda looked displeased. "Maria, you need to apologize. We don't treat people like that in this room. I raised you better."

A woman stood up at the table in front of them. "That skinny girl was rude to all of us and she always is. She acts like we're the bad guys because we don't understand what she is going through, but we all think she doesn't belong here. She isn't even overweight." The woman next to her gave her a high five, and she sat back down with authority.

"That is the point of this class. We can't always see the struggles other people are going through. Maybe instead of judging her like you all hate when people judge you, ask her what she struggles with. We are supposed to be a family, supporting one another. She's guarded and everyone here needs to give her a chance."

Maria got up and walked out of the meeting. I followed, but Saffron was nowhere to be found.

"I know you meant well. Let's do a workout, okay? That will help. Your mom doesn't get how superficial and horrible Saffron is. She shouldn't be a part of our group, anyway."

Maria nodded. "She's a diva, that's for sure. My mom and I don't always see eye to eye on things. She fought to get skinny and in shape and I keep struggling."

We both changed and found open elliptical machines next to each other. Maria put in her ear buds. I got to a steady pace and imagined the weight falling off to stay motivated. I really needed to lose weight, and I promised myself I would not eat fast food tonight or carbs of any sort. I had a salad in the fridge with my name on it, and I was going to feed my body less and using portion control. I wanted to see the look on Eric's face when I had skinny jeans and a tight sweater on without a muffin top. I was going to lose the weight and throw it right in that slutty girlfriend's face. Then watch and laugh as Eric pushed Cinnamon to the curb and came crawling back to me.

He used to look at me with the same eagerness he now looked at Cinnamon. Every time I used to walk past him, he would playfully slap my butt.

The sex stopped ten years after we were married, but I did not notice enough to care. How bad was that? We were too tired most nights, and sometimes it was a headache or a backache, but who was I kidding? It was just an excuse.

We stopped going to bed at the same time and took turns going out when Alex was little so we could both get out of the house, just never together. I did not want someone else watching my baby, and Eric felt the same way. He seemed so content with having sex once every couple of months. Sure, he complained sometimes, but I thought he was joking. If I knew he would end up leaving me, I may have responded differently.

We had always been parents first. Was that not what we agreed on long ago? I thought we agreed, but the more I thought about it, the more I realized it was my fault our marriage had failed. Had I run him right into another woman's arms? Someone who would not deny him sex? The young gold digger?

I spotted Nicholas in the weight room. He sat on a bench and put on his shoes. He took a swig of his water bottle. His Adam's apple bobbed up and down as he drank.

He glanced in my direction and waved. I pulled my hand away from the handle on the machine to wave. In the process, I lost my balance and crashed my head against the handlebar.

He came running to my side, with Maria on my other side. I looked around to see how many people saw me crash.

"Are you okay?" Maria touched my forehead. "That looks so painful."

I began laughing uncontrollably, and they both smiled and shook their heads at me. While most people would cry, I laughed at myself so others could not beat me to it.

"I'm fine, just a little bump," I said. Did Nicholas make me this nervous? What was my problem around him?

"Let's just check you out," Nicholas said. He shone the flashlight on his phone in my eyes. "Your eyes look okay. Do you remember what happened?"

"Yes, but I wish I didn't."

"Why don't you take a walk with me," he said as he took my hand.

"We need to stop meeting like this. I really am not such a klutz, I swear."

He just laughed. "You make life interesting."

We walked around the building to get some fresh air.

"I'm thinking I'm the one bringing you bad luck," he said.

My head was throbbing, but I managed a smile. "You must really think I'm a hot mess."

"Not at all. How's the head?"

He reached over to feel my forehead, and I flinched.

"That's a huge bump. We should take you to the hospital. I had no idea how bad it was."

I took a step back. "No, no. That's, um ... an old injury. I had to have twenty-six stitches in my head when I was younger. It's been a knob ever since."

"Really? That's crazy, let me look again."

"It's fine. It happened a long time ago. It's still a little tender to the touch."

"You sure have some bad luck, you know that?"

"You're telling me," I said.

I waited for him to ask me what happened, but it never came and I was relieved. I didn't want to talk about it and relive that day again.

CHAPTER 9

"You've got to be kidding me. This is your couch?" She jumped on it. "Where did you get this piece of crap?"

I threw a pillow at Maria, who caught it after it bounced off her face.

She laughed and threw it back at me.

"Tell me how you really feel," I said.

"I'm sorry, but it's hideous."

"I bought it at a garage sale."

Maria jumped off the couch. "A garage sale in October? It's probably infested with bedbugs! Who has a garage sale in October?"

"Stop, drama queen. For your information, it belonged to a little old lady who passed away. I bought it from a customer at the bookstore. I don't plan on living here very long. I'm just giving Eric some time to think. Besides, the couch may not be much to look at, but it is comfortable."

Maria grabbed my shoulders. "You need to tell him you want your house back. He cheated on you, and he should've been the one to leave."

"I know it is mine. I'm just giving him some time, that's all."

"Time for what? He has the woman he was cheating on you with staying at your house, for goodness sake, and she's sleeping in your bed. He can have this place instead."

I held my breath. "I just feel bad since he is the one who makes all the money, you know? Plus, this is my cousin's house, and she doesn't really like him that much."

"Smart girl. You were married for how long? It's not just his money and, like you said, it is your house. Your mom bought that house for you before the two of you were married. They awarded it to you legally during your divorce. I'm not sure I can keep repeating this to you, girl. You need to get your house back."

I grabbed the broom to keep my hands busy and swept the floor. "I know. I just have a feeling I'm going to get him back. I think demanding my house isn't the way to get him back."

"Look around you. What about Alexandra? You need to stop thinking this way. Girl, you live in a horrible run-down neighborhood when you have a house on the lake, and how much are you even paying to stay here?"

"Minimal. Like I told you, this is my cousin's house. It was an investment. She just wanted someone to stay here to let the neighbors know someone is living here so no one tries to break in, like squatters."

Maria got up and put her hands on her shoulders. "Squatters?"

I laughed because I had no idea what they were until my cousin explained it to me. "They are people who find houses no one lives in and illegally break in and live in them."

"That happens? In Hibbing?"

"My cousin says it does."

Maria put her hand on my shoulder again. "Get your house back."

I'm not dumb. I knew she was right, but what was a couple more weeks? I needed some time to figure out a plan so he wouldn't have to leave, and I could be back there with him again.

I pulled her hand down. "This is my house right now, so just be supportive, okay? I want my family back."

"You're right, it's your life. I'm sorry. A nice blanket will completely uplift that couch. And I must admit, it is comfortable."

I smiled because she respected my words, even if she didn't agree with them. "Thank you."

She kissed me on the cheek. "You know I'm always going to be real with you. Now, I must get going. See you in the morning?"

I walked her out, then took two steps toward the kitchen and stopped myself from my normal routine of grabbing food after a stressful situation. I would not let food define me, not anymore. I went right to the cupboard and pulled out all the chips and chocolate chip cookies and any other junk food I could find, including muffin mix and threw them in the garbage.

I carried the garbage bag outside and put it in the dumpster where I would not be able to dig it out if I became desperate.

My neighbors were outside, working on a lawn mower. I hid behind a tree and watched them.

My cousin told me the man was a retired vet who had a stroke, so she excused the junk all over their yard. Apparently, he fixed machines for a living, but as he worked on the mower, he seemed to have a hard time speaking. The yard was full of wooden boards, old machines, shingles from the roof, and other junk. I hated looking out my kitchen window at their mess while I did the dishes every day.

The power was no longer connected to their house, and no one ever went inside the house. It all seemed a little strange, but I did not know of their struggles, and tried not to judge them. I walked back into my house, first smiling in their direction, but they never looked my way.

I whipped up an omelet with mozzarella cheese. On a normal day, I would cook a juicy cheeseburger on the grill or bake a pizza, but today I was going to respect my body and feed it what would nurture it. Linda said not to treat it like a diet because diets are not forever. Yo-Yo diets only deprived the body of what it needed, and the weight loss was only short term. Diets were to speed up weight loss for a head start on the journey to a healthy body. I wanted to do it right by eating healthy and eating less, a lot less.

For the first time in a long time, I did not feel lonely while eating by myself at the table. Nicholas's kiss hung on my mind. That kiss was not meant to be romantic, and I loved Eric.

Was Maria right? Maybe I should have insisted Eric left instead of voluntarily leaving my home, but he was the breadwinner of the family. This was all just short term. He would wake up and realize how much I did for him, wouldn't he? He had to pick his family over an affair. He just had to.

What kind of name was Cinnamon, anyway? He would soon realize the grass was not greener on the other side. I finished my last bite, but I was still hungry. I opened the fridge and then shut it. Instead, I went into the bathroom to brush my teeth and ignored the temptation to stress eat.

The gym was quiet, but I scanned the room for Nicholas, anyway. He was nowhere to be seen. I was the first to arrive at the meeting.

Linda came over and smiled at me, her entire face filled with joy. "Hello, Valarie, so great to see you back again. How is everything going? I see here you weighed in at one hundred and ninety-five pounds last week when you started."

I felt my face grow hot. "Don't remind me."

"Oh dear, that is nothing to be ashamed of. It is just a starting point. It is all about getting healthy. You need to be confident in who you are and weight doesn't define you."

Linda could see right through me. Sure, I shared a lot with the group, but Linda listened and she cared. She made me comfortable stepping on the scale in front of her and not worrying about judgment. This was just a number on a scale. A starting point, like she said. So why was I so nervous then?

"Thank you. I've been working really hard."

I stepped on the scale. Linda nodded in approval and turned the screen to block my view so only she could see it.

"Wow," she said in disbelief.

Linda wrote the number in my booklet and gave it back to me. "You are down five pounds. How do you feel?"

I beamed. Five pounds was an impressive start for me. It meant my hard work was paying off. "Like I won the lottery."

"You didn't win, you worked hard. It's all in here," she said, pointing to her temple. "Did you sign up for a personal training session?"

I shook my head, but held back that I was nervous and self-conscious. An image of my fat flopping around as I did jumping jacks while my pants fell down below my stomach or falling on the elliptical when a trainer pushed me to go faster was the reality of why I was not on board to schedule a session yet.

"Look here, there is an opening tomorrow morning at six with Nicholas." She leaned closer to whisper. "And between you and me, he just happens to be the best trainer."

"I was hoping for maybe a female trainer," I said. I had promised I would do a session with him. I just could not get myself to, not when all I could think about was those lips on mine.

"He is the best."

"Let me think about it, okay?"

Linda put her hand on mine. "Take the leap. I'm certain your hard work will show on the scale next week."

Linda was right. Linda was always right. Maybe I would feel more confident next week.

The room filled up. Maria and Saffron were the last two to come in. They stood on the scale and then made their way to the table and sat next to me.

Saffron slammed her purse down and crossed her arms. Her lip jutted out in an impressive pout. "I gained a pound."

"I'm sorry. Next week," Maria said.

There did not seem to be any animosity between the two of them. I would have to ask Maria after the meeting if she found Saffron and apologized. I was glad today did not seem to be awkward between the two of them.

"I'm down two pounds," Maria said. "How about you, Val?"

"Well, I was pleasantly surprised because I lost five whole pounds."

They both gasped.

"Congratulations. I thought your face looked less pudgy," Saffron said.

I would not let her get to me. Saffron was just being Saffron.

Maria leaned in. "Tell me your secret? Please. I am so proud of you. Aren't you glad you came now?"

"I'm not really sure what I did. Just focusing a little more on what I put into my body and how often, I guess. I'm really trying hard not to overeat."

"Just wait until you start working out more. I can't wait to crush that scale, too," Maria said.

"There's going to be a speaker on intermittent fasting next weekend at the conference. You guys are still planning on going, aren't you?" Saffron looked at the both of us.

Maria looked at me. "Yes, we're going, right?"

"Yeah," I said. "I still plan on going."

Saffron squeaked with excitement. "We should all ride together!"

Hell no.

"We would, but we already have a full car," Maria said. "But we'll meet you there."

"Too bad, we're going to have a fabulous drive up there. My two best girlfriends are coming. You guys are going to love, love, love them. We like have been best friends since high school."

I forced a smile. "Yay," I said with little enthusiasm.

"Can't wait," Maria said.

"So, who are you riding with, then? Don't tell me your hot brother who keeps turning me down to go out on a date."

I gasped and put my hand in front of my mouth to silence it.

"Don't tell me he's gay. He isn't gay, is he? Oh, that makes so much sense."

Saffron seemed to be deep in thought.

"Calm down, Saffron. He isn't gay, and yes, he is coming with us," Maria said, obviously annoyed.

My chest fell. I was riding all the way to The Cities with Nicholas? Here comes another embarrassing moment.

Maria looked at me. "What are your three goals this week?"

Saffron flipped her hair behind her shoulders and answered. "Not to forget my lip gloss at home on my next date. Buy a new outfit for the conference next weekend, and of course, no eating past six at night. What about you?"

"Well, to not feel bad when I come to the gym and have to leave my kids behind crying for me," Maria said.

"Ouch, that really happens?" Saffron said with a look of disgust. "I'm so never having kids."

"Ok. Anyway, next is working out at least three days and not missing the two Calorie Counter meetings. And last but not least, stay within my thirteen hundred calorie budget each day for the next seven days."

I nodded. "I think I'm going to steal the calorie one from you as my first goal. Goal number two, no fast food or sugar. And for the third one, no talking about Eric for the entire week because that is what leads me to binge eating."

"Amen to that, sister," Saffron said with her hand in the air.

"That's going to be tough," Maria said.

"Yeah, I'm sick of hearing about him," Saffron said. "Loozer. If I met the guy, I'd probably kick his butt for you. Don't waste your time or energy."

The meeting was a success. Everyone was excited about the conference the following weekend.

"Are you going?" Erin from the front table asked Linda.

"I am. I'm going with my kids, actually," Linda said, looking at Maria. "I may even show off a few backflips there to surprise the young people. The surprised reactions are always worth it."

We all agreed.

"Your mom is coming with us?" I whispered to Maria.

Maria got up and pushed in her chair. "Well, she's a speaker, so she's taking a van with a bunch of other trainers, but she's riding back with us. Is that a problem?"

"Are you kidding? I love your mom. I can't wait."

"Oh good. I don't want to you to have any last-minute excuse not to come."

"Me? Nah," I said.

Now I couldn't make up an excuse to cancel last minute. Oh well, it couldn't be that bad, could it?

CHAPTER 10

"**A**re you sure you're going to be okay running the store by yourself for the weekend, Mom?"

"Oh please, Valarie, I do own the place."

It would be nice if she acted like an owner and was a little more responsible. "I know, Mom, I just want to make sure. Is there anything else I can do before I take off?"

My mother dusted off the top of the bookshelf. "What do you think about having new and used books in the store?"

I laughed. "I've been telling you that for years. It would be a great way to get more people in and make the books more affordable, but you always said there wasn't enough space."

She waved me off. "Oh please, we have plenty of space. I would never say that."

"Okay, well, go for it. Let's talk more about details when I get back."

"Sounds good, dear. Be careful, the snow is really coming down out there."

"I will."

I left the store with a list in my head of all the things I

should be doing instead of going on this trip. But when was the last time I did something for myself?

I really should be celebrating because I dropped another five pounds for the second week in a row. I was now down to one hundred and eighty-five pounds. Never did I think I would celebrate that weight, but I never weighed myself before the divorce, so I did not know how heavy I was. I was too busy being a wife and mother. Not that Eric cared.

The week went well. I focused on my well-being, working out, and eating right. Alex actually noticed, too. She even complimented me on the healthy meals and how much happier I seemed lately. But I struggled when she begged me not to go away for the weekend. She was sick of Cinnamon, and I felt guilty. She wanted to stay at home with her mother and not deal with her father's young girlfriend. I had to stay strong because I needed to do this for myself. I did nothing for myself.

"Mom, she's not much older than I am, it's sick," Alex said to me one day.

The hardest part was when I had to suck it up and tell her, "Just give her a chance." I hated being an adult at times. Why did I never get to be the fun parent? Oh yeah, because I wanted to raise her to be a good person instead of an enabled child. It was easy being my daughter's friend, but man, was it hard to have to discipline her for her own best interest.

I headed home through the thick snow, hoping the weather forecast had been wrong about the eight to twelve inches of snow. I prayed it would miss us and not come until tomorrow, when I was safely in Minneapolis with my friends. But no, here I was, watching the beautiful snow as it came down. I shrugged off my worries because I was told I worry too much and it was true.

At five thirty, I stood by the front door waiting for Maria to pick me up. Halloween was next weekend, and I admired the witches I had lined up next to my back sidewalk. They were made of straw and had sparkly black hats.

My phone chirped in my pocket.

"Hey, Val, I am so sorry, but Mikey has a fever of one hundred and three, and I have to take him in to the ER. I know Mark could take him, but I can't leave him like this. You go without me, and I'll try to make it up there tomorrow afternoon if he's better."

I tried to hide the sadness in my voice. "I'll wait until tomorrow, too. I'm not the best winter driver, and I do not know where I'm going."

"No, no. I talked to Nicholas, and he's going to pick you up. I promise, I'll be there first thing tomorrow, once poor Mikey's fever breaks, okay? We can ride home together, I promise."

"Nicholas? No. I don't think—"

"Please, I don't want him driving by himself, and anyway, he's on his way to pick you up now. Please, please do this for me? Pretty please? I feel just terrible about ditching out on both of you at the last minute. It'll make me feel better. Pretty please."

I groaned. "It's weird that I am going to The Cities with your brother when you aren't even going to be in the car."

"I'm begging you. Please."

"Fine."

"Thank you, thank you. I owe you. You are the best."

"Yeah, whatever. You owe me."

There was a loud scream in the background

"Listen, Val, I have to go. Mikey, it's okay, it's okay, sweetheart. Nicholas will be there in five. Have fun and see you tomorrow."

"But..." I looked at my phone screen. Maria had hung up already, obviously not taking no for an answer. Three and a half hours in a car with Nicholas terrified me. What would we even talk about? Maybe I would just sleep.

Nicholas pulled up in a Ford Taurus. Where was his truck? I threw my suitcase and bag in the back seat and got in.

Nicholas smiled.

"Where's your truck? Don't you know it's a snowstorm out there?"

His eyes twinkled at my cross words. "Well, hello to you, too."

I knew I was being rude to him for no reason. It wasn't his fault Maria cancelled. Maybe he was just as nervous about it being just the two of us as I was.

"I'm sorry, I can't believe Maria cancelled on us at the last minute."

He pulled out onto the road. The storm was worse now. All I could see was bright lights and the whiteout ahead.

"It's just one night. Mikey wanted his mama. She'll make it tomorrow, don't worry."

Why did I feel so uneasy about being alone in his car? In just a few hours, we would be in our own separate hotel rooms.

"I know. Poor little guy. I'm sorry, I was just a little shocked."

He took a right and went down the ramp toward Walmart.

"Where are you going?"

"I'm taking seventy-three."

"But don't you think the interstate is a better idea? There are more gas stations and places to stop in case the roads get bad. This way is just too rural."

"The roads are already bad. Plus, I'm an amazing driver."

He shot me a sexy grin, as if that would make me trust him. He likely used that smile on a lot of women, but it would not work on me. My heart was taken, and I was not a fool.

"How is your head?"

He was trying to change the subject, but I was not giving in.

"If you go this way, you're risking my life and yours. We're not even in a four-wheel or all-wheel drive vehicle. I'm scared of icy roads."

He put his hand on my leg and gently squeezed it, making my body overheat.

"It's okay, I'm a great driver. Trust me."

I took his hand off my leg. "Fine, but remember I warned you."

I really wanted to be wrong.

Thirty minutes out of town, the road was covered in deep snow, and visibility was down to a few feet. We could not make out the sides of the road, and there were no longer any tire marks from cars.

"Maybe we should turn back and get your truck," I said, although I knew it was too late to turn around.

He turned toward me. "My truck's in the shop getting the dent in the door fixed."

My mouth opened. I was the one who dented his door.

"I dented your door, didn't I?"

He nodded. "It's fine. I've got it handled. I'm just giving you crap."

"I'm sorry, but you told me there wasn't a scratch." My stomach was on fire, and I was having trouble breathing. "I don't want to be stranded in the middle of nowhere. Please turn around."

He turned to look at me. "It's too late now. It's going to be—"

Before he could finish explaining once again how everything was going to be fine, the car spun in a circle. The front end went right into a snowbank and buried the hood of the car. He grabbed my hand as I held my breath, just waiting for the airbags to go off, but they didn't.

"Are you okay?"

I took a minute to get my lungs to work because I wasn't breathing.

"Yeah, I'm okay." Not.

"I'm so sorry."

I chose not to speak yet.

He squeezed my hand. "Are you sure you're okay?"

"I'll be better once we get out of here."

He put his weight into his door and pulled on the handle several times. Nothing.

"Try yours."

I put all my weight into my shoulder, holding the door handle, but the door would not budge. He unbuckled his seatbelt and climbed over the seat.

The funny thing is, I felt oddly calm despite our predicament. "What are you doing?"

"I'm going to see if I can get out through the back doors."

He pushed and then kicked the door while pulling on the handle, and it finally opened. Snow came in and covered him like an avalanche.

"Nicholas, are you okay?"

"I'm ... fine ...the snow is ... heavy. It must have fallen down from the top of the car," he said breathlessly.

I followed him into the back seat, and he held my hand as I climbed out of the car. He was such a gentleman, even if he was stubborn.

"I'd leave it until we figure out a plan."

I followed him through the deep snow and up to the road. "What are we going to do now?"

I relied on his response and hoped he had some kind of

plan because my cell phone had no service, and I doubted he did either.

Nicholas's eyes narrowed, and he shot me another smile. But it was more protective, caring. "Give me a second to think, it's going to be okay, I promise."

That was too easy. He was obviously as stumped as I was. "But there aren't a lot of people that live on this road, especially in the summer."

He looked into my eyes. "Do you trust me?"

I nodded because, for some reason, I did.

He got back into the car and climbed over the front seat. The headlights and flashers started up. He climbed out of the car. "Now we need to dig it out enough so a passersby can spot our car."

"And then?"

"And then we head for a house around here or best circumstances a car goes by. If a car sees our car in the ditch, they might stop or call it in down the road. We'll be okay, just don't panic."

I nodded and walked back into the snow to follow his lead.

He dug in the snow until he found the front of his car and then we wiped off the headlights on both sides. He led the way down the road.

"Why this way?"

He stopped walking and looked at me. "I'm really not sure. Do you want me to be honest with you?"

My toes were numb and cold. "Yes."

"Okay, I do not know where we're going, but I know this area has a lot of hunting shacks, so just keep your eyes open, okay?"

"Okay." I tried to act calm, but inside I was terrified. I was just glad I wasn't alone.

I pulled up my hood to block the wind.

"Someone else has to be dumb enough to drive in this snowstorm in the middle of nowhere," I said.

He stopped and picked up some snow and balled it in his hands.

"What are you doing?"

"I'm protecting us," he said.

"With a snowball?"

He dropped it and grabbed my hand, placing the pocketknife inside my mitten. "You're right, you need to protect us."

I shook my head.

We walked for what felt like hours, but my watch said it had only been ten minutes.

"Stop," he said.

I stared ahead and then turned back to him. "What?"

I couldn't hear a thing. Did he have super hearing or something?

He pointed up the road and into the snow. Luckily, the snow kept the skies bright, so we weren't walking in darkness.

"I think I see a gate up there. You see it?"

I squinted through the falling snow. Was his body temperature too low, and he was hallucinating? My insides churned with dread because I couldn't see anything. Were my senses failing me?

"No. I don't see anything," I said finally.

He walked faster, and I followed. I was impressed as we approached the gate. The wind blowing the snow so hard in our eyes, we had to turn our heads as we walked. We climbed around the gate and followed the opening in the trees.

"Are you sure this leads to something?"

"No, I'm not, but we have to have faith."

He stopped and grabbed my mittened hand in his and gave it a squeeze, which surprisingly did calm my nerves.

I looked into his glossy eyes and his abnormally red, rosy cheeks and nodded. We continued to walk for quite a while, deeper into the woods.

"How do we know this doesn't just lead to a hunting stand or something?"

"Trust me," he said. "I know the woods."

Not much farther up the road, I looked up, and we both cried out in happiness. A small log cabin stood in front of us like God placed it there on purpose.

I couldn't hide my amazement. "A cabin. I can't believe it!"

"I told you. I grew up hunting with my dad," he said.

I nudged him with my shoulder and with all the energy I had left; I forced my frozen thighs and feet to run until I reached the old cabin. I turned the handle, but it was padlocked. I pulled on it and when it didn't budge; I hit it.

"It's locked! Unbelievable! Are you kidding me?" I started kicking the door and banging my shoulder into it while pulling on the handle in a panic.

He waited until I was exhausted and stopped freaking out.

"Do you feel better now?"

I nodded my head and wiped my tears of frustration.

"I have an idea," he said.

He pulled a large branch off a tree and set it on his shoulder like a baseball bat. He bent his knees and swung it at the window. The sound of broken glass hitting the floor inside was the sound of hope. He broke the rest of the glass off until the sharpness around the sides of the window was gone. He got on his hands and knees in front of the window.

"You want me to stand on your back and climb through the window?"

"That would be helpful. You don't want to stay out here all night, do you?"

I shook my head and stepped on his back, holding onto

the side of the cabin, and peeked my head inside. It was pitch black. Perhaps there were mice or bats hidden in the darkness. I had to be brave, so I did what any other person would do. I dove in headfirst.

The sharp pain in my stomach burned, but it was small compared to the happiness I felt just being inside and out of the cold and wind. I touched what felt like a couch. I let go and cut my finger on a piece of glass from the floor.

Nicholas climbed in after me and I will not lie. It was pretty impressive.

I used the flashlight feature on my phone and found a candle on the wall.

"You don't happen to be a trainer that smokes, do you?"

"Nope, I guess not. Why?"

"There are candles on the wall."

I checked my phone again, but there was still no signal. I tried calling Maria just in case of a small miracle, but the call would not go through.

"No service?"

I shook my head. "How about you?"

"Nope, I've been watching my phone this whole time. Nothing. It's a dead zone. I'm not sure if it's because of the storm or that we're in the middle of nowhere."

I opened a drawer and found a box of matches. "Bingo."

Nicholas lit the candles on the walls.

I opened up the cupboard and found some canned food. "You hungry?"

He picked a log off the floor and placed it in the fireplace and began adding more wood to it. "What did you find?"

I turned the can of beans toward him. "Well, we have some beans here, and they aren't even expired."

He looked back and made a face. "Isn't there anything other than beans?"

"A box of rice, some oatmeal, and spaghetti o's."

"Spaghetti o's, huh?"

The fire blazed. I moved close enough to warm my frozen hands and body.

Snow was blowing through the broken window and gusts of wind threatened the fire. "We have to do something about the broken window," I said. "But how are we going to fix it?"

"I've got it. You just stay here and warm up, okay?"

He took the comforter off the small bed. The cabin was just one room with the fireplace, a twin-size bed, a dark leather couch, a wooden end table, a small kitchen table with two chairs, and deer antlers that hung across the ceiling in a line.

A "Welcome to The Shack" sign and a drawing of a man, woman, and two boys hung on the wall. It looked like the picture was taken twenty or thirty years ago, maybe more.

Nicholas found a chisel and climbed out the window. Ten minutes later, he broke the padlock and opened the door. He was sweating when he came back in. He took the shade off the window, found a board in the corner, and nailed it to the open window.

I immediately felt a difference, but I was still shaking even though I was standing in front of the fire. My pants were wet, which made it impossible to warm up. The chill was deep in my bones. The shack was poorly insulated, and all I really wanted to do was cry.

Nicholas cooked rice over the fireplace in a pot with melted snow from outside.

"Where did you learn to do that?"

He shrugged his shoulders and said, "I'm making it up as I go."

CHAPTER 11

She was so beautiful all bundled up, her hair peeking out from the side of her hood as she leaned in to eat.

"What do you think? Is it okay?"

She swallowed her food and smiled at him, making his body shiver.

"I was starving. I would have eaten pretty much anything at this point, but it isn't that bad. I'm slightly impressed. But next time you make me dinner, I'd prefer a steak with my rice."

"Next time, huh?"

Humor always helped Nicholas relax. He was nervous about being stuck at this shack in the middle of nowhere, but he had started a fire and the cabin was warming up so at least they would not freeze to death.

Val's hands shook as she took her last bites, and she wrapped the blanket tighter around her body and moved closer to the fire.

"Still cold?"

He groaned inwardly. What a stupid question to ask. Of course she was cold, the poor girl was shivering. He felt like a real jerk for not listening to her when she said he should have taken highway thirty-five in case they had problems. That road was the interstate and more likely to be plowed. He cursed under his breath. His truck never would have spun out like that and if it had, he would have driven right out of the ditch. He had done it before, many times actually. He just wasn't used to driving his car in the winter.

"Yes, I just ... can't seem to warm up. Are you still cold?"

He nodded. "A bit. We weren't exactly dressed for going in the ditch, but who plans that, right? At least we both had boots on."

He got up and made his way to the kitchen and opened a little closet he had not seen earlier. He found a bottle of whisky. "Thirsty?" He held up the bottle.

"What is that, whisky?"

"Yep."

"I don't think I've ever been so excited to see a bottle of whisky before. Anything to help us warm up sounds like a great idea."

"There are some tin cups in the cupboard, but they're full of cobwebs so I'm thinking drinking it straight out of the bottle may be the best bet."

He dragged the rocking chair across the floor to the fire and patted the seat. She wrapped the blanket tight around her body and sat down. He took the hard wooden chair and carried it in front of the fire. He opened up the bottle and took in a deep inhale. "Whoa. That's strong. I haven't had whisky since I was a teenager and now, I remember why." He handed the bottle to her.

She tipped her head back and took a big gulp. "That's terrible." She stuck out her tongue. "How do people drink this stuff?"

He took the bottle back, and they both stared at the crackling fire in silence.

"Aren't you going to have some?"

He shook his head. "To be honest, I used to love whisky, but it brings back a lot of bad memories of my younger days. I used to be an alcoholic," he said. "I have to pass. It's all you. Drink as much as you'd like."

She covered the bottle in her blanket. "I never really drank much in my younger years. I became a mother pretty young. What made you sober up?"

He seldom told anyone about his past. Regan knew he used to be an alcoholic because he liked to think if she knew he wasn't perfect, she would listen to him when he told her no in the future.

"My wife left me, and I needed to grow up and raise Regan."

She opened the bottle and took another swig. "Did she leave you because you were an alcoholic?"

He was not sure how much he was ready to share. He did not want to scare her away, or worse, lie to her.

"She left me because I had a lot of demons. I couldn't come to terms with a lot of things from my past. Regan's mom was patient with me, and she thought I would change after Regan was born, but I couldn't snap out of it."

"Why? What happened?"

She seemed genuinely concerned about him. When he looked deep into her eyes, his pulse raced. She intrigued him. She was different, refreshing.

"I was young and dumb and depressed, to say the least."

"Why? Why were you depressed?"

"Oh man, it was a lot of things back then. My dad went to jail and my mom died when I was young, so I was angry with the world. Linda took me in and she was great, don't get me wrong, but I couldn't help but feel abandoned. I may have been a drunk when I married Regan's mom, but I still don't understand why she would just take off and leave Regan like she did."

Val turned her body in the chair and leaned into him and away from the fire.

"How old was Regan when she left you guys?"

He looked down at his shaky hands and put them under his legs. "Two."

"Wow, that's horrible. Do you know where she went? Where she is now?"

His teeth chattered uncontrollably as he spoke. He tried to relax, but it wasn't working. He was cold and nervous, upset at the memory of it all. "Her name is Carla, and no, I have no idea. She has had no contact with us at all since she left. She's been gone fourteen years and the funny thing is we are still technically married."

Val got up and grabbed two pillows off the bed. She banged them against the bed frame, making a dust cloud that billowed into the air. She coughed, hit them again, and then set the pillows on the rug in front of the fire. The old braided rug looked a couple of decades old, and likely dustier and dirtier than the pillows. Val took off her boots and waved him over.

He pointed at himself and held his breath, and she laughed at his gesture.

He took off his boots and jacket and crawled under the comforter with her. They were about a foot apart, lying on their sides and staring at each other face to face. He felt her cold foot slip under his pant leg and rest against his ankle. Her foot was so cold.

"I never thought I would lay here with you, snuggling in the middle of the woods when I woke up this morning," she said with a laugh.

He put his arm around her, and she rested her head on his chest. It all felt so natural.

He was paralyzed for just a moment. It felt so good to have her in his arms, even under the circumstances.

"I couldn't think of a better way to warm up."

He ran his fingers through her hair. He could get used to this.

"I didn't expect this to be so comfortable with all your hard muscles beneath me," she said. "I also didn't expect we would get so close today, but you saved my life again."

He laughed and pulled her closer. Her hair smelled amazing, like peaches mixed with roses or something just as amazing. Whatever it was, he could not get enough. He breathed in deeply, not wanting to let her scent leave his mind. Her head rose, and his chest expanded. When was the last time a woman lay on his chest when he did not tense up and roll away, wishing she would leave?

"I wonder how long it will take before people start to worry about us," she said.

"I think when we don't show up at the hotel tonight, Linda will probably start worrying about us. I just wish we had enough reception to call them," he said. He took his phone out and looked at it again. "Have you looked at yours lately?"

"Yep, nothing. Maria will definitely worry tomorrow if we aren't there."

Val was shaking a bit underneath the covers. Nothing a warm shower would not fix. The thought of her in the shower made his body warm all over.

Being stranded with Val was not all bad. This would give him the opportunity to get to know her better. If they didn't end up starving to death, that is. He closed his eyes and all he could see was her. The way her yoga pants clung to her thighs, and the way her baggy shirts would sometimes tighten with the way she moved, showing off her natural curves. Her clothes were baggy but always left him imagining what she hid beneath them. She was not like the other women he dated in his past.

Sure, he was young and drunk throughout most of his relationships, but he did date two or three girls after Regan's mother left them. None of them were real, none of them were Valarie.

Regan's mother was thin and always worried about gaining weight. She never ate carbs or sugar, not because she wanted to be healthy, but because she worried she would gain a pound. She talked about other women and put them down, and she expected him to agree with her insults and judgments. She spent most days at the gym or shopping, spending more money than they had until she pretty much left him bankrupt. Though his father came from a family of wealth, he refused to support them financially because she was so disrespectful toward him.

He was drinking anything he could get his hands on, preferably whisky, when he was with Carla. He was a horrible father and husband at the time. They were both equally selfish. When she left, his world changed. It was a wakeup call, and his father was there to guide him.

The women he dated around the time Regan was ten were beautiful, but with no brains or self-respect. He never brought them home or introduced them to Regan because he did not want a serious relationship. They were all a lot alike, superficial with dull personalities. They were not anyone he could see settling down with, or even anyone he wanted his daughter to meet. There was just no spark.

Valarie was different from any woman he ever met. She was beautiful and smart, kind and real. She was still in love with her ex, but if all he could be was friends with her, he would be happy. He just wanted her near him somehow.

He squeezed her a little tighter, enjoying their bodies being entwined.

"Did you always know you wanted to own a gym?"

"Not exactly. I ran a gym in Grand Rapids, but I never thought I would be able to actually own my own gym. If it wasn't for my dad's help, I wouldn't have had the opportunity, to be honest. I decided to move to Hibbing so Regan could be closer to her grandfather and there aren't any gyms here with pools, except the schools, of course, so it was a great opportunity. We found this huge building not being used and decided why not? My father loved my business plan so he invested in it."

"He sounds like a good guy," she said.

"How about you? Did you grow up dreaming about running your family's bookstore?"

"More than you can imagine. I grew up working at the bookstore with my parents. I always loved books, and I even preferred them to traveling and still do. I hate to fly."

He felt the passion shooting through her veins as she talked about the bookstore.

"I could sit there for days, reading books, organizing and reorganizing the display shelves. It may not seem very special, but I never wanted to do anything else. I'm hoping my mom passes down the bookstore to me soon so I can take it to a new level. I have so many ideas, but she is not exactly on board with them."

"Tell me about them."

"I want to put in a better play center for kids, have book club meetings, and maybe even book signings, but my mom is a stickler. She's not around much, but she won't adopt any of my ideas. Except earlier today, she finally said she was thinking about having used books in the store. I'd asked her for years, but today she acted like it was her idea. I just don't get her."

"That's too bad. Why do you think she doesn't want change?"

"She wants everything to stay the way it was when my dad was alive. But he died before Alexandra was born, so it's due for some updates. She still decorates for holidays, but she definitely struggles with change. She's very critical of me and refuses to talk about my dad at all."

"Why?"

She shrugged. "I'm not sure. She disappears and is hardly ever at the store. I don't even know where she goes, to be honest. I worry about her. A guy from some bank came in the other day to speak with her, but my mom said it was nothing when I asked her about it. I worry she is in some financial trouble or something. She won't talk to me about it, believe me, I've tried."

"And you have no idea where she goes or what she does?"

"Not even a guess."

"That's crazy."

She yawned and stretched out. "Sorry, I'm so tired, I can hardly keep my eyes open."

"Same here," he said, but he could stay awake listening to her talk forever.

Within seconds, she was snoring softly. Her hand was on his chest, and he ran his fingers through her hair again, careful not to wake her. He lay awake listening to the sound of her breathing until he could no longer fight his exhaustion, and he drifted to sleep.

CHAPTER 12

For being stranded in the middle of the woods in a blizzard with a man I hardly knew, I slept really well. Although after last night, I felt like I had known him forever. I woke up and for a second did not remember whose body I was entangled with, nor where I was. But once I remembered, a smiled spread across my face.

We made oatmeal for breakfast over the old stove and talked about his plans for the gym. I loved the animation of his hands and the expressions on his face when he talked with such passion about the gym and Regan. He was smart, confident, and damn, he was good looking.

He saved my life and heard some of my deepest, darkest secrets. Now I could add that we snuggled in bed together, and relied on our body heat to keep us from freezing to death.

"It looks like the snow is dying down a bit, and I found a couple pairs of oversized snow pants. You want to go for a walk with me and see if there is any way for us to get out of here?"

"That sounds like a good plan. How oversized are the snow pants?"

He threw me a pair after comparing them. Was he throwing me the bigger or the smaller pair? With my luck, my big butt wouldn't fit into the oversized pair and that would be embarrassing. I took off my jacket and slipped them on. They were a little big, and not snug at all. They were definitely too long. The man who owned them must be a giant. I tucked the bottoms of them into my boots and put my jacket on over the straps.

The cold air felt very refreshing, and the biggest snowflakes I had ever seen drifted to the ground in front of me. I caught some in my hands and stuck out my tongue to catch one.

Nicholas laughed and did the same. "Who knew this would be so fun? I don't remember the last time I really enjoyed the snow. Probably not since Regan was a little girl."

"Same here. I've been so caught up in trying to be super-mom, I haven't taken a moment to really see what's right in front of me."

He led the way into the woods. I stepped into his large footprints in the snow. The tall trees came together like they were holding hands with their branches. The snow stuck to the trees, and they looked as though they were putting their heads together. It was a breathtaking view.

I needed to reserve the battery power left on my phone, but I was dying to get a picture of the breathtaking forest before me. I snapped a quick photo and looked back up at the tunnel-like view of nature.

Nicholas followed my gaze. "This is beautiful, isn't it? Let's take a picture together. This is an adventure we will never forget." He took out his camera and put his arm around me before snapping a photo.

If Eric were here, he would have laughed at me and told

me the only time winter was beautiful was when he could follow in an animal's footsteps in the snow after he shot it.

"It almost doesn't seem real."

He snapped another photo of us, getting the tops of the trees in the background. "Of all the trees I've seen in Minnesota, I've never seen them so perfectly placed. It's as though we are alive in a painting that hangs on the walls of dentist offices and restaurants around town."

"Well, that sounds boring."

He tilted his head sideways. "I guess it does. How about like a picture you would see hanging in one of the beautiful homes in Side Lake?"

I nodded. "Now that sounds impressive. Right on the wall next to an enormous bay window overlooking the lake. I just found the perfect place to hang it in my place on the lake."

He laughed. "Do you paint?"

"God no, but if I did…"

We walked beneath the tunnel of trees, hand in hand. Once the path ended and the trees were scattered through the woods, our hands dropped. I knew he was holding my hand to steady us both, but I wasn't ready to let go.

"I'm pretty sure our car is up this way," he said.

We stepped onto the road. Tire tracks from luckier vehicles broke up the deep snow, but we were so far out in the middle of nowhere, the roads had yet to be plowed. We pushed through the deep snow on the road to the ditch and found his car right where we left it. Flashers still blinking.

Nicholas and I uncovered most of the car. He wanted someone to see the car and stop or send for help if we weren't close by.

The snow was coming down harder now, and he finally gave up.

"The snow is covering the car faster than we can dig it out."

He got the door open, but closed it again.

We walked back into the woods, following our fading footsteps. He hardly said a word, so disappointed and angry at himself. We entered the tree tunnel on our way back to the cabin, and I knew I needed to cheer him up. I grabbed snow off the ground and made a snowball and threw it at his head.

Nicholas put his hand on his head and cried out in pain, then bent over with his hands on knees.

I was surprised I could throw so hard. I walked over to apologize. "I'm so sorry, Nicholas. I didn't mean to throw it so hard. I was trying to make you laugh." I put my hand on his back.

His motion startled me. One minute I was standing next to him, and the next I was being carried over his shoulder toward a giant snow bank.

I laughed, hitting his back and kicking my legs. "You tricked me! I thought you were hurt! Put me down!"

My screams were playful and only further challenged him.

He tried to put my head in the snow, but I was not letting go of his neck so he could drop me. There I was, dangling over the snow, my legs tightly wrapped around his waist. He tried to get me off, but he grunted as his strength weakened until he finally fell over with me still in his arms.

We were both silent, staring into each other's eyes as we lay there on the ground, snow on our faces. I reached out to his swollen lips with my finger. I wanted to touch them, make sure they were real. I closed my eyes so I could feel the nerves in the pit of my gut, the electricity as our lips met.

Our lips were frozen together, neither of us wanting the kiss to end. Being stranded in the middle of the woods made it appear as though we were the only two people left on Earth. We locked eyes and took in the moment.

He reached out to grab a piece of hair that was hanging in front of my eye and tucked it behind my ear. Such a small touch, but it left me breathless.

He leaned in to kiss me again and I pulled away, getting to my knees and then on my wobbly feet. Reality hit me. I needed to get my family back. "I can't, I'm sorry."

"I'm sorry, I didn't mean to…" Nicholas held his arm in front of me, and stopped me from taking another step. I was confused and sad the excitement had to end.

"I shouldn't have let the first kiss happen. I'm so sorry. It's not you, I promise."

"No, I'm sorry."

We both looked around awkwardly.

"Look," he said, pointing into the woods.

I gasped at the exhilarating sight. A buck with huge antlers stared back at us. I focused on counting the points on his rack before he ran out of view.

"It's at least a ten pointer," he said.

The buck stopped running and locked eyes with me. It was nothing I had ever felt before. My heart started pounding, the blood raced through my body, and I did not breathe or move because I didn't want him to run and risk this moment ending before it had to. I watched his head move back and forth, but I was no longer fixated on counting his rack.

"What a sight," he whispered so close to my ear I felt myself blush.

"That was unbelievable," I said after the buck ran out of sight.

"It was beautiful, wasn't it?"

"I don't think I spend enough time in nature. I've never felt anything like that. I still have goosebumps."

He smiled. "That feeling never stops. It was breathtaking, wasn't it?"

The way he took in everything around him made my heart flutter.

Eric would have run after it to scare it away. He shot a deer every year in November during deer hunting, which gave us enough venison until the next year. I wanted to go hunting, but I just couldn't bring myself to shoot a deer. I would probably cry for a week. I left that for Eric to do with the guys.

Did Cinnamon cook venison the way he liked it? Did she even cook at all? I hoped she was a vegetarian. That would show Eric. I laughed at the thought.

Once we were back inside the shack, I lay down on the bed and wrapped myself up in the blanket. It smelled like dirty socks, but I was in no position to be picky.

The sound of heavy breathing woke me from a nap. I turned onto my side and saw Nicholas on the floor doing push-ups. The muscles in his back were pulled tight across his shirt and bulging. I couldn't take my eyes off him. I counted twenty-five and had no idea how many he had already done. He was so hot. I had to stop him, stop the feelings that brought on so many sexy thoughts inside my head.

I jumped to my feet. "Are you hungry? I'm hungry."

He stopped and wiped his brow and the back of his neck with a grimy hand towel. "I have definitely worked up a sweat. What shall we have for dinner tonight?"

I laughed. Did he have to be so likeable? It was as though we were playing boyfriend and girlfriend, living in this home in the middle of the woods together. It was a fantasy, not reality.

He returned to the push-up position, and talked while he grunted, down up, down up. I imagined being underneath him, and the way his warm lips felt when they were locked with mine. I shook my head, trying and failing to clear the naughty thoughts that circled in my brain.

"I haven't had spaghetti-o's since I was a small child," I said.

"Spaghetti-o's it is then," he said. "Once the snow lets up, I think we should walk to the road again and start heading north. It may seem deserted, but a lot of people drive down this road and live this way. They have to be going to work or something."

"On a Saturday?"

"Oh yeah, it's Saturday, isn't it?"

I put my hand on his. "We'll find a way to get out of here, I know it."

"I have no doubt we will be out of here by tomorrow, that's for sure. It can't snow forever."

"You just tell me what you need me to do, and I'll do it."

He stopping doing push-ups, sat up and wrapped his arms around his knees, and rocked back. "I know you will. I'm just out of ideas right now."

I nodded.

"Val, you're sure beautiful, you know that?"

"Stop," I said. I was never good at accepting compliments. "I'm not, but thank you."

He leaned in and dropped to his knees, just inches from my face, and flipped my long hair behind my shoulders.

A chill started in my neck and ran down my arms and legs.

"How do you not see it? You're stunning."

I was overweight, and when I sat down, my stomach bulged over my jeans. I didn't exactly feel beautiful, plus I hadn't taken a shower and was probably not smelling the best at the moment.

I shied away from him. "Thanks."

"It's true," he said, clearly not dropping it.

The moment was getting too intimate. I needed to distract this attraction again or within moments we would be on the floor, rolling around, unable to keep our hands off each other.

"Enough about me. Tell me about Regan. She sounds like a really sweet girl."

He sat back and frowned. "She struggled so much when her mother left, and at times she becomes angry. She loves swimming, and she seemed happy to move here and be closer to her grandpa. But once we moved, her attitude worsened. I worry I made a mistake moving her away from the town she grew up in, you know."

"I wouldn't worry too much, she's a teenager. I'm not saying she isn't devastated that her mother left her when she was just a baby. I'm sure it's difficult for her never getting to know her mother, and she probably will always have some issues from that, but she loves you. You never let her down. She may not realize it because teens don't think with their full brain. It's that transition between being a sweet child and wanting to be an adult without acting like one. They want us to respect them, but they continue acting childish, impulsive."

He chuckled. "Isn't that the truth?"

"Do you ever worry her mom is going to show up at your door out of the blue and turn your lives upside down?"

Nicholas got up and grabbed a bottle of water out of his bag. "Every day since the day she took off."

"I'm so grateful you are a workout addict who carries your own water around with you or we would be very thirsty."

He handed me a bottle. "Fiji water is one of the best bottled waters you can find in this country. It doesn't have all the crap in it the others do, and it's good for you. People don't realize the harm other waters can have on their bodies overtime if they don't know what's in what they are drinking."

I could tell he didn't want to talk about his ex anymore, and I respected that. He was clearly changing the subject for a reason.

I couldn't help teasing him. "Is there anything you don't know?"

"Many things. Not to brag, but I have been known as the king of useless information in the past."

I smiled. "That was not useless information, it was highly informative."

He raised his eyebrows and shot me another sexy grin.

"I think we need to toast," he said.

We clinked water bottles as if they were flutes of champagne.

"To being stuck in a hunting shack that has a port-a-potty, we couldn't be luckier," he said.

"And toilet paper."

"And toilet paper."

"So, tell me about your parents. You talk a lot about your dad, but not your mom."

He cleared his throat. "My mom passed away when I was quite young so my father raised me on his own."

"I'm so sorry to hear that."

I could not imagine not having my mother around when I was growing up. Losing my father was hard enough, and I was close to adulthood when it happened. "How did she die?"

"Cancer," he said, staring into the darkness.

"My mother could hardly go on after my father died. She changed completely. What is your dad like? Did he remarry?"

"Linda is my father's sister. She adopted me. When I was older, my father got... hurt, so I went to live with my aunt Linda and Maria, of course. My dad never remarried. He said he only had one true love."

"Did you like living with them?"

"They were good to me, but that was when I truly became an alcoholic, and I didn't stop drinking for five years."

"So, how did you meet Regan's mom? Carla, right?"

He cleared his throat. "Yes, Carla. Okay, well, like I said, my dad got hurt, but I was almost eighteen. He gave me everything I wanted and if I did something terrible, he never punished me. I think he was trying to make up for the loss of my mother. Anyway, I moved in with Linda, who is a saint if you haven't noticed. She had a home on Big Sturgeon out in Side Lake." He was silent for a moment.

"Don't feel like you have to—"

"It's fine. I don't mind talking about it, really. Carla, Regan's mom, lived next door to Linda in the summers. When I was young, Maria and I would play over at Carla's all the time or she would come to our cabin. When I moved in with them, Maria had already moved out and gone to college. Carla was at our cabin most days, trying to stay away from her parents. She was beautiful and smart. She was three years older than me, so she would buy the alcohol, and we would sit on her dock and drink a lot. It was young love."

"In the winter, we would sit by her fireplace and drink some more," he said. "We partied a lot, and when I was with her it felt like I could forget what I'd been through and just be me. She constantly worried about gaining weight so she never ate much, but I would not bother her about it since she was never on my case to quit drinking."

His eyes glossed over. I slid my fingers in his, and he squeezed my hand as if it gave him the strength to continue.

"Carla and I bonded, mainly because she was struggling, too. Her parents were getting a divorce, and they gave her their cabin. Her mom gave her a bunch of money, but she wasn't ready to go to college. She was a bartender at a restaurant in Side Lake on the weekends, and she focused all of her energy on her looks. She had to be skinny, her makeup had to be perfect, and she talked way too much about herself. She was a true snob, but I didn't care. She drank with me. When you have an addiction, you pull away from those who try to separate you from your addiction and get closer to those who join you. We broke up for a while and Linda tried to sober me up, but I had some stuff from my past I couldn't deal with. I tried going to therapy and group. I'd visit my father, but then I would be back to drinking on Carla's dock. It was a never-ending cycle. Carla and I blew through all the money that was left to her within a few months."

"But I thought you and Linda were close?"

They dropped hands, and he rested his head against the wall and put his hands in his lap. "She gave me tough love by grounding me and trying to keep me in line. I needed that, but I was far too angry to let anyone love me. And I was so angry at my dad. Carla soon became pregnant with Regan. She wanted an abortion, but I talked her out of it. I promised I would get sober, and I was clean for most of her pregnancy, with Linda's help. Linda never gave up on me. After Carla left, Linda and Maria tried to keep my mind busy, and I even bartended in Side Lake for a while. I was young and dumb and thought she would come back. Boy, was I wrong."

He closed his eyes. "I will never forget the day Regan was born. She was so beautiful and looked just like her mother. I stayed sober for the next couple of months, but then Carla started going out and not coming home until two or three in the morning. One day, she took off and didn't come home for two months. I called the police. We searched for her, and then I saw the charge on my credit card bill for cosmetic surgery."

I gasped and covered my mouth with my hand. "No. What did she have done?"

"Boob job," he said. "I started drinking, then Carla came

home for a while, but I just couldn't stop drinking. Things had changed between us. We were fighting more, and she was having an affair after affair. She became closer to Regan, and I worried that one day she would take off with Regan and never come back, but that didn't happen. She took off alone and didn't come back at all. She didn't even call. I moved back in with Linda until my dad finally got better, and then I moved to Grand Rapids with him. I went to college, and that changed my life. My dad moved back here a few years ago and bugged me to open up a gym here and now here I am."

"Wow."

He got a serious look in his eyes and took both of my hands in his. "Val, there is something I need to tell you. My dad—"

I jumped to my feet when I heard what sounded like metal hitting cement. "Did you hear that, Nicholas? I think it's a plow!"

Without another word, we ran out the door and through the snow. We were saved!

CHAPTER 13

I
t felt so good to shower and shave, take a nap, and eat a sandwich. He never realized how good normal things felt until he was stuck in a cabin in the middle of the woods with no cell phone, unable to shower or eat delicious food. Although he wouldn't take it back. Being trapped in the middle of nowhere with a beautiful woman he couldn't stop thinking about was an adventure. Why was he glad to be home again?

Both Linda and his sister were eager to hear from him. Linda called Maria and Maria tried calling both of them, only to get sent to their voicemail multiple times. The police were called, and the state patrol was on alert to look for them on highway thirty-five.

After a weekend alone with Val, he didn't want to part. He was so close to telling her the secret he'd been hiding and then, wham; the plow interrupted them. He needed to focus his energy on the gym and stop thinking about her.

He walked into the gym, worried it had fallen apart when he left, but it looked exactly the same. No one even asked him how his weekend was or where he had been. The weight room smelled of sweat and bleach. He attempted to get the smell out so many times, but it was useless. Nothing worked.

He hit the weights and pushed hard until his arms went numb. Now he felt great. Weight lifting was his favorite kind of pain. He had always been a stocky guy, but working out at the gym helped define his muscles. He pushed his clients the way he pushed himself and enjoyed the way they reacted to their new bodies. Sometimes his clients gave up, or they would argue with him and tell him they couldn't do what he asked. He hated those words. He never understood why someone hired a trainer and then hoped they would go easy on them. They were paying for encouragement and the key to a healthier body.

Every person he trained had different expectations. Some wanted to be thin, some wanted to build muscle, some wanted to feel better, some just wanted to be healthier. Some came because of their decline in health. Those were the clients who never had excuses and always gave it their all.

He looked at his watch. Three o'clock. Saffron was always at least five minutes late. She could not be on time for the life of her. He was not about to argue with her. Whatever time she showed up was her choice. She was still paying from the time she scheduled her training.

"Oh dear, am I late again? Whoops," Saffron said. She gave him a hug and cheek kisses. Her hair and makeup were perfect, and when she started to sweat, she would have to take a break. She drove him crazy. Why go to the gym if she did not want to sweat? It was always about the attention, he had no doubt.

"Saffron," he said with a nod. "Did you have a good weekend?"

"Yeah, the conference was like amazing and so inspirational. I thought you were going to come? Why did you ditch?"

Saffron was in her mid-twenties, tall and beautiful, and she knew it. She reminded him a lot of Carla when she was that age. She tried so hard to impress everyone else that she seemed to forget who she was or what she really wanted. She was too busy looking over her shoulder to see who was watching her.

"Well, the weather wasn't exactly the best when I left, so we didn't make it up there as expected."

"That's too bad." She put her hand on his shoulder and squeezed his arm. "Wow, you must work really hard to get them like this, huh?"

He brushed her hand off. "I just got done lifting. Why don't we start with some stretching, okay?"

She followed him into the exercise room and slapped his butt with a laugh. "Sorry, I just can't help myself."

He frowned. "Saffron," he said sternly.

She batted her eyelashes innocently. "What?"

He shook his head. She was not someone who could be tamed. She was inappropriate and a little annoying, but he had a business to run, so he needed to figure out a way to handle her professionally. But sometimes she really challenged his nerves.

As he finished her session and led her into a cool down, he was proud of himself for pushing her enough to sweat. Her hair was slightly damp, and she was panting. He grabbed a towel from the back wall by the window and threw it at her.

"OMG. Who knew that could be so much work? My whole body feels exhausted after that? Just wow." She dabbed at her forehead with the towel, careful not to ruin her makeup.

"Next time try coming without makeup on, and then you won't have to worry about it."

"Oh, Nicholas," she said. "You are just too funny. I think

you and I really have a connection. Drinks at six so we can schedule some more sessions?"

"Well, I ..."

"Zimmy's at six it is," she said.

She was out the door before he caught her. She stopped to talk to his sister. He did not want Maria to find out he let a date with Saffron happen or she would never let it go. Everyone knew she had a thing for trainers, but he was pretty sure she had a thing for any guy that was a challenge until he wasn't anymore.

Yeah, she was beautiful and had a killer body, but killer bodies and no personality were never a delightful combination. He needed a woman that was kind and smart and ... well, someone like Valarie.

He waited for them to stop talking and then cut her off at the exit door.

"Saffron, Saffron, wait a second."

She turned around, a big grin spread across her face. "Hey there, Nicholas. You just couldn't let me get away, could you?"

"I'm sorry, I can't meet tonight. I have to pick up my daughter."

"After, then?"

He shook his head. "It's not a good night. You can arrange your next appointment with me tomorrow after your Calorie Counters meeting. I'll be around."

"Nah, I'll take a rain check, Nicholas. I'm busy tomorrow. You owe me," she said.

How was he going to let her down lightly? He would have to lie through his teeth or she would never stop.

"I'm seeing someone," he said and then cringed. What did he just do? She would tell everyone, and it was far from true. Maybe she would leave it at that and not ask questions.

She squealed. "Nicholas Ryan, who is the lucky lady? I just have to meet her."

Nope. Who was he kidding? This was Saffron he was talking about. She would never stop bugging him until he told her about this fictional person he was dating.

"It is kind of on the down low," he said.

He tried to get away, but she grabbed his arm. "I'm not letting you go until you tell me who she is."

"When I'm ready to tell people, you will be the first to know. Maria doesn't even know, so please keep this between you and me."

He heard a gasp behind him and frowned as he turned around. "Maria, hi,"

She tapped her foot. "What don't I know? What are you hiding?"

"He's seeing someone!" Saffron announced the news for the entire gym to hear.

Three people close by came walking up.

"Nicholas, when were you going to tell me? I must know," Lilly from Calorie Counters said. Her friends giggled.

"Ugh, I have to go." He scowled at Saffron. "Thanks a lot."

She waved. "Anytime. You will tell me who it is."

He would have to explain what really happened to Maria eventually, but she was sure to let it slip when people started asking around. He would have to lie to her, too, and then after a couple of weeks, tell her it didn't work out. What was he going to tell Linda? Would it get back to his father? Val? What a mess. He was so sick of Saffron, and why didn't he tell her the truth?

Regan had put a couple of chicken breasts in the oven and was making a salad when he walked in.

He picked a tomato out of the bowl and ate it. "You're home early."

She slapped his hand playfully as he reached for another.

"I can't believe you're cooking, and I can't believe your phone isn't in front of your face."

"Ugh, can I just have a thank you? I used to cook for us all the time back in Grand Rapids, you know."

"I know, but you haven't cooked much here. I love your cooking and it's nice to be able to take a break. I'm exhausted."

"Hey Dad, can I stay at my friend Alex's house on Halloween?" She looked in his direction. "You know, my female friend from swimming."

"I guess so."

He avoided telling Regan he knew exactly who Alex was, and that he spent the whole weekend stranded with her mother.

"You owe me for making me stay with my grandpa last weekend like a ten-year-old child. You need to trust me, I'm responsible."

"It's not that I don't trust you, you are a teenager, Regan. I won't give you an opportunity you can't resist when your brain isn't fully developed yet. It's called a crime of opportunity."

"Ugh, fine. Just eat your dinner."

She had missed him, he could tell. She couldn't stop talking. He enjoyed listening to her complain about her weekend and go off about swim practice. If he said anything, she would likely scurry away, so he listened to every word.

CHAPTER 14

"You lost another five pounds this week, wow. How do you keep doing it? Usually people plateau after a couple of weeks," Maria said.

Saffron shot daggers at Maria. "How do you know that? You're not an expert."

Saffron turned her back on Maria and focused on me. "You're doing amazing, Val. I'm back to my starting weight of one thirty-five. Please tell me how you do it."

Maria checked her mid-section and squeezed it. "My mom is the professional and the teacher, remember? I listen, even if I don't always follow her advice."

Saffron ignored her. "How much are you down now, Val?"

"Well, fifteen pounds, I guess."

"Fifteen pounds?" Maria almost spit the water out of her mouth. "I'm down six."

"It's not a competition," Saffron said. "So, how much do you weigh now, girl?"

Linda came out of nowhere. "Most women don't like to say that out loud."

"I think just telling you I dropped fifteen pounds indicates where my weight is at," I said. I was proud, and I didn't want to put myself down by putting my weight out there. I wasn't exactly thin yet.

The group clapped as Linda announced my progress to the class.

Maria looked a little sad and smiled gently at me. "I would be happy to be in the one hundred club. I'm going to have to try harder."

"I'm sorry, I didn't mean to ..."

Maria waved me off. "No, no, it's not you. It's just with Mikey being so sick last weekend, I got little sleep and I gained weight instead of losing it. I was stress-eating."

I shot her a concerned look and waited for her to finish, but Linda started the class.

"What went well this week?"

Everyone was silent until a woman's hand shot up from the front row.

"I went to the gym every day this week, and I had excuses made up in my head, but I still went. I remembered what you said, Linda, about how it's harder to get to the gym than to work out once you're there, and you were right. I wasn't really motivated until I got there. I realized my mind was telling me I didn't want to go, but really my body was begging me to exercise. It felt so good."

"I'm so glad to hear that. It isn't easy to fight the self-sabotage, but Erin is right. We're our own worst enemies. We need to take a step back and listen to that inner voice and then tell ourselves to shut up." Linda made her way to the back of the room. "How about what went wrong this week? Anyone want to share?"

Saffron stood up. No one stood up during the meetings, but Saffron was really one of a kind.

"So, there's this guy," she said.

There was always a guy with her. The room groaned in

response and put their heads down, but she did not seem to notice.

"There is this guy that I really like, and I asked him out but was shocked to find out he was in a relationship. I went home and threw up."

Linda's face drooped. "How long had it been since your last purge?"

"Three weeks."

She looked at me. "I binge and purge."

"Do you really like this guy? Tell me why him turning you down hurt so bad."

Linda was so patient with her.

"Hmm, I'm not sure. He treats me differently than most men do. He doesn't act like I am just a piece of ass, you know. He sees everyone for who they are. He looks me in the eye when he talks to me, and he truly cares about people. Men just aren't like that. I mean, like I have never met a man like that before. I always thought they just wanted one thing, but even when I wear my booty shorts that seem to magnetize men, he still looks at me the same way. I don't get it. Is that a good thing or a bad thing?" She sat back down, deep in thought.

"He's seeing someone, Saffron," Maria said. "He told you that. He must really like this woman, give him some space. It isn't about you. Nicholas hasn't dated in years. Can you just be happy for him?"

Linda looked shocked. "Nicholas? My Nicholas?"

My stomach lurched. I was with him the whole weekend, and he never mentioned anything about seeing someone. He acted as if he were single. Why did I even care? Because he was a good kisser? I wanted Eric back anyway, so why was this bothering me?

"Now look what you've done," Maria said to Saffron.

Saffron shrugged her shoulders. "Whoops. I totally like forgot you were his mom. He is a grown-ass man though."

"Sorry everyone, my Nicholas doesn't really date, and he doesn't like everyone knowing his business. Let's just keep this to ourselves. Can you guys do that for me?" Linda said, as if she were talking to her best friends.

Everyone nodded or said yes.

"I guess. Fine," Saffron said with her arms crossed.

I believed everyone would keep their word because we all respected Linda. Although I was still having a hard time understanding why he didn't tell me. He opened up so much at the cabin, but obviously he was afraid to tell me everything. Did it really matter? The kiss was a mistake. It's what happens when two people are all alone and think they may be stranded forever. It's normal.

The meeting was over, and all I could think about was stuffing my face with chocolate chip cookies. Linda stopped me on the way out the door.

Did she know I was planning on cheating?

"Will you wait around so I can talk to you quick?"

How could I say no? I waited until everyone was gone, but I did not know why she wanted to talk to me. Why did I feel like a child being told to stay after class? Like I automatically felt I did something wrong. Maria was first out the door because her husband texted her most of the meeting about Mikey, only wanting his mom. I could not imagine starting all over and having more children. One was enough for me. But Maria loved the balance now that she worked two part-time jobs and got to work out and go to Calorie Counters, too.

Linda came out. "Can you sit down with me for a second?"

This seemed serious. What did I do?

"I was bummed you guys didn't make it to the conference

last weekend. I heard you and Nicholas had some car troubles, huh?"

This felt more like an interrogation. "Yeah. We didn't think we were going to make it out alive, to be honest."

"Maria tells me the two of you had to break into a cabin. That must have been so scary."

Linda was confusing me more and more. Why did it seem like she was upset with me? Did she think I did that on purpose to trap him or something?

"It really was."

"I will not go around in circles here. I think we have enough respect for each other to just say it. Is there something going on between the two of you?"

So that was what she was worried about? Linda was worried I was the one in a relationship with Nicholas? Did she not think I was good enough for him?

"No, nothing is going on between us. I have no idea who Maria and Saffron are talking about. This is all news to me, I swear."

Could she tell I was getting all worked up about this? I wanted to walk out on her. My respect for Linda was lessened by the second.

"I know Nicholas can be persuasive. Did he tell you not to tell anyone?"

"No."

I stood up, and Linda followed.

"I believe you," she said. "Did you guys maybe have an end of the world moment where you thought you were going to die so you might as well just have sex?"

"Linda! No." My face was on fire. "It wasn't like that at all. Nicholas was a gentleman and a good friend, but nothing more."

Linda frowned and sat back down. "I was really hoping to

intimidate you into telling me. I'm sorry. I'm really not good at being tough, am I?"

Was she still trying to trick me? "No, you did a good job, and if there was something going on you probably would have gotten me to talk."

Linda smiled. "He just won't talk to me anymore. Did he happen to mention another woman at all?"

I thought back to our conversations. If he mentioned someone, I would have remembered. That was something I wouldn't forget.

"The only woman he mentioned other than Regan was Carla."

"Carla? He mentioned Carla?"

I nodded. "He talked about what happened and why she left."

"Oh."

"Yeah, it's really sad."

"She wasn't a good person or an excellent influence on Nicholas when he was younger, but I think she was just really scared and confused. Thank you for telling me."

I nodded again. "Next time don't give me the third degree, just ask, okay?"

"Deal. I can really be an angry mama bear sometimes, but he is so special to me."

I understood that all too well. I knew I would have done the same for Alex.

My stop at the grocery store on my way home was solely to buy junk food to shove into my mouth after the day I had. I made my way down the cookie aisle and grabbed three boxes of white fudge Oreos. They were my very favorite and only came out right around the holidays.

I picked up chips and pop, but as I came around the corner, I spotted Cinnamon. The sight of her stopped me right in my tracks. I tried to turn my cart around to avoid her before she saw me, but we locked eyes and she came at me like a predator preying on an unsuspecting victim.

"Hi, Valarie." She smiled, showing her perfect white teeth.

"Cinnamon," I said, probably too inviting. "How are you?"

She glanced at my cart and sneered. "Oh, dear. I don't remember the last time I had Oreos. I wouldn't want to get fat. I would have to call you and find out where to find plus sizes, and I would rather die than be stuck in those clothes." She pointed at my outfit in disgust. "I'm so jealous that you carry yourself so well with all that ... extra weight. I, on the other hand, would rather die. But you really pull it off."

I wanted to punch her right between the eyes, but she wasn't worth it. I bit my tongue and smiled back instead. This was the woman my daughter had to spend time with. I knew I had to be the better person. I would not let this superficial woman get to me.

I tried to walk past her. "Okay, then. Great seeing you."

Did I really just say great seeing you? What was wrong with me?

Cinnamon's smile disappeared, and the demon within came out. "I'm so glad I ran into you. I'm just dying to find out where you bought those brown curtains in my living room. Eric said you were the one who found them, correct?"

"They were a wedding gift," I said, hoping to remind her I was the one who married Eric, and she stole him away from his family.

The thought of Cinnamon having the curtains my mother bought for us made me cringe. Thinking about the two of them sitting at my kitchen table in the morning, drinking coffee out of my favorite coffee cups and talking about my curtains, was an image that would only play over and over in my mind for weeks, I was sure.

"They sure are fabulous, but I was hoping to get them in

another color. Brown is just so ugly, you know? The house needs a little younger taste to liven it up. Anyway, good luck with your cookies. I have to get home because Eric won't stop texting me. You know how he is."

I wanted to gag. I could feel the bile rising in my throat.

"He sure is a horny thing, isn't he? Later, Bee. Have fun with your food."

Have fun with your food? Eric is horny? She was so childish! The war was on.

Who was I kidding? I would never get Eric back. I needed to stop getting my hopes up, but we were a family. I wanted my life back.

Once Cinnamon was finally out of sight, I put the junk food back on the nearest shelf. I didn't care that I was putting it back in the wrong place, but the guilt was killing me. So I walked around the store and put the junk food back on the shelf where it belonged. It sucked being a good person with a conscience.

Cinnamon would soon realize her plan of putting me down was backfiring and just gave me more ambition to get thin. I put away the Oreos. I would not give in and eat myself into a food coma. I knew what I needed to do to get him back and no matter how hard it was, I was going to do it.

I picked up my phone. "Maria, what are you doing? I need you to come shopping with me. It's time for a new wardrobe."

More like an outfit or two. Let's be real. I did not have that kind of money.

I couldn't believe how fabulous tighter clothes looked on me now that I lost some weight. I was now in a size 12, but my stomach wasn't as swollen so I had a little room in the waist. High-waisted jeans looked so good on me now, and I had to turn around just to remind myself how good my butt looked in them. It was a start on my journey to become irresistible.

"You are a hot mama," Maria said. "Look at that ass."

My face grew hot. "Eat your heart out, Eric," I said with a laugh.

"I can't believe it took you this long to get clothes that actually fit you. You have a great body, you know that?"

"I don't know if I would go that far, but soon."

Alex even looked up from her phone to stare at me when I got home from shopping. "Mom, you went shopping. I love your outfit. Are those high-waisted jeans? I may have to borrow them from you."

Coming from Alex, this was an enormous compliment. She never even noticed when I had six inches cut off my hair last month. "They would be huge on you."

"For how thin you are getting, I'm sure it won't be long until you're my size and then I will steal your clothes."

Alex was a size six. Would I ever be a size six? I liked to think it was possible, but I couldn't imagine it.

I brought the bags upstairs and dropped onto my bed with a bounce. I felt amazing and imagined what I would look like when I lost some more weight.

Alex came bursting through my closed door.

"So, I just got off the phone with Regan, and she said you and her dad were stranded in the snowstorm last weekend and had to break into a cabin together? Spill the tea! Why didn't you tell me?"

I sighed. "I wasn't hiding it from you, sweetie. I guess it just never came up. It was no big deal. A plow came and saved us, and we were never in any real danger."

"Mom, Regan thinks her dad has a crush on you. He hasn't stopped talking about you since the moment he got home. Are Regan and I going to be sisters? Because I think that would be really cool, I'm just saying."

"Oh no, he doesn't have a crush on me. We're just friends."

"It makes sense why you're eating so healthy and going shopping for cute clothes. Come on, I'm your daughter, you can tell me. Regan seems to think you two are definitely an item."

"We are not an item, and anyway, I think he's off the market. I've been married for decades. Come on, give me a break here."

"Dad found someone else before you two even broke up, Mom. I think that gives you the right to find someone else, too. I'm just saying, if it happened, it wouldn't upset me. I would love to have Regan as my sister."

"Sorry to disappoint, but Regan will not be your sister," I said with a stare to show her I was serious. "But I appreciate your support."

Alex got to the doorway and turned back. "And just so you know, Cinnamon and Dad have been fighting non-stop. She sucks."

"I had no idea. I'm sorry, honey. That must be so hard to be around."

She shrugged. "Nah. It's just karma.

I considered chasing Regan down and lecturing her about respecting her father and whomever he wants to be with, but instead I laughed into my hand once she was gone. I was going to stay out of it, but I had to admit it felt good to hear.

My stomach grumbled, but I was too tired to get up and make something to eat. I lay in my comfy bed and read the newest Elin Hilderbrand book, *Golden Girl*, that had arrived at the bookstore that morning. This was my happy place. My books were my escape from all the stress eating and unhappy days. I opened up the book and got sucked into the pages, leaving me no longer feeling hungry.

CHAPTER 15

I arrived at the bookstore a little before seven on Halloween morning with plans to get the store ready, including setting out candy for the trick-or-treaters. Maria sent a text early saying something came up, so she would not make it in for coffee. Maria never missed morning coffee.

I passed the mirror next to the stuffed spider and did a double take at my reflection. My new high-waisted pants and black long-sleeved shirt tucked into my pants, and my black cat ears definitely made me not only look the part, but I looked and felt thin. Velcro attached my cat tail to my pants. I smiled and squealed like a teenager at my appearance. I always thought I looked great until I looked in the mirror and realized how heavy I looked–until this moment.

My smile faded at the thought of skipping breakfast again this morning. I knew it wasn't healthy, but I loved the control I had over my weight and how thin I felt when my stomach was empty. Sure, it made my hands a little shaky, but I felt so much better when my stomach didn't stick out. The way I felt when it was full was an awful feeling, like a brick in my gut. I fixed myself a cup of coffee and a shot of espresso.

My morning was so relaxing, spent organizing the new shipment of books, cleaning, and vacuuming the store. A few people came in to browse, but it was pretty slow. The only sales I expected to make today were a few Halloween children's books and free candy. It was the same every year.

The bell rang just as I was wrapping the cord around the vacuum and placing it in the storage closet. "Be right with you."

I stopped in my tracks as I rounded the corner and there Eric stood with a dozen roses wrapped in a red bow. To say I was in shock was an understatement. I stood there, unable to move. I blinked, unsure if this was real or if it was a hallucination. Was Eric really there with a look of desire in his eyes?

He nodded in approval at the spider webs and decorations. "It looks nice in here."

"Thank you."

He came back.

He looked me up and down. "You look… wow."

He knew I had a hard time taking compliments, and I could not remember the last time he noticed me, let alone complimented me on my appearance.

"What are you doing here?"

He shook his head as if waking up from a dream. He handed me the flowers.

"Here, these are for you. I messed up. Please forgive me. I was a jerk."

"I'll be right back. I need to grab a vase for these."

I had to get away. This was what I wanted, so why could I not face him? I needed to breathe and think.

I hid in the back room, leaning against the wall. My heartbeat was out of control and my breathing was way too fast. I was sure I was going to pass out. Where was Cinnamon? What exactly did he want? Would he change his mind again tomorrow? I was not sure of anything. I steadied my breathing with deep belly breaths and then made my way back to him.

He was pacing and running his fingers through his hair. Our eyes locked.

He blurted, "I kicked Cinnamon out."

I rubbed the back of my neck. "Wow, okay. I'm not sure what to say. You caught me off guard, showing up like this."

"I'm sorry, I was so dumb thinking I would be happier without you."

He took a step toward me. "Cinnamon is so immature. I can't believe I didn't see it. I didn't realize what I had with you until I lost you."

I was lost in his eyes. He picked me.

"She just isn't you. I will never forgive myself for letting her talk to you the way she did at the swim meet. When I saw that guy kiss you afterward, my heart dropped. I was jealous. I knew I needed you back. The thought of his hands all over you ..."

"You were jealous? Of me?"

I had to pinch myself to make sure this was actually happening. I imagined it so many times, but never did I expect it to happen this way. For him to say he was jealous of me.

"Yes, I was jealous. I made a huge mistake. You were always there, and I guess I forgot how much I truly loved you. Cinnamon is selfish and childish. You are a woman." His eyes were filled with passion.

This time, I took a step closer to him.

"Alexandra and I got into a fight yesterday because she wanted to hand out candy instead of going to a movie with me and Cinnamon. When I said no, she got upset and told me about you and that Nicholas guy from the swim meet. I don't want you to be with anyone else. Choose me."

This was his karma. Now he knew what I felt like these last few months. A part of me wanted him to feel hurt and rejected.

"Anyway, that was the moment I knew I had lost you, and you were worth the fight. I even called Maria this morning so I could have a few minutes alone with you so I could apologize. I love you, Valarie. I love you so much."

No way was Maria happy about this.

He leaned in and kissed me. His lips were warm and soft. I pulled away. I couldn't let him off this easily. Not after what he did.

"So, where is Cinnamon?"

"She's gone, gone forever. I told her I loved you, and I always loved you. I want another chance. At this. At us."

His hands explored my body, up the back of my shirt, taking my breath away.

I missed his lips and the way he was looking at me right now, but what if he got sick of me again and went back to Cinnamon when times got tough?

"Val?"

I looked up, our eyes locking again. I thought back to our wedding, when we locked eyes just like this. The day he got down on one knee and made a big romantic gesture in front of all of our friends and family, and then he sang and danced to Bryan Adams to win my heart even more. The day Alex was born, Eric held her in his arms for the longest time until she cried and he looked so scared, like every new dad. Our trips to the North Shore, hand-in-hand as we watched the sunset and made love on the beach. There were so many good times. How could I not give our marriage one more shot? What would it hurt? This was what I wanted, after all. Wasn't it?

"What am I going to do with the house in Brooklyn?"

He squealed, picking me up and kissing me more passionately than he had in a decade.

"You are more beautiful today than you were when we first started dating. Thank you for giving us another shot. You won't regret it, I promise."

I bit down on my smile. "Hey, Eric."

"Yeah?"

"I want this moment to last forever, but I must get back to the store. Can we finish this conversation after work?"

"I'm sorry, get back to it. Let's celebrate tonight. Dinner at six?"

I shook my head. "I'll be here until at least seven for the trick-or-treaters."

He hit himself in the head with the palm of his hand. "Oh yeah, that's right, it's Halloween. I'll make reservations for seven. Should I pick you up here, then?"

"It's a date," I said.

He kissed me again, dipping me backward, then he hugged me close.

"You have no idea how much I have missed you. I can't wait to see those sexy clothes on the floor later."

I giggled and shooed him out. "Goodbye, Eric."

He beeped his horn and waved at me. I watched him from the door as he pulled away.

He was jealous. Jealous of Nicholas and me after our fake kiss. He did not know about the kiss in the woods, but that was something I did not share with even Maria. Who was the mysterious woman Nicholas was dating, anyway? But wait, why did I even care? I had my family back. I had to tell Alex.

"Are you serious? Dad? Why?"

It was not exactly the reaction I thought I was going to get from her. Was this not what she wanted?

"I thought you would be happy for us. Cinnamon moved out."

Alex stopped by to get another bag of candy for the trick-or-treaters at our house because we had a lot more kids than we expected and we were running low. Here I thought she would be thrilled to find out her parents were back together, but she was not happy at all.

"Eh," Alex said. "I thought you liked Nicholas."

I put my hand on her back. "Alex, I told you he's seeing someone else. Nothing happened between us, he's just a friend.

"Regan said he only said that because some chick from the gym tried to get him to go on a date. Some lady named Emerald or something."

"Saffron?"

"Yeah, whatever. Anyway, it isn't true."

I shook the thought away. "I'm happy. I want us to be a family again." My eyes teared up.

"I'm sorry, Mom. I just want you to be happy. If you're happy, I'm happy, okay? I just worry about Dad doing that to you again. I don't want to see you get hurt. I love him, but he doesn't exactly think before he does things."

How sad my teenager knew this about her dad, but she would see this time was different. No marriage was perfect, but she was too young to see that.

"I appreciate you looking out for me."

The bell dinged, and I grabbed the bucket of candy.

"I'll see you later, Mom," she said.

It wasn't a trick-or-treater, instead, it was Regan and Nicholas. Alex stopped to greet them at the door.

"Trick-or-Treat," he said. "Surprise."

I was definitely surprised and curious about what he was wearing. I couldn't help but smile.

"What are you doing here? More importantly, what are you wearing?"

"Well, Regan and your daughter here were planning on giving out candy to trick-or-treaters at your house, and I thought I would help you here at the store. I had this old costume, and I thought it would be fun to show it off. You don't like it?"

He distracted me with his puppy dog eyes and pouty lip.

"Bye," the girls said as they walked out the door.

Alex looked back and winked at me.

I could not help staring at Nicholas. He was a grown man in a spiderman costume with tight spandex and all. Every muscle was bulging beneath the fabric. He made that costume look so good.

"Nice costume, I like it," I said. "It takes a real man to wear spandex."

"I thought you'd get a kick out of it. I must warn you, my package isn't really this big, I'm wearing a jockstrap."

I burst out laughing and could not stop because, of course, my eyes looked directly at it. I had to excuse myself and run to the restroom so I did not pee my pants from laughing so hard. When I came back, two little princesses stood in front of Nicholas.

"Your costume is the best! Thank you for the candy," one little girl said as she skipped away.

"Happy Halloween," he said as they waved on their way out the door.

"Kids are so cute," he said. "One of the little girls actually told me to tell her dad where I got my costume because he was wearing a T-Rex costume, and he could hardly see out of it. She called him an embarrassment. He couldn't even fit in the door."

"She is right, you look great."

"Thank you. Listen, before more kids come in, I want to talk to you about Linda. She told me what happened, and I want you to know that Saffron kept pestering me and ..."

"And you told her you had a girlfriend to shut her up?" I said, finishing his sentence.

"Well, yeah. How did you know?"

"A little birdie."

"If you knew, why haven't you called me?"

"You haven't called me either."

After I said it, I realized I was not only flirting with him, but I was leading him on, too. I was with Eric now, and I needed to tell him.

"Listen, Nicholas, there's something I have to tell you."

The bell rang again.

"One sec."

I took one step before realizing I was too late. I looked at Eric and then back to Nicholas. "I'm so sorry you have to find out this way," I whispered to him.

Eric acted like he didn't even see Nicholas, but that wasn't possible, was it? He put his hands on the side of my face, and pulled me into him with such force, and then kissed me. The kiss lasted much longer than expected, and it was a bit uncomfortable. He was practically eating my face. By the time he let me go, Nicholas was already by the door, and I was out of breath and had to wipe the slobber off my chin.

I sprinted to catch up to him. "Nicholas, wait."

He was by his car, opening up the door.

"I'm sorry," I said.

He shot me a worried glance. "If this is what you want, I'm happy for you," he said. "Have a good night."

I studied him, but he did not seem angry, more surprised. I locked up the store and took Eric's hand.

"Hungry?"

"Yes," I said, but I felt sick about not being able to straighten this all out with Nicholas. He knew how much I loved Eric, didn't he? It was just some harmless flirting. He could have anyone. He didn't actually have feelings for me.

CHAPTER 16

Maybe this was the bad karma he long deserved. He told himself not to get involved with Val, but he could not help himself. At first, he wanted to get to know her better, but then he fell in love with her. How was that possible? He promised himself he would be single forever.

He took off his shoes and collapsed on the couch. He heard some laughing upstairs and then footsteps that creaked as they put their weight on each step. Were the girls here? They must have stopped here on their way back to Alex's house.

His house was enormous, built in the nineteen twenties. Eventually he wanted to move to his cabin in the city of Side Lake when Regan graduated from high school. Every summer they lived out at their cabin on Perch Lake. It was a lake of its own, not connected to any other.

It was calmer and more relaxing than the chain of lakes because it wasn't connected to another lake. But living in town was convenient for her, and he worried about her driving highway five from Side Lake in the winter.

"Hey, Alex and I are going to a movie. Can I use your car?"

Regan got her license a few months ago, but he would not buy her a car until she was more responsible. He hated when she had his car, but he only let her borrow it when he knew he was home for the night.

Alex was a beautiful young woman and looked like a younger version of Val. She had that dark Italian skin like her mother, and long, dark hair.

"It's so great to officially meet you, Alex." He shook her hand. Her grip was confident, and she smiled at him as if she knew something he didn't.

She knew a secret about him. His secret crush on her mother, which was not exactly a secret anymore. Regan knew him well, and she had a big mouth. He overheard her telling someone over the phone, and she really only talked to Alex.

"Dad, come on, we don't shake hands, that's weird," Regan said.

Alex looked at Regan. "I don't mind. I think handshakes are nice. It's great to meet you, Mr. Ryan. My mom tells me so much about you."

"Where is Alex's mom, anyway? I thought you guys were hanging out tonight?" Regan said.

"I didn't realize she already had plans, and I was tired anyway."

Regan looked at him sideways and then exchanged glances with her friend.

Alex's lip quivered. "My mom went out with my dad, didn't she?"

"Uh ..." Was she not happy that her parents were getting back together? What teen did not dream of their parents getting back together after a divorce?

"It's okay, Dad. She doesn't want them together. She

wants her mom to be happy, and we think the two of you would be perfect together."

"It's true. I see the way her face lights up when she talks about you," Alex said.

"She talks about me?"

He was surprised at the thought.

"Oh yeah. She told me all about the weekend you two got lost in the woods together. How romantic. She went on and on about you."

He sat up taller. "She did?"

"I think she thought you were dating someone else or something, so she took my dad back. It's, whatever."

"Ok, well, we are going to go. Bye Daddy," Regan said. She pushed her friend out the door.

Not five minutes after they left, he heard a knock at the door.

"Okay, Regan, you know there's a key for the house on the ..." He opened the door and stared. He could not believe his eyes. He knew that hair anywhere.

"Hello, Nick," she said. "Can I come in?"

He was blocking the doorway because he could not move. His eyes blinked rapidly. "Carla?"

She looked like Carla, but much older. She was still thin, but had more wrinkles around her eyes and mouth, and her skin looked like leather from too much sun.

"It's me," she said.

He had no emotions about her arrival. Sure, he thought this day would come, but he hoped it would be after Regan turned eighteen, when she could make her own choices about her time with her mother. This was going to be a tremendous shock to her. How would Regan react?

"What are you doing here?"

She slid past him into his house. "I'm here to see my daughter, of course."

Did she forget she had not contacted Regan in almost fourteen years? Did she think she could show up and everything would be fine? As if the last fourteen years never happened?

"Regan isn't here."

"Well then, I guess that will give me time to catch up with my husband." She tapped his chest with her pointer finger and moved closer to him.

He stepped back and removed her hand. "I am not your husband."

She laughed. "You actually are. Legally," she said, raising her eyebrows at him.

"Where have you been all this time?"

She walked over to his couch and sat down.

He threw up his hands. "Just make yourself comfortable."

She acted as though she never heard his comment. "I think I need a drink for this. Sit down, quit being so uptight."

"I quit drinking years ago, Carla. I don't have any alcohol in the house. Besides, I think you owe our daughter a sober explanation of what happened."

She stood up, her small black skirt rising a little too high.

He turned his head in disgust and shielded himself from further view of her butt cheek. "Carla, have some decency, pull your skirt down."

She looked down. "It's nothing you haven't seen before. When did you stop liking what my bottom looks like?"

"When you walked out the door years ago."

"You were a drunk, Nick." She picked up a photo of him with Regan and then put it back on the table. "She looks just like me."

"You're right, I was a drunk, and you left our child with me and took off without a word. What if I couldn't sober up?

I get why you left me. I deserved it, but not our child. Not when I was at my worst with my addiction. What if something had happened to her?"

She turned and looked at him. "It didn't and you're welcome." She tapped his chest. "You're sober, aren't you? Because you knew you had no choice, right? You should thank me. You haven't changed one bit, you know that? The only thing that changed is that you aren't a puddle, and it looks to me like you replaced the alcohol addiction with exercise."

He had probably doubled in muscle size since he last saw her. After he quit drinking, he turned to exercise. Endorphins had a way of letting out the stress without resorting to alcohol.

"It's a positive passion, not an addiction. Exercise doesn't run my life, it improves it. And it's how I make my living at the gym."

"Oh, so you work at a gym now, huh?"

She walked toward him slowly, making sure her hips popped with each step. She was trying to seduce him. That was how she used to always get her way with him. But the joke was on her now because it was not working. She could not play these games anymore.

"Actually, I own a gym," he said, sticking out his chest.

She continued walking toward him until her face was inches from his. She batted her eyelashes and kissed him on the lips. He was shocked, but he could not move away. He just stared at her.

"Sounds like we own a gym since I'm your wife and all."

She grabbed her jacket off the back of the couch and buttoned it. "I'll be back to see my daughter tomorrow. Bye-bye, handsome." She air kissed him and shut the door behind her.

They were better off when she disappeared. How the

heck did she find them in Hibbing? He picked up his phone and stared at it. He wanted to call Val, but she was with her husband now. Linda? No, she would be just as upset.

"Maria," he said as soon as he heard her voice on the other line. "Can you come over? I need you."

Maria was always honest, but kind. It was a no brainer that she was the best person to help advise him.

"She just flaunted herself and said she was your wife? That takes guts. Where has she been all this time? Did she give any explanation at all?" She asked after he told her what happened.

"No. Not a word."

"She will not get away with this. Not if I have anything to say about it."

Maria was by his side when Regan got home. He gave her a hug, but pulled away when she did not hug him back. She smelled like alcohol.

"Regan, have you been drinking?"

She looked away.

"You can't lie to me. I smell it on you. Where were you drinking? I thought you were at the movies?"

Regan rolled her eyes. "It was just a couple of beers, Dad. Get off my case." She pushed past him.

"Oh no, you will not get away with it that easily. You were drinking and driving in my car? Do you not understand what could happen to you if you were caught or if you killed someone? You'd have weeks on the swim team, which means you would have to sit on the bench and watch and be unable to swim in any meets. Did you think about that? And you would have to go to court and explain your actions. You realize you'd miss regions, right? That is the least of what could have happened to you. Did you think at all?"

When she did not respond, he said, "Regan, look at me." His hands were shaking, and he put them behind his back.

Maria got off the couch and stepped in front of him. "You know I love you, Reggs, but this is out of character for you. Why were you drinking and driving?"

"You guys are exaggerating. Fine, I went to a Halloween party with Alex. I didn't plan on drinking, but it just, I don't know, happened. It isn't a big deal. It's not like I do this all the time. I would not get caught. I'm not stupid."

"It is a very big deal, young lady. I'm really disappointed in you. You could have killed someone."

Regan let out a high pitch groan. "I'm disappointed in you, Dad. How could you let Valarie go? Alex said that her mom went back to her dad because of you."

"That's not true." Was there any truth to that? It did not matter. "Stop changing the subject. You screwed up, and you're grounded from my car. Give me your phone." He put out his hand.

"But, Dad--"

"Now," he said.

He had been so easy on her because of all she had gone through, but his patience was gone.

"Just because you were a drunk, doesn't mean I am going to be. You just don't understand what it is like and you don't even care!"

She stomped up the stairs to her bedroom and slammed the door, making them both jump.

Nicholas bit his tongue. He would not argue with her. He would not win, and he had to be the adult here.

Maria put her hand on his back. "It's going to be okay. You did well. I had no idea you were such a good parent. I'm proud of you. I know that couldn't be easy to do."

He rubbed his eyes. "I'm exhausted. I can't tell Regan her mom is back when she's drunk."

"You can tell her in the morning, but you need to tell her before Carla shows up again. I'll call Mark and stay the night to help you in the morning, if you want."

He waved her off. "No, no. You've been amazing, and I'm grateful for that, but this is something I need to do on my own. I've got this."

"Okay, sit down," she said.

He did as she asked because his legs were wobbly.

"Can I ask you something off subject?"

He let out a sigh and shook his head. "What?"

"Tell me about this woman you're seeing."

He laughed. "I'm not seeing anyone."

"Are you sure?"

"I'm very sure. Last I checked, I was single. Why? Do you think this is the best time to ask me about this? Do you not see what is going on?"

She patted his leg gently. "Yes, I'm taking your mind off things. Was Valarie the woman you were referring to when you said you were seeing someone?"

"I like her, yes, but we weren't seeing each other. I just needed to get Saffron off my back. It doesn't matter anyway, she's back with Eric now."

"So? Get her back."

He stood up, unable to sit any longer. "I'm not going after her. She has her family back. It's what she wants."

"Okay, okay. I'll shut my mouth."

He hit her in the face gently with his pillow. "Highly unlikely. I don't think you know how to shut your trap."

"That's probably true, but I wanted to be nice. But we both know she isn't in love with him, she's just used to him."

"I don't know if that is true. Can I ask you a question?"

She raised her eyebrows and put her hands deep in her pockets.

"What's going on?"

She turned her head away. "I don't know what you're talking about."

"I know you," he said. He could tell something was off. They knew each other well. Her eyes looked so sad.

"I'm exhausted. It would make me much happier if you would just let yourself be happy. The two of you were meant to be together, trust me."

She kissed him on the forehead. "Now get some sleep. Tomorrow is going to be an emotional rollercoaster."

He walked her out. He was disappointed in Regan, and he was disappointed in himself. Why did Carla have to show up now?

CHAPTER 17

I unlocked the door and set down my belongings. Everything looked different. The house no longer felt like the home I designed and made my own. Cinnamon tried to undo everything I spent years creating in her short amount of time here.

I decorated the rooms in dark brown and cream. Cinnamon's red and brown made the rooms look like crap. I should have felt better that I was here and she was not and he chose me, but I just stood there feeling lonelier than I did going home to my house in Brooklyn. I was a stranger in my own home.

My forest green and white bedroom with a cherry oak bed frame was now repainted pink, as if it was a room decorated for a small child. Cinnamon could not afford the changes on her salary, that I knew. Eric must have been in support of it. I wasn't sure I could stomach sleeping in the same room where Eric had made passionate love to another woman. Was I supposed to just move back in as if nothing happened?

I had to stop over-analyzing everything. I needed to leave

the past in the past and move on. Forgive, but never forget. A fresh start. It was the only way to move on.

I started putting away the trunk full of my stuff, but realized I could not move another thing in until Eric and I had a talk about everything.

I drove the twenty minutes back to Hibbing and pulled up in front of the house I had been living in since my world was turned upside down. The gray wooden siding was peeling off. The white garage was faded and needed a fresh coat of paint. The two-stall garage was something I was so grateful for, even if one door wouldn't open because it was dented. This house stood for a vast change in my life. I was more grateful for what I had in this rundown old house than I had been in my beautiful lake home. But why?

I walked inside my house and stared out the window at the mess in the backyard next door. Since the first day I moved into this house, I wanted to leave. The neighborhood was full of peeling paint, garbage-littered yards, and strange people wandering around, talking to themselves in the middle of the night. Every time I went for a walk with Alex, we smelled marijuana. People sat on their front doorsteps and smoked it or sat around a bonfire and passed a bong. There were some good areas in Brooklyn, but my neighborhood was horrible. The house next door had wood, garbage, and metal stacked high in a pile and random crap all over the yard. They didn't mow, and they didn't seem to care that it was, well, a dump.

I wanted to leave so badly, so why was I having second thoughts? It was my home, after all.

Despite all the craziness in my neighborhood, this house felt more like home to me than the house I shared with Eric. Was it the independence I needed? I didn't want to stay in this old house, but I wasn't sure I was ready to risk it all and move back in with the man who cheated on me. I trusted him and he broke my trust. I guess it was normal to take time to repair that. I would have to think about my feelings before I met Eric for dinner.

The peace and quiet in the house were nice, but I had to face my hungover daughter and teach her a lesson she wouldn't forget. One thing teenagers loved was sleeping in. Not today.

"Alexandra, wake up."

She covered her head with a pillow. "But it's Saturday."

"You're right, it is, but you broke the rules and drink with your friends last night, so today is the day you do chores, remember? I left a list on the table downstairs. I want you to have everything done before I get back from work. No one can come over, you're grounded."

Alex pulled the pillow off her head and squinted at me. "What time is it?"

"Nine."

"In the morning? Mom, come on, my head hurts. It's too early."

I bounced the bed. "Your head hurts because you were drinking last night. Now get out of bed and get to work. It's the best cure for a hangover, and maybe you'll think next time and make better choices. "

Alex sat up and rubbed her eyes. Her hair was in snarls, and she looked a mess. I smiled a little to myself. That will teach her to be reckless.

"Hard time sleeping last night?"

"I think I'm going to vomit," she said.

Her face looked a little green.

I put my hand on her back. "The next time you think it's a wise idea to go to a party and get drunk, remember what this feels like. You and Regan are really lucky the cops weren't involved or you wouldn't be going to sections."

I hoped this was just a onetime experimental thing. Kids had no idea how much a few drinks could affect their lives, sometimes even the rest of their lives. Drinking and driving was dangerous. Alex was lucky to wake up with just a hangover.

"You know, in my day we would have a few drinks and put our keys in a bowl and sleep over. A lot has changed because of drunk drivers. You really need to think about whether this is the life you want to live. Your grandfather's life was taken too soon because of a drunk boater. None of us are invincible."

I arrived at the bookstore shortly after Alex got out of bed, then I saw the piece of paper stuck to the door. It was an eviction notice. I tore it off the door and looked around to make sure no customers were around to see it. How long had it been on the door? I fumbled with the key, my hands shaking. This was my mother's doing, or not doing. This was a rent eviction notice. Had someone given this to us as a mistake? Was this some kind of cruel joke? My parents owned this bookstore and had since I was a child.

My mom's phone went straight to her voicemail. "Typical." I wanted to close up and search for my mother and find out what was going on, but if this was real, then we needed the money to fight the eviction. None of it made any sense to me. My biggest fear was losing this store and all the blood, sweat, and tears my father had put into it to make it this successful. I wanted to keep it thriving, just as he had. I lost my husband, my home, and I could not lose this store.

I made myself a cup of coffee and put out fresh muffins from the bakery. My mind was frazzled, but I had to stay strong.

I packed away the Halloween decorations and replaced them with Thanksgiving decorations. They were nowhere near as exceptional as the Halloween decorations, but I loved all the holidays in the bookstore. Christmas was my favorite holiday, even though it was the day I missed my father the most, except for the fifth of July. That was a sad day full of terrible memories.

Christmas was the day every year we would go on a family adventure, as dad called it, hiking through the woods to find the perfect Christmas tree. My sister and I usually argued over which one to pick, but our dad would eventually step in and point out which one he thought was perfect, and we would always agree. He had an eye for things like that.

We'd trudge back through the woods, dragging the tree through the deep snow, and lift the heavy tree into the truck box. Despite being all sweaty and tired, we still had enough energy to sing Christmas carols all the way to the bookstore where we set the tree up and decorated. At home, we put up a fake tree because my dad believed the Christmas spirit kept people coming back, and he considered his customers a part of our family. He knew every person who walked into the store by name and when he did not know their name, he chatted with them until they felt comfortable enough to tell him their name without his asking. He truly cared about each and every customer. It wasn't just about the sales to him. He wanted them to feel at home.

My dad knew all the books in the store from cover to cover, from romance to children's books. He researched and read every genre. I was the only kid I knew who did not have a television in their home. We were nowhere near that poor, but we preferred to read or tell stories by the fireplace. We didn't have time for television. We had family game nights every Sunday, and we always had dinner together after the bookstore closed. Mom left an hour early, and we helped, so when our dad walked in the door, her homemade dinner was on the table.

After he died, my mom stopped cooking, and I was left to fend for my own dinner, but she never stopped baking in the mornings for the customers. My sister had gone away to college and my mom was depressed. I got pregnant with Alex a year after the accident. I was bored and alone. Our close-knit family had become strangers within weeks due to the guilt and blame we all carried from his death. He was the glue that held our family together, and without the glue, there were just pieces of what was once the closest family.

The bell above the door rang. Eric sauntered in.

"I had to see how my wife was doing and give you a kiss."

"Well, that was sweet of you. Where are you off to so early on this Saturday morning?"

"I thought I would start moving some of your things from that ugly house in Brooklyn back to your actual home."

I kissed him, but pulled away at his words.

"Okay, what's wrong? Is it something I said?"

I looked into his familiar eyes and ran my finger down the lapel of his jacket.

"How about we start with dinner tonight like we planned? I think we need to take this slow. We can't exactly pick up where we left off. There were troubles in our marriage before, and we need to make sure our relationship can withstand what it has been through in a healthy way."

He shook his head and took a step back. "You're going to hold this against me forever, aren't you? She's gone, fired from my company. You have nothing to worry about."

"It's not just that, it—"

Before I finished, the bell rang, and a woman walked in.

"Listen, let's finish this conversation when I come over tonight, okay?"

He let out a sigh, but he wasn't happy. "Fine."

He headed for the door, but not before checking out the woman from head to toe. He tipped his hat and looked at her backside as he opened the door.

Unbelievable. Had he changed at all, or could he just not control himself? Were all men like this?

I approached the woman. "Hello and welcome. I'm Valarie, but my friends call me Val. Is there anything I can help you find today?"

The woman was tan with long blonde hair. She floated across the store on her heels. Her Louis Vuitton purse was a dead giveaway she was from out of town.

"You don't have any books on how to talk to your teenage child after taking off for most of her life and not calling, do you?"

I let out a nervous laugh. "Can you be more specific?"

Her shoulders caved in, and she no longer stood as tall as she had just seconds ago. "I left her with her father when she was just a baby and as time went by, it became harder and harder to call. Am I a horrible mother?"

An uneasy feeling was building in my stomach, and it was a little awkward that she was talking to a complete stranger about something so personal, but she obviously needed to talk to someone.

"Any idea what the title would be?"

"I'm sorry, you must think I'm crazy coming into a bookstore and spilling out my troubles to a total stranger, but I have no one else to talk to. I almost called an Uber, then I saw your store and the eviction notice. I came back because I thought the person who was running this store must be feeling stressed t like I do. You do own this store, don't you?"

I shook my head. "First of all, there aren't any Uber services in the area. We have a taxi service though."

"I must have New York City girl written all over me, huh?"

"As for the eviction notice, it's a mistake. It really makes little sense. I was hoping no one saw that. I think it was someone's idea of a horrible prank. My mother actually owns this place. "

Cinnamon was probably the prankster now that I thought about it. Getting back at me for Eric. Was I the other woman now?

She put her hand on my shoulder. "It's nothing to be embarrassed about, it's not even your bookstore. If it makes you feel any better, I'm in a bookstore and I don't even read nor do I have anyone to buy a book for. I'm pretty sure my family hates me."

"So you left them to go to New York City, then?"

"I went to Los Angeles to become a star. Can you believe it? I always thought as soon as I made it, I would call my husband and daughter, and they would move to California with me. It was stupid, I know. Time passed by and before I knew it, it was too late."

"It's never too late."

The woman laughed. "I guess so. The crazy part is I did well for myself, and I ended up on Broadway and moved to New York City. I was meant to be on stage. I finally came back and do you know what I told my estranged husband I hadn't seen in fourteen years when he answered the door?"

Fourteen years? It felt like a punch to the gut. I had no doubt this was the infamous Carla. I wanted to tell her to quit talking and to leave, but I just stared at her and listened intently.

"I demanded to see my daughter without even much of a hello. I figured he would be doing terrible without me. He was a drunk when I left. I came back, and he has this beautiful home, and he looks better than he did when I left, and I realized he was better off without me. It wasn't supposed to be this way. I must seem like a real bitch to you, wishing he was miserable without me?"

"I don't even know you."

I wanted to tell her off, but I knew it wasn't my place. This was a battle Nicholas needed to fight, and I was staying out of it because I had my own family.

"What advice do you have for me? I need to win back my husband."

CHAPTER 18

"Regan, we need to talk."

"What, Dad? Don't you think you screamed at me enough yesterday? I'm never going to drink again, okay? I feel just terrible."

Nicholas felt that way so many times when he was younger. He would mask his headaches by drinking first thing in the morning. He thought the best way to cure a hangover from drinking too much was to drink himself sober. He was so young and dumb back then.

"Actually, it's about your mom."

She sat up in bed. "What do you mean, my mom? You never want to talk about her. You think that just because I drank one night, I'm going to end up like her? Weren't you the alcoholic, Dad?"

"Yes, but no," he said. "Actually, your mother showed up here last night."

"What? Here?" She jumped to her feet. "You have to be kidding me."

"I'm not kidding. She wants to see you, and I think you should at least give her a chance to explain herself."

Regan turned and stared out the window, her arms crossed.

He walked over to her and put his hand on her shoulder, but she shook him off.

"Tell me how you're feeling, please."

She groaned. "I don't know. I guess I always dreamed about this day, but the years kept coming and going and she never came home. Where has she been all of this time? Why now? Does she even love me anymore?"

She turned her head, but he saw the tears in her eyes. He pulled her head onto his shoulder and wrapped his arms around her.

"I'm so sorry, sweetheart. I know it's been really hard for you. It was quite a shock for me, too."

"I need some time, Dad. I can't believe she thinks she can just show up like this without warning."

He grabbed a tissue off her dresser and handed it to her. "I get it, but I'm not sure when she'll be back. She's your mother, even if she did screw up. I don't want her to leave and then you regret not seeing her or giving her a chance to talk. But it's up to you, and I support you no matter what, okay?"

She nodded. "Please give me a minute. I don't want to flip out at you, but if you stay here I might. I just need to think. Alone."

"Okay. I'll let you know if she comes back. You know where I am if you want to talk."

She turned around. "If? Really, Dad, if? You want me to give her a chance, and you don't even know if she will show up twice? Do you not see the whole problem here? I don't want to worry about whether she's going to disappear and never come back again. Do you know how horrible that is? You don't understand what I'm going through at all. Your mom wasn't like mine."

She had been mad at him before, but she never screamed at him like this or treated him this way. This was how other teenage girls treated their parents, not his girl, not his Regan. He would normally put her in her place, maybe even ground her for talking to him like that, but not today. Today, he needed to give her space. She warned him and he should have just let it go. He understood. Carla was his wife. She left him, too.

Instead, he said, "You're right."

He shut the door. What he needed right now was a shower, a very cold shower, even if it was November. He left her phone by her door. She was supposed to be grounded, but she probably needed a friend to talk to, so he let it go.

After his shower, he headed for his bedroom. He opened the door and jumped. Carla was sprawled out on his bed.

"Really, Carla? What are you doing here? Why are you in my room?"

She was on her side, her head resting in her hand. She swung her legs and scooted her way toward him on the edge of the bed.

"Damn, you look good." She licked her lips and bit down on her lip.

She stared at his towel as if to magically make it fall. He held onto it tighter and grabbed clothes out of the dresser. The springs squealed as she got off the bed. He tucked the clothes under his arm and took off in the opposite direction.

"Oh, come on," she said. "You're my husband."

He turned around and glared at her. "If I had a way to get a divorce, I would have," he said through clenched teeth. The words came out in a loud whisper. "You're not my wife and haven't been in fourteen years. I despise you, and I don't love you at all. The only reason I let you in—wait, I didn't let you in, you just broke in. Anyway, the reason you are here right now is for Regan, and I don't even know if she wants to see you."

She moved closer to him and clutched his chin between her fingers. Her touch made his chest hurt.

"What's going on, and why are you in a towel?"

"Regan," he said.

Carla turned around and looked at her daughter.

"Regan, my sweet girl. Look at how big you have gotten." She walked over and ran her fingers through Regan's hair. "Your hair is so dark, like your dad's. I always thought you'd be blonde like me."

Regan's arms were still crossed, and she looked far from happy to see her mom. He had hoped she would snap out of it and at least give her mom a chance, but how could he blame her? Carla abandoned her, abandoned them, and she didn't even start off with an apology.

Regan took a step back to get out of her mother's reach. "Where have you been all these years? Why did you leave?"

"You sure are sassy, aren't you? I love it." She turned to Nicholas. "That she gets from me."

He wanted to say; she is nothing like you, but instead he bit his tongue.

"I've been waiting so many years to ask you, and I need some answers."

A wide smile spread across Carla's face, like she wasn't catching on, or just didn't care. Regan was hurt and her mom wasn't addressing anything. Why didn't Carla understand what Regan needed? But then again, she did not know her daughter at all because she never cared enough.

"What do you want to know, dear?"

"Aren't you even listening to me?"

She sighed. "I went to California. Your dad and I ..."

Regan was all attitude like he had never seen before. She

had every right to be, but he did not know what to say to help her, so he just stood there in silence.

"Your dad was a drunk. I couldn't take it anymore. He was horrible to me, and I'm sure he's been horrible to you, too."

Regan's face flushed, and her hands clenched. Would he have to step in and stop her from punching her mother? Her mean comment did not phase him one bit. He was not an alcoholic anymore. He worked really hard to get to where he was, and he forgave himself a long time ago.

"My dad is a great father, it's too bad you weren't around to see that. I don't know why you came back at all. Answer my question, Mom." She emphasized the word mom as if she did not believe the words to be true. "Oh my, is that seriously a Louis Vuitton purse? You can afford a purse like that but yet you missed every one of my birthdays without even a card or a phone call?"

"Oh this, yeah. The truth is, I went to LA and, well, I had some success and made it to Broadway in New York City. It's been amazing. You should come visit," she said. She had perfect pose and her nose was in the air.

He could not believe she was so dense. Did she have a clue at all? She was too busy being a self-centered, selfish woman. It took everything for him to hold back. He wanted to tell her to get out, but he supported Regan and was ready to step in if she needed him. He knew she needed to get this all out in the open.

"Good for you. I'm glad you have everything you ever wanted. Then why are you here?"

"To see you, silly," she said, like it was obvious.

She was clueless.

"Why?"

Carla laughed nervously. She looked to him for help. He stayed silent.

She shook her head, and a smile crossed her lips. "I see

you aren't ready to talk yet. I'm staying at the Hampton so if you decide you're ready to have an adult conversation, you know where I'll be. I'm very disappointed in you, Regan."

Regan groaned and disappeared behind the door after she slammed it.

"Wow, teens are so ... difficult," she said.

He fought to control his rage. "How dare you? She has every reason to be angry. How could you care so little? You never even sent a letter or called her to say you care. Do you realize you never even apologized to her? Somehow, it's all about you and your success. What did you expect her to do, Carla? Wrap her arms around you and thank you for finally coming back after all these years? She doesn't even know you."

She shook her head and glared at him. "What does it even matter? She would never give me a chance. You brainwashed her."

He laughed in her face. "You have to understand, it's going to take time. You're Regan's mother, but she's afraid you're going to leave again. If you want to be back in her life, you need to stay and fix this."

She was crying now. "I don't know how. I have to go back. I live there. Maybe you guys should come with me. Please come back with me, I still love you, and I'm sorry I've a hard time with my words. It has never been my strong suit, you know that."

"Carla, you can work on building back your relationship with Regan, but I don't love you anymore. I've moved on. I told you that, and I mean it. I'm not moving to New York so don't even get your hopes up."

"Is that what this is all about? You want a divorce, don't you? Is there someone else? Is that it?"

He put a hand on her shoulder. "There is no other woman, not that it is any of your business, but we will never be together again. We haven't been together in fourteen years and even when we were together, our relationship was not built on a good foundation. I'll help you with Regan, but stop trying to win me back, okay? And don't come in unless I open the door. This isn't your house."

"Fine," she said. "Am I that hard to love?"

He tilted his head. "How did you find out where we lived, anyway? Last you knew, we were in Rapids."

"Oh, Nick, I googled you, of course. Not that hard."

Google? Why did he not think of that? Maybe because he stopped caring and didn't want to know.

"Didn't you ever Google me?"

He did not care where she was or what she was doing. He never hunted her down. She made her choice. "No. I didn't."

She looked hurt. She walked toward him in slow motion and kissed him.

CHAPTER 19

The snow was falling gently as I stepped out of my car, bottle of vodka in hand. Eric loved vodka almost as much as I loved books.

I saw a shadow waving next door from the corner of my eye.

"Val, is that you?"

"Emily! How are you? I'm so sorry I haven't called."

Emily and her husband had moved from across the lake to next door the previous year. Emily worked in town as a PSA for the Hibbing school district, and her husband, Dawson, was a teacher. They had two children and shortly after they moved in, Emily announced she was pregnant with twins, a boy and a girl. Emily and I were together all the time before Eric kicked me out. I shook away the image of the day that changed my life.

"No, I'm sorry. I should have stopped by your new house," Emily said. She opened her door and poked her head in. "I'll be right in, Irene."

"Is Josie coming for Christmas this year?"

Her daughter Josie lived with in San Francisco with her

sister who had adopted Josie as a child because Emily was too young to take care of her.. Emily looked past me. I followed her gaze behind me and found Eric waiting in the doorway without a jacket on, his arms crossed.

"Are you just going to sit out here all night? Dinner is getting cold," he said and pointed inside.

"I'll be right in, okay? I'm chatting with Emily for a minute."

"Hi, Emily," he said in an annoyed tone. "Tell that husband of yours to call me back. I've been trying to get a hold of him for a week now. I want a gazebo put in this summer."

"I'll let him know."

He went back inside, and Emily closed the gap between us. "How are you? How is ... everything? Are you back together?"

"I don't know. Have you seen Cinnamon around lately?"

"I worry that you even had to ask that question. It's going to take time to trust him again. If you need anything, you know where I live, and you know whose side I'm on."

Irene called out the door. "Mom."

Emily hugged me close. "I've got to go. Good luck, let's chat soon, okay?"

Eric had the fire going, and the wonderful smell of cedarwood greeted my senses at the door. I breathed deeply and remembered why I loved this house so much. I could also smell oregano and tomatoes. He must be making some sort of pasta.

"What did you make? Spaghetti?"

He took a spoonful out of the pot, blew on it, and put it in my mouth seductively.

"Wow, you look amazing. Why didn't you lose this weight when we were married?"

Same old Eric. "Thanks, I think."

He dropped his head onto my shoulder. "Really? You know what I meant. How much do you weigh now, like one hundred and fifty pounds?"

"A girl never tells her weight," I said with a smirk. Flirting with him seemed so forced, but I wanted to show I could be fresh and new.

He just looked back at me, his face a mask of confusion.

"Okay. I just thought that now that you've lost the weight, you wouldn't need to be so secretive."

He took my jacket and hung it on the coatrack, which gave me a minute to think about how to reply without him breathing down my neck.

His head peeked around the wall. "Have a seat, I'm going to grab something, be right back."

Instead, I went into the kitchen. My brown bear cookie jar sat on the counter. When was the last time I ate? My head peeked in the jar with memories of all the cookies I baked for my family and put in the jar over the years.

At Christmas and every weekend throughout the year, I refilled it with home-baked goodies. I put my hand inside and pulled out Thin Mints. My very favorite kind of Girl Scout cookie. My stomach growled in response. Did I really want to ruin my diet by eating spaghetti or a cookie?

I returned the cookie to the jar and sat down on the couch. Sure, my energy was down, but Eric loved the way I looked. I didn't want to fall back into my old habit of eating everything and anything in sight until I was ready to explode.

The quilt on the back of the couch was as foreign to me as Eric seemed to be. I suspected it was another thing Cinnamon added to my home. Would I ever get rid of the evidence of Eric's infidelity?

Eric carried bowls to the kitchen table and lit two candles. It was such a romantic gesture. He was trying.

"Hungry?"

My head nodded in response, but I had no intention of actually eating anything. I finally got my husband back and if I started eating, I would lose him again. He poured us each a glass of Merlot and raised his glass.

"To a new, fresh start with my beautiful wife. May you decide to forgive me and come back to our home and spend the rest of your life with me."

I nodded and took a sip, but my focus was on how many calories and sugar there were in a glass of wine. It would be rude if I didn't take a sip, so I did and swooshed it around in my mouth for a while to savor it.

I pushed the noodles around the plate with my fork, but couldn't put the food in my mouth. What if I did, and I couldn't stop eating again? I loved that my stomach wasn't swollen anymore and that I could wear tight clothes without tying a sweatshirt around my waist or adding a cardigan to hide the extra pounds. I was far from my goal weight, and eating would only draw out the process of losing those unwanted pounds. My nights were spent at the gym after work and it took so long to burn off just one meal. I'd have to hit the gym on my way home.

Eric frowned. "What's wrong? Why aren't you eating?"

I set my fork down on the table beside my plate. "I just have a stomachache, that's all. It smells delicious."

"I bet it's nerves. I hope you still feel comfortable here."

No, I did not feel comfortable. There were bits of Cinnamon sprinkled all over the house, but Eric wanted me. Eric picked me over Cinnamon. Finally. I had everything I wanted, so why was I having such a hard time at the thought of moving back into this beautiful house? I hated my house in Hibbing and had a hard time sleeping at night with worries about the drugs in the neighborhood or someone breaking in.

"I do." I lied.

"I've missed you so much, and I hope we can move on as if it never happened. All these months apart, I've realized you are truly the person I want to spend the rest of my life with."

Eric was not exactly a man who caught a woman's attention in passing, but he was confident and, at times, loving. He never saw the inside of a gym or ate healthy, but I loved him the way he was. We had been through so much together, and I could only hope this hiccup would strengthen us.

He pushed back his chair and made his way to my side and put his hand out for mine. I slipped mine inside his, and he gently pulled me to my feet and kissed me. The kiss was wet and unfamiliar. Out of nowhere, he bit my lip. I cried out and jumped back. My finger touched my lip and returned bloody. "What the hell, Eric?"

"I didn't mean to bite it that hard. It was meant to be playful."

I laughed at the craziness of it all. He handed over a clean washcloth and stepped behind me. He put my hair behind one shoulder and began kissing the side of my neck.

I closed my eyes and tried to calm my beating heart. I longed for his touch for so long, but I couldn't relax no matter how I tried. He licked my neck, which was creepy and slobbery. I turned around to face him, and wrapped an arm around his back. My other hand held the washcloth to my lip. It was so uncomfortable.

"What's wrong? You're so uptight sometimes. I'm trying here."

Frustration flashed in his eyes.

"It's not that, it is just different. You're different."

"You never pulled away before," he said.

My lip finally stopped bleeding, and I set down the washcloth on the table. "It's just going to take time. Let's take it slow, okay?"

What was wrong with me? Why wasn't I into it? Our next

date would have to be somewhere that Cinnamon hadn't erased all memories of me.

We moved to the couch and watched what I wanted on television for the first time in a decade. I chose a romantic comedy to see his reaction. I was not coming back into this relationship without fighting for my happiness.

He held my hand, and I squeezed his hand gently. I put my head on his shoulder and then pulled it back up to kiss him. I couldn't feel his lips on mine because my lip was swollen and numb.

"I still can't believe you bit me." I

"I can't believe how swollen it is," he said, touching it gently. "Do you maybe want some ice for it?"

"Then I wouldn't be able to kiss you anymore," I said.

He smiled at that. "This is so nice, just having you here again, in my arms."

We kissed again, and his hands traveled up the back of my shirt. Really?

"Stop," I said and stood up.

"What's the matter? Why can't I do anything right? The last time I tried to put my hand up your shirt, you said you were too fat, and it made you uncomfortable. Look at you, you're thin. Thin! Don't you want to make love to me with the lights on now?"

"It's not that. I told you we need to move slow," I said. "Just because I lost weight doesn't mean I'm suddenly this confident woman. I'm still the same person in here." I placed his hand on my heart.

He pulled away and stood up. "How slow, Valarie? You're my wife, come on. A man has needs."

How dare he? I was offended, hurt, and angry. He would never change. "Goodbye, Eric."

Without even the slightest bit of hesitation, I went straight to the coat rack for my jacket.

"It's this Nicholas guy, isn't it? I know all about him. You love him, don't you?"

I was holding my breath and biting my tongue to stop myself from making this even worse.

"Are you kidding me? You're sad. You don't think it could be because Cinnamon's stuff is all over the house? And what is a name like Cinnamon, anyway? You cheated on me, so excuse me if I need a minute to take it slow because I never thought we were getting back together and to be honest, I think the only reason you want me back is because you don't want anyone else to have me. Nicholas and I are just friends, Eric. And you haven't changed one bit. Do you hear yourself?"

"I cheated on you because you were distant and unattractive. You stopped wearing makeup and giving me attention. You let yourself go, and you didn't care how that would affect me."

The fire was burning in my chest. I did something I never expected I'd ever do. I raised my hand and released it, slapping him right across the face. Hard, too.

He held his cheek. "Okay, I deserved that."

"I'm sorry, I don't know what got into me."

I wanted to laugh right in his face, but I held back. Instead, I tried to apologize. I'd never hit anyone before. I just couldn't take any more of his crap.

He pushed my hand away and held his face still. When he removed his hand from his cheek, he had a perfect handprint on his face. I couldn't look directly at it or I would start laughing.

"Tell me the truth about Nicholas. Did you sleep together?"

"Eric, how can I get through to you? You cheated on me, moved the woman into my house and into my bed, while it was still warm by the way, and then you dumped her and came running back to me for some reason. You seriously expect me to come back into this relationship like nothing ever happened? What happened or didn't happen between me and someone else is really none of your business."

I was acting like a jerk now, and I needed to save myself. "If you really want to know, I did not sleep with Nicholas."

I never saw him get this angry before. He was just inches from my face and, for the first time ever, I worried he might hit me.

"Stop lying to me," he yelled, spitting as he lost control.

My voice squeaked. "I'm not lying. You cheat on me and you can't believe me?"

Instead of hitting me, he surprised me by pulling me in and kissing me so forcefully it took my breath away. I tried to pull away, but the force of his hands pulling me in tighter made it impossible. He finally pulled away, his eyes intense.

"Don't tell me you didn't feel anything."

I started laughing and couldn't quit. I fell to the ground and dropped to my knees right in front of him. It was terrible, but I couldn't hold it in any longer. I couldn't control myself. The laughter was non-stop.

"What's so funny?" he said in a stern voice, which only resulted in more laughter.

Finally, I composed myself enough to speak. "Was that supposed to be attractive? Do you know me at all? By forcing me to kiss you, I'm supposed to feel something? I don't know what kind of kinky messed up relationship you had with Cinnamon, but you will not be getting that with me."

He collapsed to his knees beside me. "I'm sorry. I'm just so jealous. This isn't me at all, you know me."

He was crying, and I was laughing. It was a hot mess of emotions.

"We're pretty messed up, you know that? Well, I want you

to know you have nothing to be jealous of. You know what I talked to Nicholas about? How much I wanted you back."

"Really?"

"Yes," I said. "I want us to go back to the way things used to be, but it's going to take some time to get there. Can you be patient?"

He looked me in the eye with love. "I'll do anything to make this right. I know it won't be easy to trust me again, but I promise to be faithful to you. I screwed up majorly, and I've learned my lesson."

Maybe we needed to put it all out in the open so we could rebuild our relationship. I had to trust that he really did want to make this work, and that it would get better between the two of us. It just had to.

CHAPTER 20

Maria shot me a surprised look. "So, how was your week? Did you eat well? You sure look good."

I had just stepped on the scale, and it horrified me. I didn't lose one dang pound. This week I worked harder than ever by counting every calorie. I hardly ate anything, and worked out at least an hour a day, every day. I could even see my collarbone, but it wasn't enough. I wanted to see hip bones, and have a gap between my thighs. I wanted to walk and not worry about them rubbing together and chafing or putting holes in the fabric of my pants from all the friction. Was that so much to ask?

Not eating gave me a new sense of power I never had. But today my hands were shaking terribly. It happened sometimes, but today was definitely the worst, and it was so hard to hide. Sometimes I had a hard time thinking, too. I didn't have a problem, I intended on eating again soon. This was just part of the fasting process, that's all. Wasn't that what religious people did? Fasting was better than throwing food down my throat until my stomach was so swollen, I had to unzip my pants.

I looked out the gym window and checked for Nicholas. Was he back with Carla?

According to Alex, Regan was devastated that her mom was back in town.

I tried to act like I was interested, but not too interested, or Alex would get the wrong impression of my relationship with Nicholas. I just wanted to make sure everything was okay, that's all.

My hands were trembling, but my stomach finally stopped growling. I had to eat something, so chicken broth and lettuce was my diet. A few more pounds and I would start putting more solid foods into my diet. Maybe just five or even ten pounds. Who was I kidding? More like thirty or even fifty. Obviously, I wasn't withering away or anything.

"I didn't lose any weight this time. It just doesn't make any sense." I mentally recalculated the calories from yesterday.

"Well, you've had a lot going on, and you're probably just at a plateau. What's your calorie intake?"

I hesitated. I didn't want to lie to my best friend, but I couldn't tell her the truth either.

"Good morning, ladies. How was your week?"

Linda was as joyful as always, but even her backflips could not pull me out of my foul mood. I was going to be fat forever. Either it was genetic or I was cursed.

"I lost two pounds this week," Maria said.

"That's great news. What seems to be working for you?"

"I think staying at twelve hundred calories a day and a low carb, high carb alternate diet has really helped. Like you suggested, I've been limiting my sugar intake. At first, I felt exhausted but now I'm feeling much more alert. You don't realize you have a problem with sugar until you live without it in your diet."

Linda lightly clapped. "I've been telling you that since you were in diapers, I'm just glad you finally did it. It isn't easy, is it?"

Maria shook her head.

Maria's excitement didn't offend me one bit. I was happy for her. I wanted her to be able to lose weight almost as much as I wanted me to.

I avoided eye contact with Linda so she wouldn't ask me any questions before class started. I did not want to lie about my two hundred calorie intake. It probably wasn't the healthiest way to lose weight, but I was in fear of eating my favorite foods and being unable to stop binging. That only led to being so full I felt sick and unproductive the rest of the day.

Not again. The only reason Eric came running back was due to me losing the weight and having self-control, and I was proud of how far I'd come. I sure missed having energy, though. The four cups of black coffee a day made me shakier, not more alert.

Linda turned to me and glanced at my shaky hands, so I sat on them.

"How about you?"

"I would love to tell you about my week, but I really have to go to the bathroom."

I could not look at my friends as I spit out the lie so I could get away. Before they had a chance to second guess me, I ran straight to the restroom at the end of the hall. I happened to pass Nicholas's office and saw him sitting at his desk with a stack of paperwork in front of him. He looked deep in thought.

I knocked gently, and he looked up and smiled. It was a genuine, cheerful smile that brightened us both up a little.

"Val, come on in. How are you?"

It was time to lay it out there. "I want to apologize for Halloween. I know it seemed like I bombarded you or like I was keeping Eric a secret from you, but—"

He held up his hand. "No, not at all. It's fine. I understand. This was what you wanted, right?"

I wanted Eric back, but I never expected it to happen that day like it did.

I shook my head, as if to wake up from my jumbled thoughts. "Yes, it is. He loves me, Nicholas. He feels terrible for cheating on me, and I know it sounds weird, but I think this may help our marriage grow stronger in the end."

I left out the part about us fighting and me slapping him in the face, but some conflict after what happened was inevitable. We had a long list of issues to resolve, but what couple didn't?

He nodded, but I was pretty sure I offended him somehow. My words just came out so wrong around him.

"Is there anything new with you?"

Would he be honest with me about Carla? Did he trust me enough to tell me? Sure he must have figured out that Regan would tell Alex and she would tell me. Teens never kept secrets from their best friends.

"Actually, there's a lot new. Are you in class right now?"

Crap! I needed to get back to class before Maria came looking for me and found me in her brother's office. She would be so angry and think I was leading him on. I couldn't seem to walk away and leave him hanging, though, but I had to.

I looked toward the closed door where the meeting was being held. "I am, I better go. How about coffee after?"

He looked surprised. "I'll still be wrapped up in this paperwork, but a break is just what I'll need. How about lunch instead?" He stared at my hands. "Val, you're shaking. Everything okay?

"Oh, yeah, I have a protein bar in my purse. I guess I forgot to eat before the meeting. No big deal."

He looked concerned.

I hesitated. How could I go for coffee and hide the fact that I am currently not eating? I didn't want to lie to him, but I also didn't want to pass on a chance to find out what the scoop was on Carla and to spend some time with him. He was my friend.

"We'll meet up after," I said with a wave.

Linda was talking about eating food slower and chewing more to savor the taste of the food and to give the brain time to feel full when I walked in.

"When we eat our favorite foods, we want to enjoy them. Try putting down the fork in between bites and not worrying about the food running out before we can eat more. We need to really enjoy our food and not just shovel it in like it's going to run out. We're so busy eating to feel better, we aren't even conscious about what we're putting in our mouth."

Saffron looked over at me and giggled. She was so immature. This was all a big joke to her.

She whispered, "What?"

"Next week, we have a surprise guest speaker. She's a celebrity most of you probably haven't heard of. She's new in the area and wants to meet all of you and tell you her story of how she's maintained a small waistline and success in life."

Linda's smile seemed a bit forced.

"Oh yay," Maria said under her breath.

Linda passed out journals and told everyone to keep track of their calories each day and not to weigh themselves at all this week.

"This journal will help you build your self-esteem by

logging three things you are thankful for this week. Write down your weekly goals. We will discuss them in the next class."

Linda held up her hand. "One more thing, I don't want to see one empty seat next week unless you're in the hospital, okay. It's very important to me that you be present when we discuss the journal and other news. Thank you and have a great week everyone."

Maria turned to me. "Want coffee or a workout?"

"Actually, I told Nicholas I'd go out for a bite to eat with him after the meeting."

She looked angry and confused. "I thought you were with Eric now."

"I am, your brother and I are just friends."

"Oh," she said, no less angry. "Well, you best get going then."

I was not sure if I needed to stay and talk to Maria or find Nicholas. I was torn, but my feet took me toward the open door. I was shaky and cold. Was the heat broken in this place, or did they keep it this cold on purpose for people exercising?

Nicholas was waiting for me right outside the door. Maria glared as she passed us.

Nicholas's eyes followed his sister. "What was that all about?"

I shrugged. "Who knows?"

He gave me the choice of restaurants, and I decided on the hotel restaurant well known for their steaks and salads. He ordered a steak cheese French which was a sandwich with salad on the side instead of fries. I ordered a dinner salad.

As the waitress walked away with their menus, he gave

me a questionable look. "Aren't you hungry? You look a little pale."

"I'm going back to work out at the gym after this so I don't want to be too full."

He nodded, with a glimmer of curiosity in his voice.

"Finish telling me what you were saying at the gym."

He fidgeted, and his dark gray shirt was wet under his armpits.

"You won't believe it. Hell, I can't believe it, but Carla showed up on Halloween."

"You've got to be kidding me," I said, trying to act surprised. "How did that go? How's Regan doing?"

"You don't have to act shocked. Regan told me Alex told you."

Now I looked like a liar. Maybe I should have been more upfront with him. Did he know I talked to Carla in my bookstore, too? Did he know my bookstore was possibly being foreclosed? Did Carla talk to him about me? Probably not. I had a problem overthinking everything, and that was exactly what I was doing.

"I'm sorry. I didn't know if it was a secret or what."

"I get it," he said. He ran his fingers through his hair.

How had I forgotten how handsome he was? I suspected he was giving Carla another try, just like I was giving Eric. Still, I felt a pang of jealousy, but I was happy for him. Fourteen years is a long time for a wife to disappear. A part of him must be happy she returned.

"Are the two of you back together?"

"No."

Relief flooded over me. Why was I so relieved, and why were his eyes so beautiful and yet so lost today? He was struggling. Was that why he wanted to go to lunch? So he could talk to someone about Carla? I wanted to hear what he had to say, but maybe I wasn't ready for that yet. We spent a beautiful weekend at a deserted cabin in the middle of nowhere, and I loved being with him. The vivid memory of us snuggling on the floor and in the bed to keep warm gave me a shiver. The way he smelled, the way his eyes wrinkled up when he smiled.

"Regan is having a hard time with her just showing up after all of these years with no explanation. I told Carla if she wants a relationship with Regan, she needs to let her know she isn't going anywhere."

"What did she say?"

"She said she had to go back to New York because she's in a show on Broadway. She wanted us to go with her."

A sharp pain stabbed my gut again like a game of ping pong. Was he going to go with her? Would he move across the country for his wife? Leave his gym behind? Was it a good idea to move Regan again? Was this really any of my business? I liked to think it was, for Alex's sake.

"Are you?"

"Am I what?"

"Are you and Regan moving with her to New York City?"

As the words left my lips, I knew I should shut up and let him talk, but I had to know the answer even if I was making this about me. Alex would be devastated. Did Regan even know what was going on? He said that Regan wanted nothing to do with Carla, so why would he say yes? Because it was New York City. Who wouldn't want to go to New York City?

"No. I have my gym here, and Regan is settling in here."

Was he trying to convince me or himself? I could not be certain.

"You could make it work if you wanted to. Just saying."

Our food arrived, and I had to force myself to eat. I took a bite of my salad and slowly chewed.

Nicholas stopped eating and stared at my plate. "Don't you want any dressing on it?"

I looked down at the dressing in a cup on the side of the plate.

"I think I asked for the wrong kind of dressing. This is Ranch but I wanted French."

He got up and walked over to the bar. He came back with a container of red dressing. "Here you go."

I slid my tongue over my teeth. "Thanks."

He had to be the nicest guy and a great friend, just like Maria. Carla was lucky, and even if he would not admit it, they would end up together in New York. Maria or Linda could run the gym, while he opened a new one in The Big Apple.

Living in Hibbing was too city for me. I preferred the lake in my backyard and the wind in my face. We had neighbors next door on Big Sturgeon, but they weren't just any neighbors, they were my friends. It was small town enough for someone like me. The people came in the summer, but in the winter, only a few lived there. Maybe a quarter of the population.

I poured the dressing Nicholas so nicely retrieved for me on my salad, and moved it around my plate to make it look like I was eating, but the more he talked about uncertainty, the more I put the lettuce in my mouth. How dare he even consider letting Carla back into his life? Carla would never stay, inevitably, she would disappear again.

Nicholas went to the bathroom, and I ordered a piece of cake to go. It felt good to fill my stomach, and I even ate my roll. A big brick of carbs and it felt good. I wanted more food, anything and everything. It made me feel better, and I had forgotten how much better food made me feel, for a moment anyway. Food was my reward for all the emotions and let downs of life.

He walked me to my car. "I'm not going to lie. It hurt to see you and Eric back together, but I'm really happy for you. I hope everything works out for your family, and if you say he's changed, I believe you. All that matters is that you are happy."

"Thank you, Nicholas. I am."

He nodded and kissed me on the forehead, like a friend. I shivered at his touch.

"Bye, Valarie. Don't be stranger, okay?"

I said goodbye, then went straight to the nearest fast-food restaurant, ate too much, and threw up.

CHAPTER 21

Valarie's car pulled away. He wanted to chase her down and tell her he was the man for her. Tell her she deserved better than Eric, but that would be selfish. She loved her husband, and she said she was happy. Although it was hard, he had to respect that. Her family was back together now. She did not seem upset that Carla was back, and she thought it might be a good idea for him to move to New York City with Carla.

Regan was sitting on the steps in front of their home when he pulled up.

"Hi Dad, can you let me in? I forgot my key again."

He shook his head. "Oh, Regan."

"Mom told me about New York. What do you think?"

All was well with her mom already? That didn't take long. Of course, Carla told her about New York without talking to him first. She knew Regan was his world and if she wanted to go, he would come, too. Did she think they would magically pick up where they left off after she took off for all those years? All would be fine and they would pack up and follow her across the country where they would live happily ever after? Life did not work that way, and he did not feel that way about her. Not even a little. Not anymore.

After she left them, he dreamed she would come back and tell him how sorry she was. He loved her, and he thought she loved Regan, but no mother would take off and leave their baby behind with an alcoholic without even checking occasionally to make sure everything was going okay. He could never do that. How was she able to sleep at night? Regan was everything to him.

"I'm proud of you for talking to her. I know how angry you were."

She followed him inside. "Well, she is my mom. I was hoping maybe you would consider moving to New York City."

He spun around. "Regan, it isn't that easy. I can't just get up and move across the country. I have a business here, and I'm not in love with your mother."

She nodded, excitement shining from her eyes. "Please, Dad. I'm not saying the two of you need to get back together or anything. Mom feels terrible for what she did. She loves us, she wants to give it another try. She's changed, Dad. She came back."

"I'm sure this isn't easy for you. You love your mom and I get that, but you don't have to move across the country to bond with her. Take it slow, finish high school. I get she is a big shot in New York and that must seem really exciting to you, but this is where our life is, Regan."

"How would you feel about me moving there with her by myself, then? She can afford to put me into a private school, and I could go to college at NYU in a few years. Please Dad, it's my dream."

Her hands were folded together as if in prayer as she begged him to say yes, and it broke his heart. He wanted to say yes, but he knew nothing about her mother's lifestyle.

"I'll tell you what, you finish high school here and then when you graduate you can move in with your mom and go to college at NYU, okay?"

"No, I want to move now.".

"No. You aren't moving to New York, Regan. This discussion is over."

Her voice turned screechy. "Why, Dad? I'm sixteen years old, and I want to live with my mom. I need my mom. I'm going to New York, and you can't stop me." With that she let out a frustrated groan, stomped up the stairs and slammed her bedroom door.

"Over my dead body," he said to himself.

He needed to give her some time to really think about this. She would come to her senses eventually.

Someone knocked at his door. Carla came walking in before he had a chance to open it.

"What did I tell you about barging in?"

"It was unlocked," she said with a shrug and a bat of her lashes. She had on bright red lipstick and a white dress that exaggerated her curves. "Where's my daughter?"

"Upstairs, let's talk."

He led her into the dining room, where they sat across from each other at the table. She grabbed an apple out of the fruit bowl, inspected it before grunting and putting it back. "These aren't fresh."

He laughed. "It's November in Minnesota. Where do you expect me to get fresh apples? I know there aren't fresh apples in New York right now."

"There are in California, I can bet on it," she said.

"But you aren't in California, so I'm not sure how that is relevant."

"You have all the money that I left you, you could order your daughter fresh fruit."

He was so angry he started laughing and the more he tried to stop, the harder he laughed. His stomach hurt and he burst out laughing even harder when he saw the annoyed look Carla was giving him. She was truly a snob if he ever saw one. Was she always this way, and he never saw it before? What a joke.

"The money that you left me? You didn't leave me crap."

She sat up a little straighter. Her poise had definitely changed. He could rest a book on her head and it would not fall down.

"You're still impossible," she said. She put her hand on his thigh.

He pushed her hand away. "It's over, Carla. Why would you bring up moving to New York with Regan without talking to me first?"

"She's my daughter, too. I will not keep this from her."

"Keep what from her? Are you kidding me? You can't just come barging in and turn her world upside down. I'm her parent, I've been here for her."

"She told me about your girlfriend."

He could no longer control his anger. He barked out, "What the hell are you talking about? Who told you about what girlfriend?"

She tapped his nose with her finger. He wanted to tell her to leave and never come back. To go back to where she had been hiding all these years and quit confusing their daughter, but no, he was a nice guy. He would not stoop to her level and hurt Regan.

She put her hands on his chest, and her lips were just a whisper away. He did not want to pull away too quick or he might hurt her in the process. He stood there and glared at her, frozen in place. She dragged her fingers up his chest, getting even closer, so close he thought she might kiss him again.

"The bookstore lady. I met her. She's cute."

She slipped her hands under his shirt collar. He grabbed her hands and pulled them out, then stepped away. She twirled her hair around her finger.

"Val? Don't you dare—"

"So it is true, huh? She broke your little heart and now she's back with her ex. You poor, poor baby."

"Get out," he said. "Just get out and don't come back. You don't care about Regan, so quit acting like you do after all this time. You never would have left her like you did."

He heard a voice behind him, but it took a minute for him to register that Regan was standing there. He meant to hurt Carla, and he was sure he did if she had a conscience at all, but he never meant for Regan to hear.

"If you are making her leave, then I'm leaving, too," Regan said. She walked behind her mother and hugged her. "I'm so sorry, Mom, he's not normally like this. I want to leave with you."

"You aren't leaving," he said behind clenched teeth.

"Watch me," Regan said. "You're acting like a jerk."

He let her go with Carla because they both needed time to cool off. It was not like she was going to New York City tonight. Carla was staying at a hotel, and he would let them bond tonight, but tomorrow he would be there with a clear head and be tough enough to make her come home. That was the only way to keep the situation from blowing up.

Carla looked at Regan. "Do you have a suitcase?"

Regan walked over to the stairs and picked it up. It looked heavy.

"Goodbye, Dad," she said.

"This isn't goodbye. I'll come by tomorrow when you and I both have time to think about this, okay?"

"Whatever," she said with a roll of her eyes. "Come on, Mom."

Carla followed Regan out the door, and he was left alone. It took him five minutes before he moved and seven minutes before his eyes filled with tears. Everything he did for her all these years did not seem to matter. Her mother swooped in and all was forgiven in a day. He lost both Val and his own daughter this week. Would he ever get a break?

He could sit home and cry, or he could relieve the stress with a workout. He grabbed his gym bag and keys.

He stepped on the treadmill. He would prefer running outside when he was this upset, but the streets were still icy from the last snowstorm, and his yak-traks were nowhere to be found.

By ten in the evening, he was alone in the gym. He was just cooling down when the door dinged, and a shadow moved in the locker area. He saw a flash of brown hair. Valarie. She swung her hips just enough to gain attention, but not in an overly confident way. She likely did not realize she was doing it. She had her head down and was untangling her headphones when she looked up and locked eyes with him.

His heart skipped a beat. "Hey."

She smiled, a confused expression on her face. "Nicholas, weird time to see you here."

"I'm surprised you aren't at home with your daughter and husband. Why are you working out so late?"

She squinted her eyes.

"I'm so sorry, that came out wrong."

She laughed at his mistake. "I'll let it go this time," she said. "I just needed to clear my head, which I'm sure is the same reason you came here. Am I right?"

"Yes, actually. Carla got to Regan, and she thinks I should let her move to New York City. Can you believe that?"

"She's a teen, of course she thinks it's a good idea." A

guilty look crossed her face. " I need to tell you something. I met Carla at the bookstore on Halloween."

Val met Carla? "What did she say?"

Valarie got on the treadmill next to him, but he was stopped. "She never said who she was, but she asked me for advice."

"What do you mean?" Why not tell Val who she was and how did she find out about her in such a short time?

"She saw our bookstore was being foreclosed, and she thought whoever owned the bookstore was worse off than she was, so she asked me for some advice."

He shook his head and wiped the sweat off his forehead with a towel. "Of course, she did. Typical Carla. You aren't losing the store, are you?"

"I'm not sure exactly. My mom said she handled it, and I hope she did. Anyway, Carla said some things about leaving her daughter, and I realized she was talking about Regan. She talked about how she said some terrible things to you, too, and that she wants you back. I just thought you should know. I don't want any secrets between us. I respect you too much."

"I appreciate that. She has been a real pain in the butt. I enjoyed catching up with you at lunch the other day. I miss our conversations."

She smiled, and a wistful expression crossed her face. "Me too. Do you ever think about that weekend at the cabin?"

All the time. "Yeah, it's kind of hard to forget. How about you?"

"Sometimes. Other than the fact that I was worried we were going to freeze or starve to death, it was nice to be away from all the stress in the world, you know?"

He nodded. "Yeah, I know."

"I've never met anyone like you, Nicholas Ryan. When I'm with you I stumble a lot, but I know I have a genuine friend."

He smiled. "Me too. You are one of a kind."

She took off her sweatshirt, and he couldn't help but stare. She looked even more confident now that she was working out, but the gray color on her face and her shaky hands had him worried. "Valarie, are you eating okay?"

She frowned and shot him a sharp look. "Excuse me?"

"I don't mean to be rude, but your face is kind of gray."

She turned away. "Not you, too." She put in her ear buds and began running.

He took that as a cue for him to leave, but he was worried about her. He walked to the back of the gym, but monitored her from afar.

While he was putting a weight on the bar, he heard a bang. He found her lying on the floor, the treadmill still on.

"Valarie, Valarie, can you hear me?" He put his head on her chest. Her breathing was shallow. He fumbled with his cell. "9-1-1? I have an emergency to report at the gym. A young woman has collapsed."

He gave the dispatcher the address.

He held Val in his arms and rocked her back and forth. "Come on, Val. Don't quit on me now. I can't lose you."

The ambulance was there within minutes.

The paramedics came running in. "What happened?"

"She was just running on the treadmill and then she collapsed. I was in the other room, but I don't think she's really been eating much. Is she going to be okay?"

The paramedic knelt beside Val. "We'll take good care of her."

He watched them work quickly. He didn't move except when he had to peek around them to see Val was moving. Her eyes opened, but she wasn't talking. She picked up her hand as if she wanted him to hold it. He slid his fingers in hers.

"They are taking good care of you. Just relax. I'm here."

"Don't leave," she whispered.

"I'm not going anywhere."

The paramedics hooked Val up to an IV and lifted her onto a cot and into the ambulance.

He jumped into the ambulance with her and grabbed her hand again.

"Sir, are you a relative?"

"Yes, I'm her husband. Now, drive!"

They didn't question him again, because why wouldn't he be her husband?

CHAPTER 22

Nicholas was holding me in his arms, and I was staring into his eyes. We were happy and everything was perfect. He was wearing a tux and the biggest smile. I put my hands around his neck, and I felt such peace with him.

"Everything is going to be okay, sweetheart."

I was in my wedding dress. He pushed open the bedroom door with his foot and smiled like he had just defeated Bowser and he was saving me again. I was now Princess Peach, and then the whole Mario gang surrounded us. The craziest part was, it didn't seem weird at all. Like Luigi and Yoshi were always just around, and this was normal.

"Val, Valarie!"

I opened my eyes. My hand hurt where an IV was attached, and the pain in my head was instant as the lights in the room shone through my eyes. Someone needed to turn down the lights. Then my eyes found Nicholas, and all the pain subsided. Did we get married? Nope. I kept replaying the treadmill fall in my head. Why did this keep happening to me?

He was leaning over the side of the bed and squeezing my hand. Why was he still here? Then he said, "You're awake."

How long had I been sleeping?

"You took one hell of a fall, but you're lucky, just a few stitches and a big egg on your head. How are you feeling?"

I let go of his hand to shield the light, then instantly regretted pulling my hand away. My hand fit perfectly in his.

"Is the light too bright?"

Before I could answer, he was over by the door, switching the light off. He sat down next to me. "Do you remember what happened?"

"I'm not sure exactly. I remember the treadmill was going, and I was going down. I flew right off the back."

"And hit your head on the floor. Luckily, it wasn't a cement floor. The doc said you were extremely dehydrated."

Then it got quiet and a little awkward. I'm not sure if it was because we had nothing to say or so much to say that we knew we couldn't.

I winced from the pain. It came in waves and it happened right in the middle of the awkward silence.

"Close your eyes, Val. is there anyone you would like me to call? They're keeping you overnight."

I shook my head and closed my heavy eyes. I could not call Eric. It was too soon. He would ask too many questions, and I was in no mood to talk to him right now. I just wanted to close my eyes.

I hoped he was wrong, but they kept me overnight for observation. No concussion, but I had a bump on my head, and low blood sugar. They wanted to monitor me and make sure I ate solid food before they would discharge me.

The doctor came in early the next morning. Nicholas was asleep in the chair next to me. Why did he stay?

"I'd like to talk to you. Do you want him to leave?" The doctor nodded his head in Nicholas's direction.

"No, he can stay."

Nicholas grinned and squeezed my hand in response.

"Are you her husband?"

"No, he's just a good friend," I said.

"I see here you've lost quite a bit of weight since your last appointment with your primary doctor. Is that correct?"

"Yes, I attend Calorie Counter meetings, and I work out a lot."

The doctor was broad and close to sixty. He had glasses and a big, round belly.

"Your body isn't getting enough nutrients, and you fainted due to low blood sugar. You don't have a history of diabetes, correct?"

I shook my head.

"You need to get more fluids and have you been eating?"

He looked at me and then at Nicholas for some acknowledgment.

"It's important you are honest with me."

Nicholas looked at me and smiled as if he was saying, be honest. "It's okay."

"I've always had a problem with overeating when I'm stressed or anxious. I've been trying to eat less, and I guess I went a little overboard."

"Do you purge after you binge?"

He had to sound so technical. "No, I felt better when I stopped eating, but I know now that wasn't a smart idea. I don't do it all the time or anything."

He nodded as if he understood.

Nicholas smiled genuinely, like Nicholas always did. He was so supportive and sweet, never any judgment in his eyes.

This doctor obviously didn't understand what it was like to be an overweight woman with all the judgment and expectations that were put on us. Sadly, it was mainly from other women, like other mothers, friends, and family. It wasn't until it came directly from my husband that it really hit me that I'd let myself go. I couldn't let myself go again. I wouldn't.

"You're beautiful just as you are," Nicholas said, as if he could read my mind.

The doctor frowned. "I recommend you seek a therapist. There are classes in the area for people just like you, suffering from all kinds of eating disorders. How long has this been going on?"

"Not long at all," I lied.

"It sounds like you're replacing binge eating with not eating at all. It's another kind of eating disorder. With the help of a professional, you could control your weight without harming yourself. Think about it."

The nurse came in with some brochures and a number for a therapist who specialized in eating disorders.

"Can I give you a ride home? Or would you like me to call someone? Eric or Alexandra? Maybe your mom?" Nicholas said.

"No, you can go. The sun is rising, and I'm sure Regan needs you."

He looked at his watch and jumped up. "You're right. I have to go. You sure you're going to be all right? Regan is with her mom at the Hampton, and I need to talk with her about everything before they run off to New York City."

"Go, go," I said. I wanted him to stay, but he had a life of his own. Regan needed him. He was a good man, too good for Carla. He deserved better.

He kissed my forehead. "I'll call you later. Are you sure you don't need anything before I go?"

I shook my head, ignoring the pain this time. "Thank you for being here. Good luck with Regan. Remember, she's just a lost teenager. No matter what, she loves you."

After he left, the doctor discharged me. I had no other choice than to call Eric because no way would I call my mom. I would hear her nag me for weeks.

"Hi, I just wanted to let you know I had a minor accident. I fell on the treadmill."

"Are you all right?"

"I mistyped and hit my head on the floor pretty hard. They had me stay in the hospital overnight just for observation."

"That sounds bad. You should've called me."

I did not tell him, nor would I ever tell him about my eating disorder.

"I'm on my way."

"Thanks."

I felt a little guilty that I didn't ask him to be with me last night, but I didn't want Nicholas to leave. I felt safe when he was near, like he would take care of everything, and he always did. It was about me when he was around. When Eric was around, it was always about him. But I wasn't being fair to Eric, and I needed to think differently if I wanted this to work.

The ride home was quiet. My head hurt too much to talk.

Alex was at home when we got there.

"Mom, where have you been? Did you stay at the lake last night with Dad?"

I groped for a kitchen chair. "I had a gym accident and spent the night in the hospital. Your dad picked me up this morning."

"Are you okay?"

"Yeah, just a freak accident. I'm absolutely fine."

Alex retreated to her bedroom once she knew I was going to be okay.

Eric made some tea and stood looking out the window. "I think you and Alexandra should move back in with me."

My head was throbbing, and I was in no mood to fight with him right now.

"Eric, can we talk about this later? I'm so tired."

"I can't even look out your kitchen window. That yard reminds me of where you live. All that random junk all over the place and footprints through the snow, but the footprints don't go up to the house. Do you realize that?"

"No, I didn't," I lied. "I really need to lie down, let's talk about this later."

Alex came walking down the steps, eavesdropping as she made her way into the kitchen. "That's because they live in their shed."

His brows furrowed, and his eyes sparked anger. "They live in their shed? You've got to be kidding me."

I wanted to sleep and not listen to him complain, so I did. I walked into the living room and dropped onto the couch. My neighbors, for once, were the last thing on my mind. All I cared about was staring at the back of my eyelids and waking up feeling normal again.

When I woke up, Eric was watching television on a kitchen chair he dragged into the living room. At least he stuck around. That was a start.

"I thought you were going to sleep all day. You feeling better?"

I sat up to test my nausea. "Yeah, I'm better. My headache isn't as bad as it was."

"I'm glad to hear that. I had a little chat with Alexandra while you slept. I found out who spotted them alcohol for their friend's party on Halloween, and you will not believe it."

"Who was it? Who?"

"Cinnamon and her sister, Saffron."

He couldn't be talking about the Saffron I knew, could he?

"Your Cinnamon? I think I know Saffron," I said.

He paced in front of me and bit his nails. "She's not my Cinnamon, stop using that against me. And there is no way you know Saffron. She's not someone you would be friends with. She's the kind of person you would stay away from. She only cares about herself and honestly; I don't think she has any friends. She's only into males. She hit on me right in front of Cinnamon."

He laughed, and I tried to figure out what he meant by the laugh exactly.

"That sounds just like the Saffron I know. She's not my friend, she goes to my gym."

I had just started to like Saffron, or at least feel like maybe I understood her attitude was more about insecurities, but then she went out and bought alcohol for two teenage girls?

Was it possible she knew Alex was my daughter? I had talked about Eric with Saffron, and Saffron told me he sounded like a loser and to stay clear of him. Did she tell Cinnamon everything I was saying at the meetings? Was that why Cinnamon was always throwing my weight in my face? Would Saffron stoop that low? Maybe for her sister. How did I not know they were sisters? Did they look alike? They were both thin, but it wasn't an obvious resemblance.

"You really know her?"

"Not really know her know her, but we've talked, yes."

He moved my legs and sat down on the end of the couch. "Let me get this right, you're friends with my ex's sister? Sounds a little ironic. I bet her and Cinnamon have been in on this together the whole time. You didn't talk to her about me, did you?"

"No." Yep.

CHAPTER 23

Getting her hotel room number from the front desk was easier than Nicholas expected. He told the receptionist he was her husband and needed a key card to the room because he did not want to wake her. That did it. Luckily, the man at the desk was a young teen, probably not much older that Regan, which made it easier.

He slipped the card in the door and the light turned green. They were sleeping on the queen-size bed, the television still on. He had to admit, the view warmed his heart. Carla's hand was wrapped around Regan, and they looked so peaceful, like a mother and daughter should look. He was happy Regan had forgiven Carla. He just wished she was more reliable and did not stir everything up the minute she arrived.

Regan was a good girl, and responsible, but her mother wasn't. Even though this scared him, every teenager needed their mother. Although he did not agree with Carla's choices, Regan should be able to make her own decision when it came to her mother. He turned on the light. "Good morning."

Regan wiped her eyes and squinted at him, and Carla rolled away from the light and onto her side.

"Rise and shine, ladies."

Regan sat up. "Dad, what do you want? I'm staying with Mom. I'm not leaving with you, and you can't make me."

Carla sat up, too. Her mascara was smeared under her eyes, and she looked like a train wreck with her hair standing up all over the place. She had on Regan's Christmas flannel pajamas. This would not be easy, but he needed to do what was right.

"Regan, you're sixteen years old, and if you want to live with your mother, then I support you."

She looked confused. "What? Really, Daddy?"

He loved it when she called him daddy. She only did it when he made her really happy or when she was excited about something.

"Really. You will miss sections, but I think you're old enough to decide which parent you want to live with. Do you still want to live in New York with your mother?"

"Yes, Daddy, yes, thank you, thank you," she said.

She wrapped her arms around him in a big hug, and he squeezed her back. He hoped he was doing the right thing, but this was what he had to do.

He loved his little girl so much, and hopefully she would be safe with her mother. She was smart and honest, but she had been so angry about the absence of her mother in her life. He was a drunk and changed his ways, so why couldn't Carla? Maybe Regan would be good for her.

"So, when are you leaving for New York?"

Carla yawned. "Not for a few days."

"Okay," he said, turning to his daughter. "I expect you to attend school until you leave then." He turned to Carla, "And you'll take care of enrolling her in a school in New York?"

"Yes. Did you really need to ask me that? I'm perfectly capable, thank you very much."

He held up his hands in surrender. "I don't doubt you. I'm just making sure. You ladies have fun, and I will probably see you when you come home to pack, right?"

Regan's smile widened as she nodded. "Thank you, thank you, thank you! I can't believe I'm going to live in New York City! Alex is going to be so jealous, I have to call her."

This was the hardest thing he ever had to do. He loved his daughter so much. This better work out for her. He felt sick as he shut the door and made his way to his truck.

He drove by Val's house and saw Eric's truck in her driveway. His chest ached at the thought. His baby girl was moving across the county with the person he least trusted in this world, and at the same time, he lost Valarie.

The gym was packed for a Sunday afternoon. Only one treadmill was available and only two machines remained open in the whole place. A woman ran on the treadmill Val had wiped out on just a little over twelve hours ago. The vivid image of her body laying on the floor and the loud thump when she fell was vivid in his mind. His heart raced as if it was happening again. He looked at his phone. No message from her yet. He wanted to call her, but Eric was likely still there. He wanted her to be happy, even if that was not with him. Would she be happy? It was what she wanted, and that was all that mattered.

He had three appointments today. Maybe working would take his mind off Valarie.

Saffron was his last appointment of the day.

"Hey, handsome. You ready to get my butt in shape?"

She bent over to tie her shoe and stuck her butt in his direction. She stared back at him, raising her eyebrows and flashing him a flirty smirk.

The woman was just too much. No matter how many times he turned her down, she took it as another challenge and pursued him harder.

Ten minutes later he received a text from Val telling him Cinnamon and Saffron were sisters and that Saffron played a part in buying their girls alcohol.

He remained professional during her session, but he was angry at the thought of her buying his daughter alcohol. This was low, even for Saffron. He took it out on her during the workout, pushing her hard and silencing her when she complained.

He gave her instructions for her to cool down and went to the front room to grab a towel and wipe the sweat off his forehead. Carla was sitting on the bench outside his office with a water bottle in her hand.

"What are you doing here? Where's Regan?"

"Oh, hi Nick. She's at your house packing. I came over to check the place out. I'm meeting Linda to talk about her Calorie Counter meeting. Did she tell you she wants me to speak to the class about how I stay so thin? It'll be great."

"No, she didn't." She just happened not to mention that to him because she knew he would be angry. He was a little surprised since Linda was not a fan of Carla either, but befriended her for Regan's sake. Linda was direct, but forgiving. She never held a grudge, but she also never forgot.

"Well, if you need anything, my office is in the back."

He turned around to leave, but stopped when she called out to him.

"I'll draw up the paperwork before I leave so our divorce can be finalized, okay?"

It paid to be nice. "That would be great, thanks."

Saffron was on her phone, sitting on the floor in the empty room when he came back to check on her. She looked up right away.

"We need to talk."

She followed him into his office.

"I knew it, you want me."

There she went again.

"Not even close. Like I've told you before, Saffron, our relationship is completely professional and I don't like you like that. I brought you in here because I wanted to talk about you and your sister purchasing alcohol on Halloween for minors, including for my daughter. I don't understand why you would do that. That is low, even for you."

She screeched in response. "I don't know what you're talking about. I would never do that."

"Saffron, you owe me an explanation. I'm not calling the police, and my daughter is the one who decided to drink, but I don't understand why you would put yourself in that situation, so drop the act."

She rolled her eyes and crossed her arms. "Fine. My sister was dating the father of the girl that asked for the alcohol, and she was hoping if she bought alcohol for the girls, it would put her in good graces with his daughter. I don't even know the guy. I met him once, and I did not buy the alcohol, she did. I told her she was going to get caught, and I wanted nothing to do with it. I waited in the car. This is my sister's mess. She always gets herself into these situations. She pretended to wipe lint off of his shoulder and took a step closer to him. "Forgive me?"

He stood up taller, stiffer. "Valarie is really upset with you, too. Her daughter was also the girl you guys supplied with alcohol."

"This is not on me. My sister was the one dating her ex, not me." She flipped her hair behind her shoulder.

"If this ever happens again, I will press charges, understand?"

"What eva," she said. She looked around and leaned in closer. "You sure seem to care a lot about Valarie, huh?"

He shook his head. She was not getting it. "Saffron, you know she's back together with Eric, right?"

"I had no idea," she said. "I mean, I knew he dumped Cinnamon, but I didn't know Val was dumb enough to take him back. You must be really sad, huh? The two of you were a thing, weren't you?"

She was always gossiping. She wanted him to say something so she could create more drama.

His office door opened and Maria peeked her head in. Thank goodness.

"Hello?"

Her eyes narrowed, and she eyed him and then Saffron. "Carla is out here, and she wants to talk to you about something, but she won't let me help her. I'd swear she thinks she's still married to you."

"Carla? Married?" Saffron leaned around Maria to see for herself.

Nicholas frowned at Maria, and Maria looked at him as if to say sorry and then shut the door.

"It's no one that concerns you," he said.

"We'll see." She slipped out the door. "I have a feeling this Carla and I will be great friends."

She couldn't do any more damage, could she? He was not playing her game. And if Carla wanted to see him, she could talk to him after work. They'd already talked today. What else did she have that couldn't wait?

He stared at the wall in his office, and then his eye caught the picture on his desk of him and Regan at Disney World when she was five years old. She had on Mickey Mouse ears, and she was hugging his leg. It was them against the world back then, and now she was leaving him. His house would be so empty without her in it. He was going to miss the swim meets and their nights playing board games and UNO. Maybe he should have put his foot down. What if something happened to her? Being a parent was the hardest thing in the world, and Carla had no clue. He might have made the wrong decision, but he could not go back on it now.

CHAPTER 24

The doctor popped out the final stitch from my hairline. "There you go, all five done."

"Thank you."

"How are you feeling?"

"Like I'm back to normal."

"Good, good. You'll be all right as long as you eat to nourish your body instead of using food for comfort. Have you made an appointment to see a therapist yet?"

"I saw the therapist you recommended yesterday. I'm learning a lot about my food addiction and myself. She helped me change my diet, and I'm writing down everything I eat. I'm supposed to feed my body what it needs, and to think of food as a way to survive instead of as a way to feel better." I sighed. "It's much harder than it sounds."

The doctor laughed and patted my knee. "You'll get the hang of it."

Earlier this morning, I ate a cheese omelet and a glass of almond milk. I didn't eat it all because it made my stomach feel a little queasy, but I was on my way to a healthier and happier life.

I couldn't get myself to call Maria back, but I explained the low blood sugar and hospital visit in a text. When I arrived at Calorie Counters that evening, I took my normal seat in the back.

Linda came in and sat down next to me.

"How are you doing? Everything going better?"

Nicholas told her. Of course he told her, she's his mother. A hot flush crept up my neck. How humiliating. This was a nightmare I couldn't escape. "I can't believe Nicholas told you. I'm fine, just a minor cut on the head. Don't worry, I ate breakfast this morning, and I'm seeing a therapist."

Linda blinked and shot me a questioning look. She opened her mouth to speak but Maria came in and saved me.

Her confused look made me second-guess if she really knew what was going on or not. Or maybe she was trying to pretend she didn't know.

"Hi. So, Saffron and Carla have literally been together since yesterday, and I think she's coming with Carla to this meeting today. My mom asked Carla to do a motivational speech, but I think she's trying to keep the peace, you know. For Regan and Nicholas."

"You have to be kidding me." I was in no mood to listen to Carla, not after the week I had. I wanted to avoid the drama, and Carla and Saffron both came with so much drama.

Linda overheard Maria. "We need to forgive and move on. Take a deep breath and don't let them get to you, okay? Now, did you two weigh yourselves yet?"

We shook our heads and made our way to the head table. While we waited in line to weigh in, Carla and Saffron walked in together. They were deep in conversation and once they got to the table in the back, Carla picked up my purse and sat down in MY spot.

Touching my stuff and sitting in my spot? I clenched my

teeth and tried to look away. Why did I hate her so much? Why couldn't she sit up front or something? No way was I going to talk to her or even acknowledge her presence, not after what she did to Nicholas.

"Valarie," Linda said.

I smiled at Linda and stepped on the scale.

"Don't let her get to you. She's just jealous because you and Nicholas are close. Don't let her push your buttons. She'll back off and out of your space once she knows you aren't a threat. Plus, she will be leaving in a couple days."

Linda did not seem to be her normal optimistic self, but she was the one who invited Carla to the meeting and to speak.

"I just wish she wasn't taking my granddaughter with her, but I have to grin and be nice or I'll lose them both. Poor Nicholas."

Regan was moving back with Carla to New York? What made Nicholas decide to let her go? What changed from when I last spoke with him? "That's terrible, what happened?"

"I don't know. Nicholas thinks it's for the best. You, my dear, are twenty-five pounds down since your first weigh in. Should I be worried?" Linda looked at me sideways, her eyes wide and suspicious.

Then it hit me. Linda had no idea about what happened to me. Nicholas obviously hadn't told her, but what was it she was trying to ask me then?

Twenty-five pounds. I worked so hard and now that I was eating again, I would probably start gaining back all the weight I worked so hard to lose. The thought made me sick.

"I guess the hard work paid off," I said.

"That is amazing."

Linda quieted down the entire room to announce the news.

"Ladies, I have an announcement to make. Valarie has lost twenty-five pounds."

She clapped her hands, and the whole room followed her lead.

"Was it the journaling? Is that what helped you this week?" A woman named Julie asked from the front row. She had to be in her sixties and was always taking notes at the meetings. She was very serious all the time, and I don't think she ever smiled.

My eyes landed right on Carla, and I didn't want to answer any questions. I saw her with Saffron and was disgusted by the thought of her being Cinnamon's sister and buying young teenage girls alcohol. My daughter in particular. Puke.

Linda filled in the awkward silence. "Let's talk about our goals this week, starting with our superstar, Valarie."

I sat down next to Carla in the only open spot that was at least also next to Maria.

"The bookstore girl," Carla said. "So great to see you again."

So fake. Her smile, her clothes, her heels. Didn't anyone else see it?

Saffron began whispering in Carla's ear, and she shot me an evil look. What the hell did I do?

I acted like I hadn't noticed. I opened my journal and read my goals for the class. "The three things I'm thankful for are my daughter, Alexandra, my friends and family, and Calorie Counters because it helps to hold me accountable each and every day. My weekly goals were to lose two pounds, which I did. To work out for at least an hour a day, which I had to miss two days, but I'm still proud of myself. My last goal was to do a cartwheel."

There wasn't a person in the room that didn't crack up

about my cartwheel comment. I just hoped they were laughing with me and not at me. I held my head high.

Lucky me, because Linda loved my cartwheel goal so much she did a flawless backflip. That never got old.

Linda bowed at the reaction and then turned back to me. "What is the story behind the cartwheel exactly?"

"I don't know, I just haven't done a cartwheel since my daughter was five-years-old or so. I don't take enough time to loosen up and not be so serious all the time. I've been a responsible adult most of my life, and I think it's a great way to turn my day in a more positive direction."

"I love it," Linda said. "Did you do your cartwheel this week?"

I shook my head, and instantly regretted it. I should have known what was coming next. Linda was like a little kid, happy and smiling all the time. She motivated the whole class every day. When I left the meetings, I felt like I could take on the world because of Linda's motivational lectures and positive speeches. Not today.

"Well, don't we want to see Valarie do her cartwheel, ladies?" Linda said while walking in between the tables.

Everyone stood up and started chanting "Val, Val."

I was mortified. My face got all warm, my hands shaky, but instead of chickening out, I got up in front of everyone and tucked my shirt into my pants. I put my hands in the air before rocking back and forth like a teapot. I went for it and it was probably the worst cartwheel of any cartwheel ever done, ever. I landed on my butt instead of my feet when my arms collapsed because they couldn't support my bodyweight. I was not strong enough to hold my own weight, and I wiped out, practically hitting my head on the floor. I hopped to my feet and did a crown and press, like I learned in gymnastics when I was like five years old and bowed confidently. Everyone stood and cheered. I somehow pulled it off. Well, with humor anyway.

"Calm down ladies or Nicholas is going to yell at us."

We all laughed because he looked so confused when he glanced at us through the glass window. He smiled and turned all red. I had to admit, it was kind of cute. I thought he would walk away, but instead, he opened the door and came in to say hello. The younger women smiled and sat up straighter, and the older women welcomed him with warm smiles. It was obvious to me everyone in the room was already smitten with him.

"I'm trying to work, but it looked like you ladies were having so much fun, I had to join you."

Linda pointed to me, and my face grew hot again.

"Valarie here decided to do a cartwheel and well, she kind of bombed it."

I laughed nervously and covered my face. "No I didn't."

Nicholas's eyes flashed. "Oh, I'll be the judge of that. Show me how it's done."

I shook my head. No way was I going to go out there and embarrass myself again.

"I'll do one," Carla said. She jumped out of her chair and sprinted to Nicholas's side. She did the best cartwheel I had ever seen, and everyone clapped and cheered. She bowed in response and smirked right at me.

"Everyone, this is Carla. Carla is our guest speaker today."

Nicholas waved and left quicker than he arrived. I followed him out, not too concerned about missing the speaker today. "Nicholas, wait."

He turned around with a smile that made me weak in the knees.

"How are you feeling, Val?"

I bit my lip. "Much better. Why do I continue to have so many embarrassing moments around you?"

"They aren't embarrassing. Come on. I was really worried about you. How was Eric when you told him about everything?"

"Umm..."

He put his hands on his hips. "Tell me you told Eric about what happened. Val?"

"I couldn't. It's complicated. It's too soon. We just got back together." The words popped out of my mouth without realizing I was saying them out loud. It was so hard for me to hold back around him.

"You should talk to him."

My eyes burned with tears, because I knew I couldn't. He would never understand. "I know and maybe I will with time," I said, blinking away the tears. "Anyway, I just wanted to tell you thank you."

His hand touched mine for a second, but then he pulled away.

I grabbed his hand and squeezed it. "I don't know what would have happened if you hadn't been there." I looked down. "Thank you, again."

Then he looked at me. Like really looked at me. His eyes looked so sad.

"I heard about Regan. You okay?"

"I'm numb, it's so painful, and I worry I made the wrong choice. I didn't want Regan to resent me for the opportunity, you know? And Carla is her mother, I just don't trust her."

I understood more than he knew. Raising a teenager was the hardest thing I ever did. I'd been a mom most of my life. Eric was never what you'd call an active parent, more like a fun uncle. I always had to be the responsible one, the disciplinarian, and he was the parent who got a free pass every time he did not make it to her meets or games because he was busy or working. Alex never expected Eric to show up, but if I could not make it, my daughter took it to heart.

His hair seemed grayer today than it had been the last time I saw him. This was taking its toll. "I get it, but I think you made the right call. It will be good for her. And to be honest, I give her a couple months before she is begging you to move her back home."

His eyes brightened a little. "You think so? It is New York City, and her mom is a Broadway star."

Every time we ran into one another, it was never awkward. He was always so easy to talk to and really listened to me and cared about my opinion. He made me feel as though we were the only two people in the world. Just to think not that long ago he was saving my life in a grocery store parking lot. I shook my head at the thought.

"I better go. It was so great seeing you," he said and walked back into his office.

I got my jacket and left, stopping at the bookstore to pick up the book I left there. Mom's car was out front. She was only there in the morning, but sometimes she would cover for Maria and me if we were both gone. She wasn't answering my calls or texts since I asked her about the fore-closure sign on the door. She promised she had taken care of it, but I was not so sure.

The door handle wouldn't budge. It was locked. I dug in the bottom of my purse for my key, but realized I forgot it at home. I knocked on the door to get my mom's attention, but she didn't answer.

"Mom, Mom!"

I dug through my purse and found my phone. The sound of her phone ringing inside the store without an answer made me angry. Why wouldn't she answer my calls? With my face against the glass and my hands cupped around my head, I could see my mother and what looked like a man next to her. Were they kissing? It looked like they were kissing! And they were laughing.

I knocked again, and this time she stood up and looked around. "We're closed." She said with a laugh. She was sitting on the man's lap. The streetlight was now on my mother's back as she unbuttoned her shirt and threw it across the store.

I covered my mouth and turned around in fear of seeing anything more unravel between them. My mother with a man, kissing? I was angry, embarrassed, but also kind of happy for her. After all of these years, she finally let herself love again. Why did she keep this from me? How could I be angry when my mom finally found her happiness? My father was gone, and I truly wanted her to enjoy the life she had. This explained why she was not answering her phone, but it hurt deep in my bones that she would not tell me about him. Who was this mystery man, and how did she let herself fall in love without me finding out?

CHAPTER 25

I fished my phone out of my purse once I got home, still a little shaken. Right there in the side pocket were my keys. I was grateful I hadn't found them earlier. What I saw happen between them in that store, I could never unsee that shirt flying across the bookstore. I was so glad I didn't get there a minute later, or I probably would have seen way too much. Who was that guy, anyway?

Because of my mother's striptease, I waited until seven in the morning to go to the bookstore, just in case. I prayed they were both up and dressed by now. My mom knew I always came in early, but I did not want to chance it.

She had fresh cinnamon muffins and peanut butter cookies on a plate when I got there, and she was alone. How were they fresh? When did she have time to make them?

"Mom, I've been trying to get a hold of you, what's going on?"

"What do you mean, sweetheart? I just got back from the casino this morning," she said.

I could play this game. "Oh, really, the casino, huh? Did you win?"

"Not this time." She was quite convincing as she arranged the cookies in a perfect circle.

"Well, I was at the bookstore until close to midnight last night."

"No, you weren't," my mom said and then cleared her throat. "I mean, what were you doing here so late?"

"Mom, you know if you ever wanted to date someone, I wouldn't think you were like cheating on Daddy, right?"

She looked at me, almost offended. "What are you talking about, dear? I love your dad, and there is no one who could ever compare to him."

Enough. "Oh, cut the crap, Mom. I know a man was here last night, and I saw you kissing him."

"Excuse me? I was not here with a man."

How could she deny it? It was obvious I caught her in a lie.

"Mom, come on, I saw him."

"Sounds like you're a bit confused. Are you sure you weren't dreaming? Out drinking last night, maybe?"

She was so convincing, I almost believed her, except I had seen it with my own eyes.

"Fine, Mom. Answer me this, though. The foreclosure sign that was on the door. Are we in serious trouble? I need to know if we're losing the bookstore and if we really own it. I don't believe that you took care of whatever was going on like you said you did."

She wiped the espresso machine and avoided eye contact. "I told you that was a prank."

"Mom, what is going on? I can tell you're lying. Did you sell the bookstore? I have the right to know because I do work here, and the minor fact that I'm your daughter and the bookstore was going to be passed down to me."

"Fine, we may have gotten into a little financial trouble, but I handled it."

I let out a deep breath of frustration. A pile of business cards lay on the floor next to my mom's bracelet. The same business card that banker gave to me. What were they doing here? "Financial trouble? So that foreclosure sign was right then? We don't own the bookstore?"

I put my hand on her back and forced her to look at me. "I'm not a kid anymore. Tell me the truth."

"What does it even matter, anyway? It's my bookstore."

She was impossible and closed off. She had so many secrets.

"Fine, don't tell me. I respect your privacy, Mom, but I want you to know I support you one hundred percent. Just tell me what I can do to help."

She waved me off. "Oh, I have it all under control. Trust me."

I picked up the pile of business cards from the floor, along with her bracelet.

My mouth dropped open as I finally made the connection. "Mom, are you seeing the banker?"

"Me and the banker? That's just insane."

She wouldn't even look me in the eye. It was so obvious. She opened up the register and dismissed me. I turned my back and walked away to organize the shipment in the back. The bell rang up front and I let my mom handle the customer.

She was talking to the man for a few minutes. She came into the storeroom and stared at me after the customer left.

"What?"

"I left you in charge of this place. You should get off your lazy butt and help the customers. You're supposed to be showing me why you deserve the store."

That was it. I had enough of my mother's unreasonable behavior and lies, and how she always treated me like I was a child.

"Seriously, Mom? I run the store. You're never here. You're off gallivanting around, having sex with that banker, and only showing up to put out baked goods." I went too far and did I really just say gallivanting? I sounded just like her, but maybe I was acting like her because the roles were reversed, and she was acting like a child.

"If your father were here, he would--"

"If my father was here? Really, Mom? You would not be acting this way if Dad were here. You weren't even on the boat when it crashed. You think it is all about you, but what about me, Mom? I was the one on the boat that day. I hit my head and woke up next to him on the dock, remember? Don't you think that was hard for me, too? You took off for months after his death and Sabrina, well she just vanished right after the accident."

I was now screaming at my mom, but I couldn't control myself anymore.

"Your sister went on to be an attorney. You know how busy law school is, and being an attorney is even more challenging. She did not leave because of your dad."

Why did she always defend Sabrina? My sister would no longer answer her phone. The only communication she had with us was through social media and texting and even that took years to accomplish.

"When was the last time she answered your calls? You act like the two of you talk every day, but really you just stalk her social media like a hawk."

"You don't know what you are talking about, Valarie."

My mom's hands were shaking and her left eye was twitching, but I was sick and tired of tiptoeing around her. Enough was enough.

"Who was the guy, Mom? Admit it was the banker. Please don't tell me you were having sex with him to save the store."

She snapped her head away. I waited for an answer.

"I'm not that kind of woman. We met up and he fought so hard for us, sweetheart. He promised he would do whatever it took to keep the store from foreclosure, but I just don't know if there's anything we can do anymore. It's too late." Her mother wiped her tears.

"Mom, do we not own the bookstore anymore?"

"Chad Simonson owns the bookstore now."

The man who caused the boating accident that killed my father.

I will never forget how bright the sun was shining that day, not a cloud in the sky. It was humid and sticky. We spent most of the weekend tubing and waterskiing on the chain of lakes in Side Lake. We had just dropped off my mother and sister at the beach with our picnic basket full of snacks. My dad and I were going to the landing on the connecting lake to pull the boat out of the water and then drive back to park and eat lunch.

We came out of the channel when a boat came flying at us. Dad had no time to turn the boat out of the way, nor did we have the speed to hurry in the opposite direction. I stared straight ahead, just waiting for the impact. A part of me hoped they'd somehow go around us, but they didn't have time.

Next thing I knew, I was lying on a dock next to my father and a man I'd later found out had been driving the boat. The details were still blurry, and I had no recollection of the man who pulled us out of the water, nor where he came from. I remembered seeing a man run, but I never saw what he looked like. Someone later told me the man who ran away was the man who pulled us out of the water.

The doctors said if that man hadn't pulled me out of the water when he did, I would have drowned. He pulled my father out of the water and even pulled the man who killed

221

my father out of the water. The police said he ran to call 9-1-1, but we never found out why he didn't come back. The police were searching for him. They wanted to question him about leaving and wondered why he was in such a rush to take off, but instead, we were left with so many unanswered questions.

Sabrina was so angry she stopped talking to us after that day and moved to The Cities, Minneapolis/St. Paul area, without a word. She attended the University of Minnesota and cut us out of her life.

I thought Sabrina would come around after a while, but we haven't seen her since. I was sure my mom blamed me for Sabrina taking off, and I never understood why.

I was dating Eric at the time, and two years later, I became pregnant with Alex. I still have nightmares of what happened that day, including the man who saved me, but he never had a face. We tried looking for him and even put out a reward. The police never found him. My mom eventually sued Chad's insurance company, and he went to prison for a few years for his reckless boating. I knew he had a lot of money, but how did he end up owning our bookstore? It made little sense, like he hadn't done enough to our family already and now this.

"I spent a lot of money after your father died. On the bookstore, paying for your sister's college, buying you your lake house. Your dad was always in charge of finances, and I admit I was horrible at it. I started getting into terrible debt and then when Chad was released, I called and told him he owed it to your father to save the bookstore and he did, but I still paid rent."

"He kills dad and makes you pay rent on your own bookstore?"

Her mom shrugged her shoulders. "He never meant to kill your father. It took me a long time to admit to myself it was an accident. Yes, he was going too fast, but he's a good man, Valarie, and I needed to forgive him because it was only hurting me. I never should have asked him to buy the bookstore, but I knew he would. He had money and a guilty conscience. He tried to gift it to me, but I wouldn't let him. Your dad wouldn't have wanted that."

I wanted to disagree with her, but I couldn't.

"He killed your husband, Mom, and your children's father. The bookstore is all we have left of him, and we're losing it now because you couldn't accept the gift."

"He didn't ruin our family. Quit being so dramatic. It was an accident."

"You and I both know dad would still be alive if it wasn't for him. He was reckless. Who do you think is responsible, then?"

My mom sobbed into her hands, but I didn't feel sorry for her. I wanted answers, and after all these years, she was finally talking about it. I was sick and tired of pretending it didn't happen, walking on eggshells around her all the time. I was hurting, too, damn it!

"I haven't paid in months. He's going to take the bookstore and sell it. I'm sorry. He asked me again if he could gift it, but I don't want it anymore.

I got right up in my mother's face and finally lost my temper with her. "Take the gift, Mom. I want the store. You never stopped to consider how I would feel about it. You may not care about the bookstore, but I do! I'm going to talk to him."

"It's a done deal, Val. The bank is taking it. We set up a deal that I would pay the bank directly and I haven't. Chad didn't want to be the middleman anymore. I had to make a choice, and I did what I thought was best."

"I can't believe you. You're so selfish. This store means everything to me." I threw the dust towel down on the floor.

"I quit and I'm done talking to you. How could you do this to me? To Dad? Did you ever love him?" I didn't wait for her to answer as I speed-walked out of there.

My mother called out. "No, Valarie, please don't go."

I picked up my pace and whipped open the door. I was so furious, I almost ran into a man in a wheelchair. "Sorry," I said and continued walking. The man was familiar to me, but I was too mad to give him a second thought. My heart was broken, and I was too busy wondering where I was going to work now that I had quit the only job I ever had.

I stopped for fast food on the way home. Chicken nuggets, two cheeseburgers, and French fries with two cinnamon rolls and a chocolate shake. I opened up the wrapper for a cheeseburger and took a deep breath. I moaned with pleasure. It smelled so good.

"Mmmm."

I opened up my mouth to take a big bite.

I threw all the food in the garbage after eating the burger, fries, and milkshake. My stomach was so swollen I had to undo the button on my pants. Once I threw the rest of the food in the garbage, I got into my car and drove straight to the gym. I was glad I listened to Linda about always having a gym bag in my car, so I never had an excuse not to go. I must have consumed as many calories as I should have had in an entire day, and I felt so guilty about it. Although I knew I'd be sick working out with a full stomach, I had to burn off some calories and the stress.

I put on my gym clothes in the bathroom and stared myself down in the bathroom mirror with disgust. My clothes were freezing cold from being in the car in twenty-degree weather and left me with goose bumps. My shoes froze my feet when I slipped them on and tied them. A woman behind me cleared her throat, and I turned around to see who it was.

Carla.

"Hey, it's Veronica, right?"

"Valarie."

"Oh, right?"

She looked like she had just finished a workout. Her tan skin was damp and sweaty, making her look even more bronzed and beautiful. She was thin and probably didn't have an ounce of fat on her body.

I looked down and wondered how some women stayed in such great shape. Were they born that way? Did they starve themselves? There must be a master key somewhere, and it was this giant secret these women hid from the rest of us.

"I hear you're a friend of Nicholas's?"

"Kind of, yeah."

"Don't worry about offending me if you like him. He made it very clear we were over, and I'm pretty sure he has a crush on you, anyway. I must have made it awkward for you at the bookstore. Who knew the one person I asked for advice would be the woman chasing him?"

I was unsure how to respond to that double-barreled insult. I kept my head down and put my hair in a ponytail.

"You aren't going to deny it, are you? Well, I'm just surprised you even talk to him. You know, being that his father killed your father in that boating accident."

My world swirled, and my lungs no longer worked as if someone were squeezing the life out of them. Carla could not be telling the truth. No way was Chad Nicholas's father. He would have told me, or I would have known that, wouldn't I?

I tried to pass her to make my way to the treadmill. "Excuse me."

She stepped right in front of me so I couldn't get past her. Her tiny body blocked the way.

"I'm so sorry. I thought you knew. He goes by Nicholas

Ryan because Ryan is his middle name, but his last name is actually Simonson. I wouldn't worry about it; it was an accident, right? I'm sure he wouldn't keep a secret like that from you."

Carla looked at me with pity and patted me on the shoulder, then stepped aside. "It was so great meeting you, Veronica. Have a great day."

Her smile was in no way sincere, and it made me sick.

Could Nicholas be the son of Chad Simonson? The reckless driver who killed my father and was responsible for everything bad that has happened to my family? I could not work out today after this news. I switched into my outside shoes. I needed to find out the truth, and I deserved answers.

A truck was parked in my mom's driveway when I pulled in. I debated whether or not to knock. What if it was the banker's truck? Most likely, it was his truck. I knocked anyway and walked in. Mom never left the door open, so they were unlikely to be having another rendezvous.

"Mom, Mom, are you here?"

A flash of light from the living room caught my eye. There on the couch sat my sister.

"Sabrina?"

What was she doing here?

She stood up.

"What are you doing here, Valarie?"

"I'm looking for Mom. I didn't expect to find you here. I'm so confused. Why are you here?"

Sabrina's hair was a mess. She was in sweatpants and a purple sweatshirt. She looked terrible, and her mascara was smeared across her face. She had changed so much since I last saw her. We were getting older and her age showed in the wrinkles on her face.

"Mom isn't here."

"Where is she?"

Sabrina shrugged. "I really don't know. We got into a fight and she stormed out. I had nowhere to go, so I stayed here."

Even though my sister had disowned our entire family, my heart softened, and I felt kind of sorry for her. "Why did you show up after all this time, anyway? How did you expect her to react?"

"Adam left me. I want to start a practice here, where I grew up. I don't want to live the rich life anymore. I screwed up, Val, and I'm not too proud to admit it. I'm sorry if I hurt you."

"Let's sit down," I said and led the way to the couch. "Mom isn't the same as when you left. After dad died and you took off, she had a breakdown of sorts. She's never around, and the other day I found out she was seeing someone and they were doing it in the bookstore of all places." I shivered, the memory too vivid in my mind. "Gross."

"Mom? She wouldn't. What about Dad? She's just going to forget about our father?"

I let out a sigh. "Really, Sabrina? You think you can come home after all this time and tell Mom how she should be living her life? You lost the right to have an opinion when you cut us out. She deserves to be happy."

Sabrina took off so she wouldn't have to handle the mess our dad's death left on the family. She left to forget it happened, and numb the pain. She was a coward in my eyes.

"I screwed up. I know that and I'm sorry. I never meant to hurt you. I never meant to hurt Mom. I was selfish."

"Yeah, but that doesn't erase all the years when you were gone, years when we needed you the most. I can't believe you had the nerve to come home and think it could just go back to the way it was. A lot has changed."

"I'm sorry, I didn't mean to. I was scared to come back

because Dad wasn't here anymore, and I didn't want to be here and remember he was gone. I always meant to come back eventually, but I kept putting it off and putting it off until..."

"Until?"

"It doesn't matter. I'm so sorry, and I hope you can forgive me. I'm your sister."

"Sure doesn't feel that way. I don't know you at all anymore."

She wiped away tears. "I'm still me."

I was angry, but she was hurting, and she needed someone to talk to. I was different than she was. I would never run from my family when they needed me most.

"What happened with Adam?"

"He's seeing someone else. When I figured that out, I realized I needed my family. I missed you guys, and I was so stupid for not seeing it before. I thought I could trust him."

"I'm sorry to hear it didn't work out." I knew my words seemed cold, but I didn't try to correct them.

Sabrina took my hands in hers. "I love you so much, Valarie. I know it isn't going to happen overnight, but if there is any way you can find it in your heart to forgive me—"

"I thought you hated me."

"Never! I could never hate you."

Somehow, I believed her.

"Well, I forgive you, and I think you need your family right now. Mom will come around. Are you going to get a divorce?"

"That means so much to me. As for the divorce, I have no choice. I just wish Mom would forgive me, too."

"Well, give her some time and hang out here until she comes back. Take my advice and don't judge her. She's obviously feeling guilty about this man in her life, and I think we need to support her."

"You're right. When did you become the sensible one?"

I laughed. "You know I went through a very similar experience with Eric except we're giving it another shot."

"What do you mean?"

"He was cheating on me and then he came crawling back after I moved out."

"Are you happy?"

I wasn't sure I knew the answer to her question. What was happiness, anyway? Instead I said, "I think so."

"Well, I'm sure everything will be okay. I think I'm going to take a nap until Mom gets back. Crying this much is making me exhausted. Thank you for being here for Mom. You really are strong, you know that?"

"Mom does her own thing. On another note, I have some bad news. The bookstore is being foreclosed and there's nothing we can do to stop it. Dad's legacy will be gone forever, and it's all Mom's fault."

"What did she do now?"

She listened intently as I told her about everything. Once I finished, she apologized.

"We will fix this, I promise. I wish I could help, but I've spent more than I've made trying to live this wealthy lifestyle. I overspent and I'm not in such a great financial position myself anymore."

Sabrina, broke? Now we had no chance at all to save the store. My dreams were over and my father's legacy would disappear forever.

CHAPTER 26

Nicholas had a hard time convincing Regan to go out to dinner with him the night before she left. They had decided to stay one more week. Carla wanted to leave on Thanksgiving morning, which was a punch to the gut. This would be his first Thanksgiving without his little girl. Maybe that was the problem. She would always be his little girl. Was he so terrible to her she wanted to get away as soon as she could? No, she wanted to get to know her mother.

Regan finally agreed to dinner as long as Alex could join them. He did not put up a fight, even if it broke his heart that he couldn't spend the night alone with his daughter. At least she did not insist on Carla coming with them.

Nicholas picked the girls up at Val's house because they wanted to be together on Regan's last night in Hibbing. When they got in his truck, they were all giggles.

"I can't believe you're going to be living in New York City. Can you imagine all the celebrities you're going to meet? I am so jealous," Alex said.

Regan had so much excitement in her voice. "You really

think so? I would love to meet Bruce Willis or Julia Roberts. You have to come visit me, bebe."

Alex laughed and flipped her hair behind her shoulder. "What's your obsession with old people? What about Ariana Grande and Tom Holland?"

"Yeah, I guess. There's plenty of time to meet them all."

"Old people," Nicholas said, shaking his head.

The girls sat in the back, making him feel like a taxi driver. Regan always sat up front with him. They pulled up at the restaurant on Howard Street.

"Yellow car," he said. They were parked behind a yellow car. He and Regan played this game since she was about four or five. Every time they saw a yellow car, they had to yell it out. They never kept score, but they were very competitive. Regan swore she was winning, but Nicholas was usually the one who yelled it out, or so he thought. Regan would usually slap his arm playfully with a loud, annoyed exhale for not seeing it and saying it first.

"Oh, Dad, aren't you sick of that game? We've been playing it forever. C'mon, it's a kid's game."

His heart fell in his chest. How did she not see that she was breaking him? Moving away was making her feel like an adult, too good to play games with her father. Didn't she see how much he loved her? That he never gave up on her? Why didn't she see he was not the one who took off and did not come back for years? But he would never tell her how he felt because he was glad she had her mother back in her life. He would never hurt her, but he was just a little jealous.

"Yeah, it is getting old, isn't it?" He opened the restaurant door for the girls.

She did not hear him. Instead, she pointed out a boy who looked to be about their age. She whispered something to her friend, and they both giggled.

"Table for three in a booth," he told the young man.

The server picked up menus and rolled silver wear. "Right this way."

He sat them down and winked at Regan. "It's Regan, right?"

His daughter blushed and nodded her head, all googly eyed. Alex nudged her with her elbow, and she gave her a warning look in return.

"I'm Josh. I'm in your fifth hour."

She could hardly look at him. "That's right."

"Are you on Snap?"

She nodded, but she looked at her dad as though she was ready to run out the door crying with nerves.

"Her username is Regz21," Alexandra told Josh.

He flashed his white teeth at Regan and said, "Sweet. You don't mind if I add you?"

She finally looked at him, nodded her head in agreement, and they locked eyes. Nicholas hated every second of it.

"That would be ... nice."

He walked away, and she let out a big breath of air. "I can't believe Joshua Wilson asked for my Snapchat, OMG."

Alex shared her excitement, and they both grinned happily.

"He is so hot! That was amazing." Alex's expression grew somber. "It's too bad you're leaving tomorrow though."

Regan hit herself in the head. "Oh, man, why now? Well, I can still snap him."

"True," Alex said.

"OMG," Nicholas echoed.

They both looked at him and shook their heads at each other as if to say, he just doesn't get it. He was the third wheel here.

Regan paid a little more attention to him during dinner. He knew she was going to miss him because she ignored

Alex for quite a while. Her friend did not seem to notice or care because her eyes were glued to her phone.

"So, Mom got me into that school."

"I'm glad to hear that. You getting excited?" he asked, careful not to show how sad he was that she was leaving.

"I am so excited. Living in a big city like New York is such an opportunity. Although I really wish you would come with, but I understand why you can't." She pushed her food around on her plate with her fork.

"I'm so happy for you and I wish I could be there for you, but I would go crazy in such a big city. You can come back for Christmas if you want."

Her eyes lit up as she continued. "I would love that. I can't wait to see Mom on Broadway, tour the Empire State Building, the Statue of Liberty, ugh, there is just so much to see there."

"I'm so happy for you."

"I'm really sorry about how terrible I acted when mom came back. I want to get to know her, you know. I see all my friends with their mothers, and I want that. It doesn't make me love you any less." She leaned in toward him, her eyes on Alex. "I will miss you the most, Dad," she whispered.

"Hey, I heard that!" Alex said as she put her phone on the table. "What about your bestie over here?"

"I will snap you every day."

"Does that mean I'm going to have to get this Snap now, too?"

The girls laughed at him.

"No, Dad, I will call you every day."

His lips curved into a smile. "You better."

Nicholas paid the bill, and they got up to leave, but not without both girls scanning the restaurant for the teenage boy. They took the long way out of the restaurant so Regan could walk by Joshua one last time.

Nicholas had done the same thing many times when Val was in her Calorie Counters class, or when she was working out at the gym. He always needed to peek at her one more time, and the butterflies were always there when he saw her. He didn't even tease the girls for stalking the boy because he understood all too well.

They pulled up at Val's house, and he had to call Regan back to give him a hug.

"Dad, it's not like you're never going to see me again."

He could not help the tears as he tugged her closer. She hardly even hugged him back. This was something new to him. He missed the days when she would call out to him when he picked her up at daycare and tell him how much she missed him. He felt like he was losing her.

"I'll miss you," he said.

"Dad, you know I'm stopping by in the morning to get the rest of my stuff, right?"

How could he forget? He was a mess. Her bags were packed, but she had one more suitcase to fill. Carla had told him not to worry about shipping the rest because her apartment was not big enough for it all.

"You know how Manhattan is," she had said, like she assumed he understood.

He had never been to New York City. He was a small city kind of guy. If he were to travel, it would be to Alaska or Montana to hunt or fish, not to an overpopulated, overpriced city.

"Love you," Regan said.

And then she was gone before he had a chance to say it back.

He headed back to his truck, but turned when the back door opened again.

"Hey, Nicholas," Valarie said.

She stood all bundled up in her poufy black jacket and pink hat. She did not have any gloves on, and her hands were pulled into the cuffs of her jacket. He was unsure if it was because she was nervous or cold.

He took two steps closer. "Hey."

"How are you doing? I can't imagine how hard this must be for you. Regan is a sweet girl, we're going to miss her."

They strolled down her driveway. "Yeah, it sure isn't easy. I just hope Carla has changed."

"Yeah, about that. I know this probably isn't the best time, but I really need to talk to you about something."

He was confused. "Does this have to do with Carla?"

"Not exactly. It has to do with your dad."

His stomach tied in knots. He had hidden this from her for too long, and now she knew before he had a chance to tell her. Who told her? They even had different last names. It had to be Carla.

He had to come clean. "Listen, I've been trying to tell you but—"

"But what? It's true, isn't it?" She scowled at him. "We were stranded in the middle of nowhere for three days. If you wanted to tell me, you would have. Is it true? Is your name really Nicholas Simonson?"

The blue in her eyes sparkled in the streetlight, and her long dark hair peeked out of her hat. There was no turning back now.

"When Linda adopted me, I changed my name to Nicholas Ryan. My father insisted that I didn't have the same last name after what happened."

"So you knew this whole time he killed my father? When, Nicholas? When did you know who I was?"

She stared at him.

"I didn't know who you were until the last day we were stranded at that cabin. My dad asked what your last name was weeks before that and when we were sitting there on the floor, it just came to me. I tried to tell you but the plow came." She would never forgive him. He was such an idiot.

She covered her face with her hands. "How could you hide this from me?"

"I'm so sorry. I couldn't tell you. I didn't want you to hate me. You mean so much to me."

"He ruined my family. He ruined everything, and you knew it. You're a liar and a fraud."

He moved closer to her. "Let me explain."

She stepped back. "I never want to see you again. When I am at the gym or Calorie Counters, don't come near me. You hear me? Does your entire family know who I am?"

He closed his eyes and nodded. "Linda does."

"I feel like such a fool. I can't believe you."

"I'm so sorry. I never meant to hurt you."

He chased after her as she sprinted to the house. She paused and stared at him with so much hate. "Goodbye, Nicholas. We aren't friends anymore, you hear me? Never talk to me again. You can tell your family to stay away, too. This whole time you pretended to be my friend, but it was because you felt bad that your father murdered my father, and he came out of it just fine. Now he's the reason my bookstore is getting foreclosed. Did he tell you that?"

"How could that be?"

"Maybe you should ask him that," she said. "Goodbye, Nicholas."

The door shut, and he was all alone outside her door. He could not change her mind. She was right, he was a liar and a fraud, and he had an opportunity to tell her everything and he froze. It was useless. She wanted nothing to do with him ever again, and he did not blame her.

He stopped at the liquor store and bought the best whisky on the shelf. He put it next to him in his truck, and as he took the corner, it fell over. He bent down to grab it and when he looked up, he saw the headlights shining in his eyes, blinding him. His body flew forward, and everything went black.

CHAPTER 27

I slammed the door and crouched down to cry. The girls were jumping around upstairs, Alex's radio on full blast. I stood up and left the kitchen. My hands were shaking, but surprisingly, I was not craving junk food. I lay down on the couch, mentally exhausted.

I woke to a knock at the door, and I wanted to hide under the table until I saw my mom's hair through the window. Maybe she was coming to apologize?

I opened the door, and she stood there with a huge grin and a fresh batch of blueberry muffins in hand. "I was in the neighborhood and thought you might like some muffins."

"Mom, you could have taken them to the bookstore."

Her smile faded. She walked in and set down the basket on the counter. "I'm glad you keep your door locked. That neighbor is so creepy. When are you moving back in with Eric? I hate to see my granddaughter having to be here any longer than she has to."

"I'm not moving in with Eric. Not right now anyway."

She shook her head. "Why not? I thought you couldn't wait to get out of here. He took you back, didn't he?"

A loud cry of frustration slipped out. "He cheated on me. How can you take his side? I've worked so hard to lose weight to be with him. Hell, I stopped eating, purged, but you are so busy hiding this boyfriend, you haven't even noticed. I lost this weight for him because he said he was no longer attracted to me and here you're asking me if HE took ME back. You've got to be kidding me. Will I ever be good enough?"

My mom studied her fingernails, unable to meet my gaze. "I think you're overreacting a bit, dear. You always think everything is about you. That's your problem."

"Mom, get out of my house. I don't need Eric, and I don't need you telling me that I'm not good enough. I've had it. You used to tell me I was overweight, and I listened to you, but why can't you just love me the way I am? I was a mother who cared so much about my family that I lost myself along the way. Until you can support me the way I am, you can get the hell out of my house. Go home to Sabrina! Your perfect child who can do no wrong."

I shooed her out and slammed the door. She didn't even fight me.

I was on a roll, finally saying what I needed to say to her. I had enough. No one was going to tell me how I should feel or that I wasn't good enough again. I was good enough, and I did not need to get my security from anyone else.

Those muffins stared at me, and the delicious scent found its way into my nose. I needed to eat one blueberry muffin, even if they were from my mom. I took a small bite and took my time chewing so I could enjoy it. For so many years, I ate fast without even stopping to think about how amazing the food tasted. It was as though I was worried someone would eat more than his or her fair share if I didn't eat fast enough.

With my coffee in hand, I stared out the window. Not going to the bookstore first thing in the morning was killing me. Today was Thanksgiving morning, and I was running out of things to be thankful for.

I was depressed with no plans for the holiday. Usually I cooked dinner and my mom would come over and eat with us, but not this year. No way was I going to be a slave to her after the way she was acting. The bookstore meant everything to me, and it would never be mine now. With thanks to my unreliable, selfish mother. I knew it was not all on her, but I wanted it to be because I was so mad at her.

The girls were walking down the stairs, so I put on my jacket and shoes and snuck outside with my coffee to have some time by myself. It wasn't as cold as I thought it would be. Frost covered the windows of my car, but it was thirty-five degrees. I leaned over the railing. A noise from the yard next door caught my attention. I walked over to their yard, deciding this was a great time to find out who these people were and why their yard was such a disaster.

"Hello," I said.

The man did not glance my way.

The woman walked up the driveway. "Are you talking to Tom, dear?"

I smiled. "Yes, well, I was trying to."

"You have to talk real loud, he's practically deaf and blind."

Deaf and blind? In all these weeks as his neighbor, I never even noticed.

"Hi, I'm Val," I said to the woman.

"I'm Alice. What can we do for you?" she said.

"I haven't exactly been a great neighbor since I moved in next door so I wanted to introduce myself."

Tom looked up at me, but then looked down. He seemed to avoid eye contact.

"I don't think he likes me," I whispered.

"Well, we both don't like you, actually."

"I'm sorry?"

Did I hear her right? How rude. Another person for my list of people to avoid. Offended, I turned to leave, but turned back when Tom spoke.

"You're just like everyone else. Leave us alone."

He didn't even know me. I was a good person, and I was in no mood. I walked up to him and stopped a couple of feet away. "What did I do to you?"

Alice was now standing next to him, her arms crossed. "I heard you talking to your friends about our yard. Maybe you should talk to people before you judge them and making assumptions."

I looked around their yard again. "If you need help cleaning up all of this junk, I can help."

The couple laughed and shook their heads.

Tom made his way to the pile of lawn mowers and boards that were stacked up and covered with a light dusting of snow. He mumbled something, but I couldn't understand a word he was saying. He didn't move his tongue when he spoke, and it sounded as though he had a mouth full of marbles. I looked at Alice to elaborate.

"Tom is telling you that this is his bread and butter. He served in Vietnam and saw a lot of horrible things, like soldiers hearing cries from babies and when they went in to pick them up, bombs were in the cribs, and they were blown to shreds for having a heart. He had PTSD and when he got back, I did not understand what he'd been through and we were fighting all the time. I started drinking, and I lost my job. You don't understand what it was like. He had constant nightmares, and he could not work. I left him and he ended up on the streets. I was luckier than he was. I lived in public housing until I got caught with meth. I was evicted and ended up at the shelter where Tom happened to be. From all his years of smoking, he was diagnosed with lung cancer and cancer in his mouth. I stood beside him as they removed half his tongue; so don't be so quick to judge. We have been through a lot."

That explained the way he spoke. My arms broke out in goose bumps from the thought of it all. He had part of his tongue cut off. My tongue felt swollen at the thought.

"I'm so sorry. I didn't know."

"The man who bought this house was a vet himself. He found us in the house and when he heard our story, he said we could live in the shed until we found another place. The last renters left the place in pretty rough shape."

I looked up at the roof of the house. Not much was left of it. The paint was all scraped off, and the house sagged.

"The people who rented this house from him were hoarders, and there was garbage everywhere." Her eyes followed my gaze to the pile of stuff in their backyard. "Like actual garbage."

I nodded. Busted for judging again. I never would have admitted to judging people. I didn't like to get involved in drama or gossip, but today this woman proved me wrong.

"We thought it was such a wonderful offer, better than nothing. We've lost everything because of drugs and alcohol, and medical bills that kept piling up. People like you judge us and refuse to give people like us a chance. Now that Tom has such a hard time speaking, it's impossible for him to get a job or assistance due to our past mistakes and criminal history. Both of us are sober now. Going on five years"

"I'm so sorry, I had no idea."

The woman only had a few teeth in her mouth, and those left were mostly brown.

"We lost our children years ago because of our bad habits and behavior. They were six and seven when the county took them away from us."

"Usually the county gives you so many chances. Why

didn't they give you a chance? I'm assuming because you didn't have a home?"

"Well, Tom and I knew we were in no state to take care of them, so we gave up our rights, and they were adopted. We didn't want them to live the life we're living. It didn't make it easier, though. I guess saying the county took them from us makes me feel a little more like it wasn't my fault, but I know it was."

Alice's words stunned me. I tried to imagine giving up my daughter because I couldn't care for her.

"That had to be so hard."

Tom nodded and grabbed Alice's dirty hand in his.

"We wanted our girls to have a better life than we have. Please, don't call the police."

"Are you kidding me? It's not my place. I was hoping the two of you would come over for dinner tonight. I'm going to make a Thanksgiving dinner, and I would be honored if you would join my family."

Alice and Tom both looked unsure and were silent at the invitation.

"Think about it, okay? Please? I would love to have you at the dinner table with us."

"Maybe," Alice said. "But why?"

"As gratitude. I had no idea what the two of you have been through, and I want to show you how grateful I am for your service, sir."

Tom raised his eyebrows as if no one had ever referred to him with so much respect. His eyes teared up, and my eyes started watering, too.

"I ... fix ... machines ...." he said slowly so I could understand him.

Alice put her hand on his shoulder. "He fixes old lawn mowers and snowmobiles people either throw out or ask him to fix. That's how we afford to eat. It may not seem that way, but we're saving up for a home of our own. Someday, right Tom?"

He nodded. "Thank... you."

"No, thank you for letting me make up for my horrible manners and judgment. You'll be doing me a favor," I said, with utmost sincerity.

"Can we bring anything?" Alice said, and then she frowned as if she knew it was an offer she couldn't follow through.

"A hungry belly," I said. "Come over when the sun begins to set. That should be a little before five. Does that sound okay?"

Tom's lips rose in response. He looked so happy. I wasn't sure if it was because of the food or my hospitality. Maybe both.

Back inside, the girls were saying their goodbyes. The basket of muffins was now empty.

"Good morning, girls."

"Thank you for letting me stay the night, Mrs. Renyalds. I'll miss you guys," Regan said.

I teared up. "Can I give you a ride?"

"My mom is on her way, but thanks anyway."

It wasn't easy to let her go. I wanted her to stay. She was a good friend to Alex and a part of me missed Nicholas and knew we were even more disconnected with Regan gone. I was still pissed off at him, and I knew I could never trust him again. I had a hard time believing the man I knew would hide something like that from me.

I took Alex to the grocery store after seeing Regan off, which left us both in tears. Shopping for Thanksgiving food would be a much-needed distraction for Alex. I needed to buy a lot of food at the last minute.

Alex was quiet in the grocery store except when she complained about having the neighbors over, and then if she hadn't complained enough yet, the dreaded, "Are you inviting Dad?"

"Yes, I'm inviting your father."

"I don't understand why the two of you are even back together. It's stupid."

"Why? Would you rather he was with Cinnamon so she could buy you alcohol?"

That wasn't fair. Alex had come clean to Eric and me about Cinnamon. I just wanted her to get off my back.

"Mom, I won't do that again. I'm sorry I'm crabby, I just don't want to spend Thanksgiving with a bunch of homeless people."

"You are acting very selfish. That is what Thanksgiving is about."

"No, it's not about feeding homeless drug addicts, Mom, it's about family."

"Sometimes you need to go out of your comfort zone, Alex."

We pushed our cart to the checkout and, after unloading a few things from the cart; I looked up at the all-too-familiar cashier and lost my breath. I did not know if I was going to cry or throw up.

"Are you okay, Mom?"

I looked at my daughter and realized what I needed to do. We finished unloading the cart, and then I stood in front of the cashier to pay.

"Hi," I said to the cashier. I wanted to give her a piece of my mind, to tell her how much she hurt my feelings.

She looked up at me with a smile. "Hello, looks like you guys are getting food for Thanksgiving, am I right?"

"Sure am." This was the perfect time to make her cry like she made me.

"This must be your daughter. You sure look like your mom."

Alex smiled.

"I have two daughters, six and ten, but they're at our neighbor's house today because I had to work. Just couldn't give up the overtime, you know?"

Her eyes were glossy, and she had such sadness in her eyes. She was hurting, too.

"That must be so hard," I said, letting the resentment go. I grabbed my bags and put them in my cart.

"Have a wonderful Thanksgiving," she said.

"You too," I said, and then I tipped the guy bagging my groceries twenty dollars.

His eyes lit up. "Thank you so much, Happy Thanksgiving!"

As we walked away, my heart felt lighter. I smiled to myself. People weren't all as bad as they seemed. I needed to stop judging before I knew the whole truth. It was harder than it seemed, but there was no better time than to start today.

CHAPTER 28

R egan walked in the front door. Carla following
right behind. "Dad, what happened to your
truck?"

"I was turning a corner, and I hit another truck. It all
happened so fast. Luckily there was little damage to their
truck, mostly just mine."

"Are you okay?"

"Yeah. I'm fine. I was lucky."

"Didn't you just get your truck back from getting fixed?
Well, I'm glad you're okay." Regan skipped up the stairs.
"Okay, well I'm going to get my stuff."

Carla walked over and rubbed his shoulder. "Are you sure
you're okay? It smelled like whisky outside, and I'm pretty
sure you're a recovering alcoholic, or were."

"I'm not going to lie, I bought a bottle of whisky
intending to drink it, but ironically it fell over when I turned
the corner, and when I went to grab it off the floor, I hit that
truck. I never had the chance to drink a drop. If there was
ever a wake-up call, that was it."

Why was he telling her this? He needed to tell someone,

but confiding in Carla was never a good idea. He had nothing to be embarrassed about. He may have intended to drink it, but he didn't.

"I don't understand. Why does it smell like whisky in your driveway then?"

He rubbed his face, embarrassed by his actions.

"I was so angry about buying alcohol after all this time that I threw the bottle against the garage and broke the bottle when I got home. Not my best moment, but at least I didn't drink it."

"I'm sure you got a nice release from frustration."

"You have no idea. I swept up the bottle, and I was going to hose off the driveway, but I put the hose in the attic for the winter and was too lazy to get it. I was planning on finding it before you guys came over this morning, but you're early."

"Well, next time, don't buy the bottle in the first place. You can really be an idiot. That probably won't be the last bottle you'll buy."

She was nice for about two seconds, but then out came the Carla he knew.

"I'm having a hard time with my daughter moving across the country. It was a moment of weakness."

"Oh, so it's my fault?" She crossed her arms defensively. "She's going to be fine. I'm her mother, and I won't let anything happen to her. She needs me."

So easy for her to say, but what would she actually do? He wished he did not have to worry about Regan. He would not have let her go except she needed this. "I know, but she's my world and has been since you took off and left us."

She took some papers out of a manila envelope and set them on the table. "Here are our divorce papers. Sign them and then stick them in the mail to make it official, or you can move to New York City with your family. We can give our marriage one more shot, and we can all be together again. It would be best for Regan if you really care enough to put her first."

He looked deep into her eyes, trying to read her. She was serious.

"Carla ... I--"

"Don't say anything." She pointed to a sticky note on top of the paperwork. An address was written on the note. "If you decide to ditch the paperwork and start over as a family, then come. If not, send in the paperwork."

"I'm signing the divorce papers," he said. "I have a business here."

She put her arms around his neck and looked deep into his eyes. "I love you, Nicky. I was so dumb for what I did, but it's never too late to try again, right? Just think about it. That's all I ask."

She gave him a quick kiss on the lips, bringing back so many good memories, and making him forget the bad memories for a quick second of amnesia.

"Nicholas," he mumbled.

She looked confused. "What?"

"It's not Nick or Nicky. My name is Nicholas. Please stop calling me Nick, it's driving me crazy."

Regan came running down the stairs with a bag in her hand.

"Goodbye, Daddy. I'll call you when I get there." She kissed him on the cheek and hugged him tight. "Thank you for letting me go."

He pulled her in for one more hug. "I love you, be careful, and don't be afraid to call if you need anything."

She laughed. "Oh, Dad. I love you, too."

He gave Carla a gentle hug, and she grabbed his butt.

He jumped.

"Sorry," she whispered. "I had to." She winked and followed Regan into the driveway. "Think about what I asked you, okay. Don't be so damn stubborn, I'm your wife."

They got into her rental and pulled away.

Regan looked at him through the car window and waved. That was it. His little girl was gone forever.

Nicholas spent the afternoon watching *The Office* and trying to laugh, but he had a hard time even smiling. He silenced his calls, not feeling like talking to his family and co-workers. His father called, but he let the call go to voicemail.

The doorbell rang, but he was too depressed to get off the couch. The door opened, and he heard wheels rolling down the kitchen floor.

"Nicholas? Nicholas, get off the couch, look at this place," his father said.

He looked around. His house was a mess, but he did not care. He was still wearing the same clothes and hadn't show-ered since the accident.

"If you don't like it, then don't come over." It was a line Linda used when people came over to her house when it was a mess.

"I get it. Regan is gone, but she isn't a little girl anymore."

"Dad, I know."

"Then get off your lazy butt, you have a company to run."

He let out a loud sigh. "My life is a mess, Dad. I fell in love with Valarie Heinz."

"Please tell me that isn't Carol and John's daughter."

Nicholas nodded. He no longer cared.

"You got too close, didn't you?"

It didn't matter now. Val hated him.

"Did you tell her everything?"

"Not yet."

He rolled next to Nicholas and put on the breaks. "You

need to let her go. It's for the best. You don't need to tell her everything, son."

"Yes, I do, and she doesn't want me, anyway. She found out you were my dad."

"How did you even find her?

He gritted his teeth. "We ran into each other a few times. I didn't know whom she was until way later on. You had mentioned something about her that day we were talking and said her last name. I realized it was her, but by then it was too late. We got to know each other because our girls are best friends."

"How did that happen?"

"Is it true you're foreclosing on their family business?"

His father shook his head. "It's not like that. Carol doesn't pay her bills. I can't eat those expenses, and she wouldn't let me give it to her. She's stubborn, and she isn't very good with her finances."

"We broke up their family. You need to make this right."

His father rubbed his fingers through his beard, deep in thought. "They sued me. I gave them so much money, it's not my fault. I can't be in debt to them forever."

"Actually, you can."

"Nicholas, I tried. You love this woman, don't you?"

Nicholas looked away.

"You don't love her, you feel guilty and it feels like love. Think about it."

"Yes, I feel guilty, so I need to tell her the truth, but I love her. You think it's easy for me? Falling in love with the one person I hurt more than anyone?"

"You can't let this break you, Nicholas. It's better if you don't tell her. You have a gym to run."

A hot flush rose to his neck from the anger he was holding in. "She isn't like the other women I've dated. I love her, but I know she'll never forgive me when I tell her. But I can't live with myself if I don't. I've been hiding this secret for too long."

"You really want to throw your life down the toilet? I thought you were smarter than that." He began rolling his wheelchair toward the door. "Do whatever you want. I'm done trying to stop you. You won't go anyway, you have too much to lose."

He chased his father and jumped in front of him.

"Mom would be so disappointed in the way you're acting right now. I've kept this secret for so long. Regan's gone now, and it's just me. Let me grow up and clean up the mess I created."

His father stared back at him. "If you go, I'm taking my gym back. You'll be cut off from your inheritance."

He stood up. "I don't care. Take it all. It's time I take responsibility for my actions and come clean, starting with the accident."

"So be it," his father said. "But don't say I didn't warn you."

CHAPTER 29

This was the first time I'd ever cooked a Thanksgiving dinner by myself. I woke up at four o'clock in the morning to begin prepping, but I should have started the night before.

Alex was up by seven and stumbled into the kitchen.

"You're up early," I said, my eyes on the potatoes I was peeling.

"I thought you might need a hand, and I couldn't sleep. I know grandma usually cooks the turkey."

Regan's leaving was hard on Alex. They had become close over the swim season. "Missing Regan?"

Alex nodded. She took the peeler from her me and tackled the potatoes with sleepy eyes. "I'm glad she stayed for sections, but school will not be the same without her."

Alex was talking to me about her feelings. Heart-to-hearts with my daughter were seldom and far between.

"You were pretty close to making it to state, but I know you'll make it next year. It may look different without Regan, but it'll be okay, I promise. Plus, now we'll plan a trip to the Big Apple."

"I guess," Regan said, deep in thought. "Mom, what happened with you and Regan's dad that night she stayed here? We heard you screaming at him."

This caught me off guard. I had hoped they were too busy to hear what was going on. How awful that Regan had to hear someone yell at her father. "Just some adult stuff."

"Sounded like a lover's quarrel to me," she said.

"Alexandra, that's enough. Nicholas and I will never be together. Your dad and I are together, and I don't want to be with anyone else. I thought you understood this."

I wasn't ready to tell her I had been avoiding her father. It had been a couple of days since I last saw him, but I needed some time to think. Now he was coming over for Thanksgiving, and I hoped it would be a better day.

Alex's arms stiffened, and she attacked the poor potato with animosity.

"I'm sorry, Alex. I didn't mean to—"

"No, I get it. I overstepped my boundaries. It's none of my business."

Was Alex going to let her off that easily? No, I knew my daughter better than that. Nothing was that easy. Sure, she was sweet and helpful, but she was still a teenager. Raising a teenager was like nailing Jell-O to the wall. She was hormonal and temperamental.

"But?"

"But I wouldn't be upset if things didn't work out with you and Dad, that's all I'm saying."

"Let's change the subject," I said, finally.

"Okay, why did you invite the scary people who live in the shed to Thanksgiving? I mean, don't get me wrong, it's fine, and nice of you and all, I just don't understand why you don't want to spend it with your family. And aren't you afraid they're going to steal something?"

"Alex, you're being judgmental. We had this conversation

yesterday. Is there something wrong with treating them with a little respect and a nice Thanksgiving dinner? I thought I raised you better than that. This is the day you're supposed to be the most thankful for what we have. Why not share that with others"

"The most thankful holiday followed by people stampeding other people and hitting them with their shopping carts as they fight for Christmas gifts for their loved ones at cheap prices? It's messed up. I don't think Thanksgiving is as great as you think."

I wasn't exactly a fan of celebrating Thanksgiving either, mostly due to the history behind it, but I believed in making it a day to appreciate everything we had and everyone around us.

Alex shrugged her shoulders.

"You're thinking about the day your grandma punched a woman in the face as they fought for your Leap pad when you were little, huh?"

I shook my head and laughed at the memory of my mother calling for a ride to the emergency room because of a shopping accident.

"She is a little out there."

"She got it for you though, didn't she?"

"At her own expense."

I brushed my hair out of my eye with the back of my hand and finished rolling dough for the rolls. "Just promise you'll be nice to the neighbors. They've been through a lot, okay?"

"Yeah, yeah, I know. He served in Vietnam and lost his tongue," Alex said. "But don't expect me to fix them a plate."

I shot her a disappointed look.

"I'm sorry, it's a horrible story, but they're homeless druggies, Mom. It's weird and I don't understand why you have to bring them to our table.

"You know, when you were in sixth grade you wrote that

letter for the children who lost their home in a fire. You donated clothes to the girl who was your age and even made her a friendship bracelet. You have a big heart, listen to what you're saying."

"That was different, and they weren't drug addicts."

"Oh, Alex," I said. "Cut up the carrots, please."

There is that moment every mother has in a conversation with her teen when we had to shake our heads and move on. They will understand when they get a little older. For me, that was this moment. It was like trying to get a small child to understand, although young children listened better at times than teens.

Eric arrived just as I was pulling the turkey out of the oven.

"Smells delicious," he said.

He came over and gave me a kiss on the lips. He smelled fruity and sweet, like pumpkin pie. I breathed in the smell of him. "What is that smell?"

He looked around. "You've been baking all day, it's the smell of your food." He laughed.

"You smell like pumpkin lotion or something."

Then I saw the bright red lipstick on his collar, and my heart sank. Dizziness washed over me, and I grabbed a banana off the table and breathed deeply as I peeled it. I had not eaten all day, but I would not binge eat nor starve myself. Was Eric seeing someone else? Was that old lipstick from Cinnamon or fresh from today?

I tried to stay calm. "Eric, can you please set the table for five?"

"For five? Who else is coming?"

I turned my back to cut the turkey. "I invited the neighbors."

He was silent for a minute too long, and then he asked, "Like Emily, Dawson, and the kids? Those neighbors?"

I would have loved to have Emily and her family for Thanksgiving, but they usually went to Duluth to spend the holidays with Emily's ex sister-in-law and their family.

"That would be way more than five. I invited the neighbors' next door to this house."

I waited and waited for it to click and knew he figured it out when I saw his wide-mouthed expression.

"Like the dirty people next door?"

Alex came up behind us. "They're dirty because they live in a shed and don't have a real place to live."

Alex meant well, but this was sure to anger Eric.

First, his face turned red, and then he threw the silverware on the table just in time for the doorbell to ring.

I shot Eric a challenging look, so he knew I wanted him to behave. "I'll get it."

I opened the door for the neighbors. Up close, they looked even older and less groomed. I wanted to offer them a shower or clean clothes, but I didn't want to scare them off. That would most definitely offend them, and I wanted them to feel comfortable. They had been through so much and surely Eric would understand if he knew their story.

"Why don't you two have a seat and Alex here will help dish up the plates."

Alex smiled. "Tell me about Vietnam," she said as she dished them up a plate.

There was a softness in her voice that made me so proud.

Outside, Eric lit up a cigarette, and I joined him on the porch.

"You smoke now?"

He let out a vicious, forced laugh. "Only when you bring in the homeless. Those people are worse than homeless, they're dirt balls. What were you thinking, Val? I don't even know who you are right now."

"You bought the cigarettes before you came, so that can't be the reason you're smoking. What is really going on, Eric?" I pulled on his collar, bringing his attention to the lipstick. "You have lipstick on your collar."

He brushed my hand off like a spider. "There isn't any lipstick on my collar. You're crazy. You don't trust me, do you?"

Really? He was going to deny the obvious lipstick stain? Did I even care? A part of me expected this to happen. Catching him in a lie was just a way to end it. I did not love him, nor did I trust him anymore. It took this long for me to realize it.

"I lost the weight and bought these clothes with the intentions of winning you back. I'm such an idiot."

He blew a puff of smoke in my face. "So this was all just a game to you then?"

I wanted to scream at him, tell him he was a loser, and this was all his fault, but I knew it wasn't.

"Eric, you're right, this isn't your fault, it's both of ours."

He raised an eyebrow and choked on the smoke he inhaled. "It is?"

I peeked in the window at the neighbors seated at my table, and a shiver ran down my spine. "I should have let you go. You fell in love with someone else because we grew apart and were no longer happy together. It's my fault as much as it is yours that you strayed. It was right in front of me all this time, but I pretended to be happy because I was scared."

"Wait a minute. Are you dumping me?"

I laughed through the tears. "We had a lot of good times. I know that lipstick and the woman smell on your body aren't an accident. I'm sorry if I made you feel trapped."

"Don't do this, Val. I love you. I was just angry because

you wouldn't make love to me, and I had to get it some-where. I have needs, you know? We were married for so many years, and you wanted to take things slow. You've got to be kidding me, was all I could think. We've been together for so many years." He held onto both sides of the deck railing and looked up at the sky as if he was searching for the answers in the sky.

"You always want what you can't have," I said. "You're my daughter's father and because of that, we will always share her, and we have a lot of history. We were married and had some good years together. I don't hate you, Eric, and we need to learn how to get along better."

He crossed his arms. "You're right, I guess. I'm not going back in there. Those people freak me out."

"That's the thing about being divorced, you don't have to."

"You're really okay with me being with someone else?"

I wiped my eyes. "Yes. As long as you're happy, and she's good to Alex."

"This isn't one of those traps, is it? When I admit I screwed up, you're going to make me pay for it like you did with Cinnamon?"

"No, but you need to be fair. Stop fighting me on the house. My mom gave it to me and you know it. I want it back. The courts even told you it was mine. Please."

"Fine," he said.

"And talk to Cinnamon about respect, okay? She can't buy our daughter alcohol, and she needs to act more like a parent."

He cleared his throat and had a guilty look on his face. He couldn't meet my gaze.

"What is it?"

"Well, don't be mad, but it isn't Cinnamon."

"It isn't?"

"No way, she's too young for me. Now, my new secretary on the other hand."

I almost laughed. "You are a pig, you know that? Please, don't bring your new woman around Alex until you're serious, okay?"

"Who do you think I am?"

"Eric, I mean it."

"Fine," he snapped. "Will you say goodbye to Alex for me? I'm going to see my lady friend."

He was gone before I could say goodbye, and I just stood there shaking my head. I sure dodged a bullet there. I felt nothing but relief. I had been living a lie, and I was finally free. The time had come to live my life the way I wanted instead of for everyone else and what looked good.

CHAPTER 30

"**M**om, what are you doing here?"

Nicholas was packing a suitcase when Linda showed up in his bedroom.

"Your dad called me."

He turned his back on her and continued to roll his clothes to save room in his suitcase.

"What are you doing?"

Of course, his father had called Linda. His dad knew he had a soft spot for her. Sure, he loved his father, but he walked out on him. His father rarely showed he had a conscious. He played dirty to get his way, and he was over-protective. He never had a chance to learn from his own mistakes because his father covered for him. Kids today would call him a Karen.

"You know what I'm doing if my dad called you."

She pulled on his shoulder and spun him around. "I just need to ask you one question. Why?"

That was the question he had been asking himself. "I can't live with this lie anymore."

She shifted her weight. "What about Regan?"

"She's with her mom now, you know that."

She put her hand on his suitcase to hold it shut. "What about if she wants to come home?"

He faced her. "She has family to help. I have to do this, for me, for Val, for Regan, too. You have to understand, I can't live my best life with this on my conscience anymore."

She bit her nail. "Did you know who she was when you fell for her?"

"No, not right away."

"How did Val find out about your dad?"

He suspected she already knew the answer, but he told her anyway. "Carla."

"Of course it was Carla. How about going to New York City and spending some time with Regan before you do this?"

She was still trying to talk him out of it.

He shook his head. "Is that a joke?"

"Just give yourself at least a day to really think about it, okay? What if Val doesn't forgive you?"

She was probably right. "That's a chance I'm willing to take."

"In the meantime, talk to Regan and give yourself some time to sit on it. I know you love Val, but this is your future, Regan's future. Everything will change."

Everything she said was true, and he did not doubt it one bit. She was trying to help him think before he made a rash decision. But they both knew he was doing the right thing. He felt it in his heart.

Her eyes sparkled, and she shrugged. "I know it must have been tough for Val to hear from Carla, of all people, that your dad caused the accident. Can you imagine what she must think? I knew the two of you had feelings for each other. Do you think she will want you back if you tell her the full truth?"

"That's not the reason. She's with Eric again. I know there's a chance she'll never forgive me, but she needs to know. I owe her that much."

She raised her eyebrows. "That's pretty brave of you. You could end up losing her forever if you tell her, or worse."

"I know there are consequences, but it's killing me. I need to get this out." He sighed. "I bought whisky the other day."

Her voice squeaked. "No! Why?"

"I didn't drink it, but I almost did. I need to clear my conscious. I need to tell her the truth, and I will suffer the consequences. If anything happens to me, promise you'll take care of the gym. You and Maria are the only ones I trust."

She did not protest or tell him that everything was going to be fine because they both knew that was not true. His family had been hiding a secret for so many years, and he needed to get it out, even if his father never spoke to him again.

"Well, promise me you'll wait a couple of days before you tell her. Don't do it today. Tie up your loose ends first."

"I can do that, but I'm not changing my mind."

He arrived at the gym on Tuesday morning when the Calorie Counters meeting was just ending. He almost ran right into Maria.

"Nicholas, hey. I tried calling you yesterday."

"I wasn't feeling well," he said and glanced behind her.

She turned her head to follow his gaze and then whispered, "You aren't looking for Val, are you?"

"No."

"Well, she called me pretty angry the other day. She's pissed off because she found out who caused the boating accident that killed her father, which I'm sure you know."

He cleared his throat. "Maria, come on. Let's talk in my office. You don't want everyone knowing, do you?"

She shrugged, but followed him in and shut the door. "Did you tell her about your dad? How did she find out?"

"It doesn't matter. I never should've kept it from her."

She put her hands on her hips and pointed her finger at him. "She's mad at me. You said you were going to tell her. I don't blame her for blaming us all. She isn't coming to the gym or Calorie Counters, and Nicholas, I'm worried about her. I worry she's binging again or maybe even starving herself. She's lost so much weight."

"She'll be okay. She has Eric to take care of her."

Maria laughed and shook her head at him. "Oh, Nicholas. You really are blind, aren't you?"

"What?"

"She and Eric didn't last very long. They broke up on Thanksgiving. Everyone at the gym has been talking about it."

"What?" He thought they were making it work. What had changed?

"She gave it another shot, but we all knew it wouldn't last."

"But he was all she talked about. Her primary goal was getting him back. She told me that."

She squeezed his cheek like he was a child. "She wanted what she couldn't have. Her husband left her for a woman a decade younger and half her size. She wanted to know she could get him back. Losing the weight made her feel good, and it made him drool over her. Don't get me wrong; I'm sure that was what she thought. It wasn't like she was lying to you, but she finally saw him for who he was. She couldn't change him."

"You women need a handbook so we can understand you," he said. "You are so confusing."

Maria laughed. "She's not mad at me anymore. I apologized, and I brought her my homemade lasagna and a bottle of merlot."

"So she may be less mad at me, then?"

She grabbed the door nob. "Not even close. Apologize."

"I'm going to tell her the truth about the accident."

Maria shut the door. "What do you mean, the truth?"

He sat down in his chair, his expression somber. "Linda didn't tell you, did she?"

"Tell me what?"

"It's nothing."

She let out a frustrated sigh. "Nicholas, what are you not telling me?"

"You need to sit down."

CHAPTER 31

Since I quit working, I woke up early every morning to take a walk past the bookstore to keep an eye on it before anyone was out and about. Then one day there was a No Trespassing sign on the door, which made me furious, and everyday, I prayed it would be gone but it never was. Alex walked with me on the weekends when I could get her up early. We enjoyed some good one-on-one time together, just catching up and bonding.

A For Sale sign showed up at the bookstore door when I walked by the previous day. I went to the bank and met with the banker who was seeing my mom. He put the numbers together and called me with bad news. I did not have enough credit to get the loan. My heart was broken. This was it. If someone bought the store. They would never keep it as a bookstore. Mom did not even get everything of ours out of the store before we were no longer allowed to enter.

This time I did not walk by. I stopped and sat on the two stairs in front of the building and cried. The bookstore was my whole life, and most of all, a part of my father and the memories our family shared when we were happy and all together. I did not want to let it go. Even if it meant losing everything I stood for in the process. If there were any way to get the business back, I would find it.

Sabrina was kneeling behind her truck when I pulled up. She looked back at me and waved, then returned to whatever it was she was doing. The timing could not be more perfect. She was alone, and my mom was not around to talk my sister out of it.

"Sabrina, what are you doing out here? You realize it's like ten degrees, right?"

She was shivering in her thick winter jacket. The sky was clear and for the first time, I really looked at my childhood home. The siding was falling off, and the shingles were peeling, but all I could do was smile at the happy memories. We never needed an expensive house or a lot of things to make us happy. My happiness was from all the memories we shared as a family when my father was alive.

"Mom really needs to replace this roof."

"Yeah. It's too bad she's so horrible with finances." Sabrina pulled out her taillight fixture.

"How long have you been in Hibbing, Sabrina?"

She popped in the fixture and stood up, unaware of the reason behind the interrogation. She rubbed her forehead with the back of her glove. "I came up a couple days before you saw me, but I stayed with a friend until I had the courage to apologize to Mom."

"I see."

"I'm sorry I left you when Dad died. You're right, I was broken and angry. I didn't blame you for the accident. I knew there was nothing you could do. I blamed myself for getting off the boat with Mom. I wanted to sunbathe and flirt with boys, and I was mad at you."

For the first time, I saw the pain Sabrina carried on her

shoulders.

The front door opened and closed. "Hey girls. I hope the two of you aren't duking it out. I'm in no mood today."

We shook our heads at Mom's comment. So like her to say something to make it awkward.

"We're fine, Mom," Sabrina said.

"Oh good. Well then, I owe you an apology, Valarie."

My mom never apologized for anything. "Okay?"

"I'm sorry I slept with the banker and lied about it, and I'm sorry I never told you about the bookstore."

My anger was gone, and just like that, all was forgiven. "I appreciate it. There isn't much we can do about it now and as for the banker, I hope he makes you happy. I just want you to be honest with me."

"He does, but he will never replace your dad. You girls know that, right?"

We both nodded.

"No one could ever replace our dad, but there is room in your heart to love them both. Just differently," Sabrina said.

"I just can't believe the bookstore is gone," I said.

"I'm really sorry. I know how much it meant to you. I know it hasn't been easy. I guess a part of me didn't want to deal with the finances anymore. I kept putting it off, you know. It was too much without your father. I should have told you a long time ago. I'm sorry. I'm going to figure out a way to get it back, I promise. I was thinking about it and I could put a bakery in the back and you could run the bookstore. Like a real bakery, it's my dream. What do you say?"

"I say let's figure out a way to get back the bookstore," I said.

"That's my girl."

I was not going to ask my sister to help save the bookstore. It was my bookstore to save, and I needed to do this without her.

CHAPTER 32

I t hadn't snowed in weeks or I would never have found the shack. I carried my backpack and made my way through the ankle-deep snow and discovered footsteps coming from the north. There were two sets.

I knocked on the door and listened. A new window had replaced the blanket. The owners had probably called the police. I should have checked on this place days ago to see if there was any way to contact the owners, or even a search online to see if I could find out who owned the shack.

I knocked again, and a man opened the door. A woman stood behind him.

He looked confused. "May I help you?"

"I'm sorry to bother you. My name is Valarie Renyalds. A few weeks ago my ... friend and I were driving down the road here in a snowstorm. We spun out and couldn't get any cell service, as I'm sure you already know. We trekked in here and stayed in your cabin for two days. Your cabin saved our lives. We broke a window to get in. I'd like to reimburse you for whatever it cost to repair it. I'm so sorry I didn't come back days earlier."

The man put out his hand to stop me. "Don't worry, your boyfriend was already here. He fixed the window about a week ago. Such a great young man."

The woman slipped by him. "Why don't you come in and have some tea. I apologize for my husband, he must have forgotten his manners." Her smile was friendly and inviting. It would be rude to turn her down.

"Nicholas? Nicholas came by?"

Why hadn't he mentioned this to me? Why hadn't he asked me to come with him, but then again, we weren't exactly on speaking terms.

"Yes. He not only fixed the window, but he offered to pay for any damages."

"He did?"

"I told him there weren't any damages. That silly dear," the woman said.

They were an elderly couple. The man seemed a little grouchy, but the woman reminded me of my grandmother.

"I apologize for bothering you. He never told me he came out here," I said.

"You got a good one there," the woman said.

Her curly gray hair was tied back, and she had on a red Christmas sweater. Every Christmas when I was growing up, my mother would buy the entire family matching ugly sweaters, and we would have a photo shoot in front of the tree. My mom continued the tradition after my dad died, even though it was just the two of us. Eric had no part in the sweaters. "Twinsies," she'd say.

Alex wore a Christmas dress until she was twelve and then she wanted to join in on the matching sweaters. She thought it was cool.

"We aren't together, we're just friends."

"That's a shame," the woman said. "He was sure smitten about you."

"He was?"

The man snickered. "Lauraine, what did I tell you about getting into other people's business?"

"Oh hush," she said. She leaned into my ear. "Don't mind my Fred, he can't spot romance if it bit him in the tush. Please come in and have a cup of tea."

She led the way to the other side of the familiar cabin. The room was much tidier than when Nicholas and I were here. There were rugs and curtains that hadn't been there before, and a stack of boxes in the corner.

"You guys decorating?"

Lauraine laughed. "No, no, dear. We own some apartments in Hibbing. We were doing some updates and had extra stuff, so we decided to make it a little cozier up here with the extras we ordered. Fred still likes to hunt with our son, Ryan, but he couldn't make it up this year. Poor dear. I tried to get Fred to hunt without Ryan, but he wasn't on board." She leaned in again and looked back at her husband, who was fast asleep on the bed. "I don't think he could stay awake long enough to hunt by himself. He would probably forget his way back and freeze to death."

"I'm so sorry to hear that. I grew up eating venison, so I know how important that deer a year is."

Lauraine poured two cups of water out of the kettle and added tea bags. "Oh yes. Although Fred hasn't shot a deer in years. Ryan always shot them, and he would give us a little bit of the meat after he cut it all up. But tell me about you. Do you have kids? I don't see a ring on your finger."

I took a sip of the tea and almost burned my tongue. "I do. I have a sixteen-year-old daughter, but I'm no longer married to her dad."

"Oh no. I'm so sad to hear things didn't work out with that handsome young man. If you ask me, he certainly seemed in love with you. It's really none of my business, but why did you divorce him? Did he work too much? He did, didn't he? Fred worked too much, and I thought about leaving him so many times, but—"

"No, no." I placed my hand on Lauraine's. "We were never married. My divorce was with another man. Nicholas is just a friend."

"A friend, huh?" She looked over her shoulder again. "Is he married?"

"Well, kind of, but it's a long story. They aren't together anymore."

"Well then, why don't you give the poor guy a chance? How many people would care enough to come all the way out here and buy me a window?" She winked. "I only know two."

I blew on my tea and took another sip. "It's complicated between Nicholas and me."

Lauraine lifted her eyebrows a few times and winked. "I haven't been romanced in so long. Do me a favor, give the poor guy a chance and then tell me all about it. Whatever it is, leave it in the past and forgive him. You only live once."

"I will keep that in mind," I said, blowing on my tea. "Can I ask you a question?"

"Anything, dear."

"Do you happen to have any extra apartments for low-income housing? I have these neighbors and—"

"I sure do! Here, let me give you my number. I have two that just opened up. Have them call me, and I can get them in right away."

"Thank you so much. You have no idea how much this means to them. I'll have them call you tomorrow."

"Yes, dear, I'll be home tomorrow, and I should have reception. Just make sure they have at least two hundred dollars for a down payment, okay?"

"Thank you so much. I must get back. Here's my number. Call me sometime. I'm so glad I met you.

Lauraine pulled me in for a hug. "You go get him, dear. You won't regret it."

Maybe, just maybe, this woman was an angel.

The next day, I saw the neighbors with a stack of metal and wood in their backyard. They were fixing a snowmobile.

Tom got the snowmobile started after many attempts, and I ran outside to give them a thumbs up and clap. He took off down the snowy road, and Alice and I both watched with smiles.

"He finally got it running," I said.

"Yeah, thank you for helping us apply for housing, too, by the way. Selling this snowmobile will be enough to pay the rest of our first month's rent."

Since losing my job, helping the neighbors gave me a sense of purpose. They were so grateful, it warmed my heart. Next, I needed to find a new job.

"I'm so glad. How about work? Did you find anything yet?"

"We're going to do maintenance at the apartments. They have a lot of work for us. I can do the talking and Tom can do what he loves. We couldn't have done it without you. I can't believe I'm saying this, but I was wrong about you."

I smiled and hugged her. "Well, if you ever need anything, don't be a stranger."

"Thank you so much. You've done enough for us. We didn't know where to start. The neighbors around here just called the cops, but you really helped us, and we are forever grateful."

I wiped my tearing eyes. "You deserve it. Just in time for Christmas, too."

Alice looked down. "I don't remember the last time we

had a warm place to sleep and celebrate Christmas. How can we ever repay you?"

"Oh, no," I said. "It is you I should be thanking. The two of you reminded me that there is more to life than just stuff. You'll have to excuse me, there is something I need to do."

It was time.

CHAPTER 33

Maria was so angry as when he told her the truth. He warmed a bowl of oatmeal and checked his phone for the hundredth time today. Nothing from Regan and nothing from Val. He opened a bottle of water and sat on the couch. Just as he put his finger on the power button, he heard a knock at his door.

He was not up for dealing with his father. Maria probably called to yell at him again for keeping the secret all these years. He opened the deadbolt and opened the door to find the last person he expected. Valarie. Her hair hung down the back of her white winter jacket, and her bright eyes flashed. His mouth curled into a smile in response to how beautiful she looked, and his heart fluttered. She came. She actually came.

Her mouth quivered. "I'm sorry, Nicholas."

What should he say? He hoped she would forgive him, but he never thought she would just show up at his door.

She walked in and made herself comfortable at his kitchen table.

He had to tread carefully. "Why are you sorry?"

"It's not your fault your father hurt us."

"Wait, I—"

She put her hand out to stop him from talking. "No, you wait. I overreacted and I'm sorry. It was an accident. I know that, but I'm having difficulty forgetting what happened. I have horrible nightmares from that day. I was on the boat with him when it happened. I'm not sure you knew that."

He nodded. She needed to let it out, but all he could do was sweat at the thought of having to tell her the truth.

"My dad was my entire world, and I'm sure you love your dad very much, too. You said he went to jail when you were young and Linda became your legal guardian. It was because of what happened to my dad, wasn't it?"

"Yes, but—"

"I was so selfish. Your father, is he a good person?"

"Yes."

"Is he okay after the accident?"

"Well ..."

"Please forgive me. I'm sorry I keep cutting you off. I'm just a mess of emotions."

She wrapped her hands around his neck. He did not want this moment to end, but he had to tell her. He pulled her hands away.

She raised an eyebrow. "What's wrong? I'm apologizing here. I thought you felt the same way I did. I'm not with Eric anymore. We don't really go together. I love you, Nicholas. I've fought it for so long, but the truth is, I can't live without you in my life. I've fought it for so long."

He wiped the sweat from his forehead and let his hand linger behind his neck as he stared at the ground. He was about to break her heart, but he had no choice.

"I have to tell you something about the accident, Val."

She wrinkled her forehead. "What do you mean? There's nothing else to say. I don't blame you."

"Well, you should. Sit down."

She sat down and stared up at him. Her innocent eyes would never look at him the same after he finished what he had to say. It was now or never.

"I was with my father the day of the accident," he said.

The color drained from her face, and her jaw dropped, but she did not say a word.

"I was just a teenager. My dad let me drive the boat for a minute because he wanted to check on the motor in the back. He was sure he had a bad prop, but he was only gone a few seconds. I wasn't paying attention and when I turned around... it all happened so fast."

She stood up, still silent, and he assumed in shock.

"I didn't see you guys. I looked back at my dad to ask him if everything was okay ... it all happened so fast."

"I don't understand. Where were you when the police came?"

"I pulled everyone out of the water and then I left. I was scared, and my father told me I needed to leave. I didn't want to, honest, I didn't. I just wasn't thinking."

Her hands were now in fists, and a blue vein throbbed on her forehead. Her eyes were glazed, and he wanted to hold her so much.

"You were the mystery hero? You? You pulled me and my father out of the water and then left the scene before the police arrived? But you're saying you caused the accident? It makes no sense to me."

He raised his shoulders and clenched his teeth in response.

"You killed my father?" Her eyes stared at him so coldly.

He chewed on his lip. He was not sure how to respond. If only he could go back in time, change what happened.

Anger flashed in her eyes. "You're a coward, Nicholas Ryan or Simonson, or whoever you are."

"I'm so sorry. It was an accident. I never meant for anything to happen."

He took a step toward her, but she pushed him back.

She grabbed the door handle. "You weren't saving me this whole time. You were trying to make up for murdering my father. What is wrong with you? How was I so stupid?"

Tears rolled down her cheeks, but she made no attempt to wipe them. It was killing him not to brush them away with his thumb, to stop the pain he was causing her.

"I will never forgive myself for what I did. I'm so sorry, but I promise I didn't know who you were until we were stranded. It was as if a light bulb went on and it all clicked."

"But why didn't you tell me?"

He stepped in front of the door before she could pull on the handle again. "Please hear me out, I'm going to turn myself in."

She glared at him with such hate, shivers ran down his spine.

"You're too much of a coward to do something like that."

He moved out of the way when she raised her hand as if she was going to punch him right in the face.

"I never meant to hurt anyone, you have to believe me. I panicked and ran."

She walked out the door, and he followed, standing on his front porch.

"I know I'll never see you again, but I promise you, I will turn myself in tomorrow after I tell Regan."

She turned around. "You think I care? I don't love you, I was wrong."

And then she was gone.

He sat down on the floor and cried. He'd let out his deepest, darkest secret and it felt good and horrible at the same time. He did not have to lie anymore, but he hurt Val so much. If only he could take it all back. He had just lost the two people he loved more than anyone in the world.

He lay in bed, unable to sleep. He was not worried about turning himself in for what he had done. He wanted the court to throw the book at him. He was worried about Regan being stuck with her mother and Val hating him forever. He wanted Val to have closure, but at what cost? He deserved whatever he got. If they locked him up and threw away the key, it was probably too soon. He killed a man and put his father in a wheelchair. He gave the woman he loved a concussion, and his poor father took the fault. What kind of person was he, anyway? He never should have listened to his father when he told him to run. But he was just seventeen years old.

He got out of bed at seven, and he even made the bed. He would call Linda when he was at the police station so she could sell his house and whatever else she needed to do. Maria most likely hated him for what he did and not telling her the truth years ago. Likely, no one would visit him in prison.

He took a hot shower, put on his best church outfit, and his whitest socks. He stared in the mirror, unable to recognize himself. He did not eat breakfast, but he brushed his teeth and combed his hair.

He was about to pick up the phone and call Regan when the door opened behind him. His father rolled in.

"Dad, I finally did it. I told Val the truth, and I'm ready to face the time."

"You what?"

"I told her, Dad. I can't hurt her anymore. She deserves to know the truth. I'm sorry."

He waited for whatever his father threw at him. He was already numb anyway.

Instead, his father rolled over and shook his hand. "I'm proud of you, son. Your conscience is clear. You love her, don't you?"

"I do, and I don't regret coming clean. That's not why I told her. I feel ... free."

"What did she say?"

He ran his hands through his hair. "What you could expect her to say, I guess. That she hates me."

He nodded. "And what did you say?"

"I told her I was turning myself in to the police. I deserve whatever I get."

His father hugged him. "I'm proud of you, but I'm probably going to get charged with perjury. What you did was brave, but do you really need to turn yourself in? Maybe you should leave that up to Valarie."

He never thought about his father getting into trouble for lying. His dad should not have taken the rap for him. It wasn't fair, not to Val and her family.

"I'm sorry, but I have to. None of this would have happened if I hadn't been so irresponsible."

"The truth is, I have been selfish. If I would have let you be honest from the start and hadn't told you to run away when the sheriff came, you could have dealt with the consequences by now. I'm so sorry. I'm a terrible father."

"Dad, what you did was brave. You served time for me. You're my hero. You literally gave up your life for me. I'm sorry I disappointed you. I need to make it right now, clear your name."

Tears ran down his father's face. "Don't do this for me. I would do it all over again if I had the chance. I'm sorry I was a horrible example by making you hide, but I did what I knew was best. You would do the same thing for Regan."

"You're right, I would." He bent down and hugged his father. "I'm a better person because I had you as a father.

Thank you for what you did. I know you thought you made the best choice for me at the time."

His father patted him on the back. "Call Regan, son. I'm going around the block to give you privacy."

As soon as he shut the door behind his father, he dialed Regan's number and held his breath.

CHAPTER 34

I heard what sounded like pebbles bouncing off my window. At first, I ignored them. Maybe it was raining. But then they got bigger and louder. I peeked out the window and saw the man in a wheelchair throwing rocks. He must need help.

I ran outside in my slippers. "Sir, are you okay?"

He looked at my outfit. "You're going to catch a cold in that. Get some clothes on."

"I'm fine," I said, continuing to walk toward him on the sidewalk.

Something in his eyes seemed so familiar to me. Did I know him?

"I'm paralyzed," he said. "So give me enough respect to let me finish my story, okay?"

"Oh ... kay." Did this man have Alzheimer's or something? He seemed confused. I looked down the street to see if anyone was looking for him.

He picked up his phone, dialed a number, and put it to his ear. I was not sure if I should call the police to help him.

"Hey, it's me. Here she is." He extended the phone to me. I

eyed him suspiciously, but took the phone and put it to my ear.

"Hello?"

"Is this Miss Valarie Renyalds?"

I pulled my phone away from my ear and glared at the man. "How does he know my name? Who are you?"

The man motioned for me to return to my call, and I complied. "Yes, this is Valarie."

"This is Thomas Ratched from Merchant and Miners State Bank. Remember, I was looking for your mother that day at your bookstore."

How could I not know who he was? This was a very weird day.

"Okay, and what do you want from me? Someone needs to tell me what is going on here."

"Well, that's why I need to talk to you. The man who is there with you wants to buy your bookstore back for you and your family. He wanted me to tell you because he was afraid you wouldn't believe him."

I pulled the phone away from my ear and stared at it for a second. "Who are you? Why are you doing this?"

He took the phone from me and put it to his ear. "Thank you. I'll get back to you." He closed the phone. "I'm Chad."

"Wait, Chad? You're Chad Simonson, aren't you?" I backed away from him.

He nodded and rolled closer. "Nicholas is in love with you, do you know that?"

"No disrespect, sir, I don't want to yell at a man in a wheelchair, but Nicholas killed my father and let you take the blame for it."

I turned around, but he whistled loud enough to make me turn back.

"He never made me take the blame for it. Do you have a child, Valarie?"

I looked away.

"Do you?"

"I'm not sure what that has to do with anything."

He wheeled himself closer to my feet. "Just answer the question."

"Yes, I have a daughter."

"I bet there is nothing you wouldn't do for her, am I correct? She means the world to you, and you would never want one slight mistake to ruin her life. Wouldn't you take that from her if you could?"

I was crying now, and I knew he was right.

"I'm really sorry about what happened, but it was an accident. I need you to stop Nicholas from turning himself in to the police. He is my only son and I can't lose him. In return, I will buy your bookstore and gift it to you."

I pointed my finger at him, angry beyond all control. "You listen here, Mr. Simonson. No amount of money could ever buy me or bribe me. Maybe you should be telling him this."

I looked into his glossy eyes, and my heart sank just for a moment.

"I tried," he said.

Accident or not, they killed my father.

"It will ruin him. He tried to save your father. He jumped in the water and pulled all three of us out. When I came to, he was in tears. Valarie, he was just a kid. You have to remember back to that day. He was like an angel swimming in the water and pulling us out one by one. Did the paramedics tell you how hard it is to pull lifeless bodies out of the water? I was paralyzed, you were knocked out, and your dad …"

"I was a child that had to grow up without the most important person in my life. My dad was my whole world and everything changed that day. I've hated you for so long.

Did you know my sister left and hardly spoke to my mother and me for almost twenty years after the accident?"

Chad looked down at his legs and slapped his thigh. "I understand it isn't easy. Nicholas lost his family that day, too. I'm paralyzed from the waist down, and I went to prison for a long time because I chose to save my son's future. Society eats people up who make mistakes. Luckily, my sister was there for him, but it was hard on him, keeping his secret. Drove him to drinking."

"He needs to take responsibility for what he did." It sounded harsh, but maybe honesty was what this family needed.

He ran his fingers through his hair, just like Nicholas always did when he was upset. "He made a horrible mistake, yes, but I made him do it. Valarie, he loves you. He had no idea who you were for a long time."

"The answer is no. I won't take your money."

"Fine, but think about it. That's all I ask."

My hands were shaking.

"He's on his way to the police station to make up for what he did so many years ago. Don't you think he's been through enough?"

"I'm sorry for all the tragedy in your family, Mr. Simonson, but I need to go now. Good luck with everything."

I heard someone behind me.

"Mom?" I said.

"Mr. Simonson," she said

My mother nodded hello to him, and he nodded back as if everything was fine between them. How was she not angry with him after what he did?

What was going on? "Mom? I don't understand. If you know who he is, why are you being so nice? His son is the one who caused the accident that killed dad."

She wrapped her arms around me.

"Oh, Valarie. I haven't been completely honest with you. Mr. Simonson apologized to me shortly after he got out of prison. He wanted to buy the bookstore, and he told me the truth. The bookstore was failing after your dad was no longer there to manage it. I forgave him and I'm so glad I did because we got so many wonderful years there together. He asked me to meet him and gift me the bookstore, but I told him the bookstore is yours, so you needed to be the one to decide what to do."

"You knew? Why didn't you tell me?"

She grabbed my hand. "Oh sweetheart, you need to find it in your heart to forgive them and move on. It was an accident and there is no way to bring your father back. I love you, and I'm sorry I haven't been there for you. I blamed myself for not being in the boat, and I carried a black cloud around until I finally forgave Chad and moved on. Give Nicholas your forgiveness. Don't you think it's what your father would want? "She sounded so kind and caring, as if the old mother was finally coming back.

"I need some time. Just give me some time," I said. "I feel like I don't know you anymore. This doesn't even sound like you."

"I screwed up, but I finally decided it was time to be happy. I'm so sorry I haven't been there for you like I should, but I'm here now to make this right."

"I know you fell in love with Nicholas. Chad told me all about the two of you. You do know he is turning himself in today after he tells his daughter what he did," she said.

Nicholas deserved to rot in prison for what he did.

"After Nicholas found out who you were, he came to apologize to me. He loves you, Valarie. Don't you want to be happy?"

"You have been the one telling me to stay with Eric when he treated me like dirt. Now you want me to be with

Nicholas and let this man from the worst day of my life just give me our bookstore? I don't understand you!"

"I screwed up, I know. But you need to do what is best for you. Don't be stubborn."

I was in disbelief, and I didn't know what to say. There were so many secrets. I ran into my house, straight up to my room, and did what any lost adult would do. I cried into my pillow, but this time I didn't reach for the Doritos, and for that I felt some control.

I heard a knock at my bedroom door and then my mom's voice. "Please think about what you're doing. Nicholas was a teenager. Do you want him to ruin the rest of his life for a mistake? He wanted to take the blame, but his dad would not let him. Don't you see that?"

"No matter what, we've lost the bookstore, and I'm not letting Chad hold that over our heads."

My mom looked so calm. "I agree."

"You do?"

"Yes, it would never be yours if you took a bribe. It isn't who you are, but Chad is desperate."

I hugged my pillow in my lap. "I'm sorry you can't have your bakery now."

"We don't need a bookstore to be happy. Your dad lives on in our memories and our heart, not in the bookstore."

Standing before me was the mom I lost so many years ago. "You're right, but I loved the bookstore. It is who I am, just like it was who Dad was."

"Your dad was a father first."

"A wonderful father."

Then my mom laid a check down on the bed and I picked it up and stared at it, trying to make sense of it.

"I told you I'd find a way to buy the bookstore, didn't I?"

"But... how?"

She held out her hand. Her ring was missing.

"You sold your ring? Mom, no!"

"The bookstore is our home. This was just a ring. Now let's get our store back. I knew you wouldn't take the money from Chad, but I wanted you to make that choice on your own."

I jumped up and wrapped my arms around her tiny body.

"I missed this so much," I said.

I looked into her eyes, and she wiped my tears and then her own.

"I can't believe I'm leaving right now, but I have to go. There is somewhere I need to be."

My mother smiled through her tears. "I'll be here when you get back. I love you, my sweet Valarie."

I kept calling him on my way to the police station, but he did not pick up. What if he had already made his statement? What if I was too late? I pulled up to the station and ran up to the police window.

"I'm looking for my friend, Nicholas. He was coming here to make a police report. Have you seen him?"

"Val?"

I turned around and stared at him. "Nicholas?"

He got off the bench and slowly made his way to me.

I struggled not to jump into his arms. "Nicholas, did you?"

"I'm waiting for Detective Anderson to meet with me. What are you doing here?"

I looked around. "Did you tell anyone?"

He shook his head. "No, but I'm going to."

"Please don't."

He stared back at me with a blank look.

"Nicholas, I love you, too. Please don't turn yourself in. Please, for me."

He smiled. "You love me, too? Even knowing the truth of

what I've done to you—to your family?" His face turned somber. "I have to do this, Val. Please don't hate me, but I have to clear my conscience."

"No, don't. Please, what can I do to stop you? I'll do anything." I was desperate for him to hear me out.

"Mr. Simonson?" The detective said from the open door.

"Be right there," Nicholas said. "I'm so sorry, Valarie. I can't live with this any longer. I need to serve my time for what I did. I'm so sorry I hurt you."

I grabbed his arm, but let go when he gave me a sad look. "I'll wait for you, Nicholas. I forgive you with all of my heart."

He stopped and looked at me. "I love you, too, Valarie." He kissed my cheek, and I knew there was nothing more I could say to stop him. This was something he had to do for him. It was no longer about me.

He shut the door, and I collapsed on the bench with a feeling of defeat.

CHAPTER 35

I went home with a broken heart. Exhausted, all I wanted to do was curl into a ball in my bed and cry until Alex came home. My phone rang from a 212 number. I silenced it and cried into my pillow until the number called again. I was going to lose my temper if it was a telemarketer.

"Hello."

Someone was crying on the other end. "Mrs. Renyalds, I'm so sorry to call you, but I didn't know who else to call after my father told me what he did to your dad. I'm so sorry. All this time I thought it was my grandpa, but it was my dad."

"Regan, dear, don't you worry. Your dad and I ... well, I forgave him. I'm so sorry he turned himself in."

"I'm glad he did. He's brave, and he did it to clear his conscience and because he loves you."

The guilt overwhelmed me. Why did I have to tell him to go? But once he made up his mind, it was too late to stop him. Could he not see I was just angry and shocked at his admission? "Here's the thing. I've tried to stick it out here in New York, but my mom is never home, and she drinks all the time. I'm not doing well in school, and I hate the kids. Most of them have a parent who has directed a movie or is an actor or whatever. I don't fit in. I know this is a lot to ask, but can I come home and live with you?"

Regan's words rocked me. "You want to move in with me?"

"I'm sorry. I never should have asked. That was stupid of me. Forget it."

"No, Regan, I would love for you to live with me, but I don't know how your mother will feel about it."

Regan laughed. "She doesn't care what I do. I was a fool to think she wanted a part of my life. I should have listened to my dad. I know she loves me, but I never should have left. Please, I want to come home. I miss my home, my friends."

"Just let me know what I need to do."

Regan sobbed into the phone. "Thank you so much, Mrs. Renyalds. You're an angel, a true angel."

"Is it true, Mom? Did Regan's dad kill grandpa?"

I put my book down on the end table and turned to my daughter. "He didn't kill him, it was an accident. He was just a kid."

"And you're really going to fly Regan here to live with us?"

I smiled. "Don't you want her to live here?"

"Um, yeah, of course I do. Are you and Nicholas going to ... you know ... be a couple now?"

I had been asking myself that question over and over again since the day I watched him walk away with the detective. How much time would he serve? Would he be a felon?

A police officer called first my mother, then me, and then a county attorney contacted me next to inform me of the situation and asked if I wanted to press any charges. Of course, I told him no, but I had heard nothing since.

I kept my phone by me, but it had been two days now. There was nothing in the paper or on the news, and still no one had heard from Nicholas.

"It's in the past, and I forgive him. We forgive him," I told the prosecutor.

In my heart, I knew this was true. My dad would have agreed, I just knew it.

I was distracted the next few days as we packed boxes and began hauling our stuff back into our home in Side Lake. Eric even drove his truck over and helped load up our things.

"Thank you," I told him as the last box was set down in the living room.

"You have a big job ahead of you," he said. "Are you sure you don't want me to stay and help you unpack?"

"You've done enough. I really appreciate it. How is your new house coming along?"

"It's nice being in town. The lake life is more you than me. I'm sorry it took me so long to get my head out of my ass. This is your home, and I'm just glad you aren't living in that run down neighborhood anymore."

I thought about my neighbors. How excited they were to have a home again. I'd grown so much in these last few months and although I would never tell Eric, I was glad for the experience I had living in the ghetto, as we called it. It made me realize there was a whole new world out there with people less fortunate, people who lost everything.

I never thought about the people who had very little, but once I quit judging and started asking questions, I realized they aren't that much different from the rest of us. I couldn't save everyone, but by helping my neighbors get on their feet and out of the shed, I'd felt good. I wanted to do more. Help others find their way.

"Mom, I forgot my charger at the house. Would you mind getting it on your way to the airport?"

"Oh Alex, what would you do without me?"

Eric laughed. "Better you than me."

"How are things going with… what's her name?"

"Libby," he said. "She's great. She's more my age and we're taking things slow for now, but between you and me," he whispered, "I think she's the one."

"Does Cinnamon know about Libby?"

"Hell no. She won't stop calling me. I'm not telling her where I live. She's crazy. I don't know what I was thinking. Actually I do, she was young and hot."

"Same old Eric," I said, patting his back and pushing him toward the door.

"See you Saturday, Alex?"

She was sitting on the couch, phone in hand. "Yep."

I grabbed the charger from my old house. When I turned around, he was leaning against my car. I turned my head sideways, wondering if it was really him or if my imagination was playing tricks on me.

"Nicholas?"

"Hi there, beautiful. I was hoping to go with you to pick up my daughter at the airport."

"The suspense is killing me. What happened?"

"It's over now. I had to get away for a while to clear my mind, but it's finally over. I'm so sorry, for everything."

I looked down. "I know."

"I really am. I love you, Val and I don't want to spend another minute without you in my life."

I ran up and hugged him. He tipped up my chin. "Me neither. I missed you so much."

He dipped his head, and our lips met. I closed my eyes

and let myself fall. The kiss didn't end, and we made our way inside the house.

"Are you sure you want to?"

I nodded and locked my lips with his again.

"Do you think we have time?"

"Her flight doesn't come in for two hours. I was going to pick up a few groceries, but it can wait."

I couldn't rip his clothes off fast enough. I pulled on his sleeve, and it got stuck on the doorknob on the way in, leaving us both laughing hysterically when he lost his balance and fell to the floor. I pulled his shirt off the doorknob and set his arm free.

We shut the door, but didn't make it any farther into the house. We made love passionately on the kitchen floor twice. We laid there afterword, panting and exhausted. He turned on his side and stared into my eyes. He kissed my neck and made his way up to my ear. It sent shivers down my back. I didn't want to get up even if my back was killing me from the linoleum floor.

"Who knew we would end up making love for the first time in this old house," I said.

"Who knew you would be the one to save me in the end," he said.

I raised an eyebrow.

"If it wasn't for you, I never would have stood up against my dad and cleared my conscience."

"So, I'm finally your prince charming," I said.

He took a peek under my bra. "You're definitely female, but you are forever my queen."

"I can't take the credit, even if I wanted to. You did this yourself. You never told me, what happened."

"Let's just say it's over."

I poked his nose. "I'm pretty sure it's just beginning."

CHAPTER 36

"I have some news to tell you girls, and I would love your help."

They put down their phones and gave me their full attention. I thought back to just a month or two ago when I could hardly get Alex to give me a minute of her time without that phone in her face. It all changed when Regan came back.

I pulled the key out of my pocket and jiggled it in front of them.

Alex grabbed the keys from me to examine them and then handed them to Regan.

Regan handed them back to me after examining them. "Did you get a new car, Mrs. Renyalds?"

I shook my head.

"We aren't moving again, are we?" Alex said.

I shook my head at her, too. "These are the keys to the bookstore. It's official. I can move back in tomorrow."

Alex gave me a big hug. "That's great, Mom."

Regan joined in. "I know how much that bookstore means to you."

I dug through my purse. I took out my checkbook, wallet, lipstick, Jill Shalvis's newest novel that I could not stop reading, and my sunscreen—it might be winter, but there was still sun and I did not want to chance skin cancer on my face. I could not hold another thing in my hands. I looked around for a place to set things down when I heard what could only be the sound of dangling keys.

"Mom."

I grabbed my car keys out of her hand. "Where did you find those?"

She smirked. "I think you are losing it, Mom. They were right here on the table."

I snatched them from her and shook my head. "It's time, let's go girls."

I stepped inside the bookstore and the aroma of books, dust, and my childhood filled my senses. The room was much bigger than I remembered. The shelves were stacked in the corner and the books in boxes throughout the room.

My mom came up behind me and put her hand on my shoulder. "How does it feel to have your very own bookstore? Are you nervous to take it all on by yourself?"

"I'm honored. I can't believe it is finally all mine. I couldn't have done it without you, Mom. I will pay you back every penny."

We stood there in silence.

I bent over, opened up the first box, and took out the first book.

"Bob Dylan. Your dad's favorite singer of all time. It's a sign."

I turned and hugged her, dangling the book over her shoulder.

"Mom, you can go on your trip now. I'm going to be fine."

My mom and the banker were driving up the north shore

to do some fishing and stay at a cabin for the week. My mom found a partner in the man and it was about time. She didn't call him her boyfriend, but we all knew. She was now smiling all the time and saying nice things. It was actually starting to annoy me. I wasn't used to this new happy person.

"Okay, well, you sure have a lot of work ahead of you. I feel terrible for leaving."

"I'll be fine. Go ahead, have fun."

It wasn't five minutes later the bell jingled. I jumped to my feet.

"I'm sorry, but we aren't opening until next week," I said.

I looked up and there were two faces I did not care to see again.

"I owe you an apology."

I could not hide my surprise. "Huh? Cinnamon? Saffron? Why are you here? We aren't even open yet."

I knew I should have locked the door when my mom left.

"Congratulations. We heard you bought the place, and we both wanted to talk to you."

The sisters stared at each other in an awkward moment of silence. They nodded their heads in my direction until Saffron pushed Cinnamon forward. A burst of giggle slipped out of my mouth at the look on her face. I silenced it by covering my mouth with my hand.

Cinnamon cleared her throat. "Like I said, I'm here because I know I've been terrible to you. The things I said at the swim meets and everything. The truth is, I was jealous of you."

"Of me?"

"Yes, of you." Cinnamon looked down at her hands. "You're so beautiful, and you eat what you want, and you don't worry about what others think."

She knew nothing about me or who I was back then. I was so insecure, but I'd come a long way in the last few months. I'd lost another five pounds at my last weigh in, but I was okay with that. I was eating healthy and trying to control my binges by eating a little of the junk food I loved but not overeating. Sure, it was a daily struggle, but I had a lot of support.

"We all have our struggles, but I appreciate that. I just don't understand why you came here to tell me that."

Saffron stepped forward. "That was me," she said, smiling her bright white teeth at me. "I knew Eric was your husband the first day I met you, and I was trying to get intel for this girl." She pointed her thumb at Cinnamon. "But then I got to know you and it made me absolutely miserable. I feel terrible and I haven't been to Calorie Counters because I couldn't face you after what I did. You're a good person and I'm sorry."

Cinnamon threw her hair back. "And I'm sorry that I flaunted my thin body around you all the time and made fat jokes. It isn't easy to look this good all the time. People are rude to me too and jealous, you know? Oh, and I'm sorry for sleeping with your husband."

Same old Cinnamon. Was that even an apology?

I studied her expression. "Is this your way of apologizing?"

"Yes. I'm sorry. I was even thinking about purchasing a book to seal the deal, but from the looks of things, I may have to wait."

"That's a good idea. I wouldn't even know where to start digging."

They both let out high-pitched fake laughs, and I smiled because at that moment I realized for the first time, we are all a little nuts and insecure. Although next to them, I felt like I was okay with just being me.

EPILOGUE

Eighteen Months Later

The bookstore was decorated in red, white, and blue in honor of the Fourth of July just two weeks away, and Regan and Alex were helping me work at the bookstore. They shifted back and forth from working at Nicholas's gym and my bookstore.

Sunday night was my favorite day of the week because it was family game night, and we all took time away from work and school to spend it as a family. Nicholas's father, Maria and her family, and Linda would come over, along with Sabrina and her husband, who were back together. I had recommended a great therapist to them, who happened to also be the therapist who helped me overcome my emotional eating disorder.

My mom and Thomas got engaged on the top of the Empire State building a few weeks ago while on vacation. Of course, the guy was a romantic and also a big Mark Dawson and Tom Clancy reader. I could tell a lot about a person by the genres they read and the authors they admired.

Even Eric would stop by once in a while to join in the fun on Sunday Funday. Sometimes my mom and Chad would get a little too competitive and Nicholas and I would have to separate them, but it was always a great time.

I was just finishing up with the last box of unopened books at the bookstore before I went home to get ready for game night. I pulled out one book at a time, taking in a deep breath of the new book smell that brought me right back to helping my father, as a child, when I took the books out of the boxes for him.

"What are you doing?"

I looked at Nicholas, who was definitely laughing at me with a strange look on his face.

"Are you smelling the books?"

"Don't knock it until you try it."

He looked at me sideways, but he leaned in, closed his eyes, and inhaled deeply. "I must admit, I still don't get it, but I have the rest of my life to understand what you mean."

"Oh?"

He got down on one knee, and I held my breath. He took out a copy of my favorite novel, *The Notebook* by Nicholas Sparks, and placed the familiar princess cut gold ring with the biggest diamond on the book and held it out to me. He was a bit shaky, so I reached out to hold the other side of the book steady.

"How? What? Nicholas, how did you find my parents' ring? It was pawned off months ago?"

"I have my ways. Now let me finish wooing you, please."

"I'm sorry, continue. I just can't believe you even found it! It means so much to me."

He raised his eyebrow, and I touched my thumb and pointer finger and ran them across my lips. He shook his head and continued.

"Val, our story isn't perfect, it's actually quite ironic, but you are the love of my life, and I want to wake up with you by my side every day for the rest of my life. Every day I get to spend with you is a miracle. I've learned so much about myself since I've gotten to know you. Who knew being stranded in the middle of nowhere when we both thought we were going to die was the best day of our lives? I can't imagine this journey in life without you by my side. Would you do me the honor and be my wife?"

I stared at the giant diamond with tears in my eyes. "We said we were going to take this slow, but I know what I want, too. Yes, Nicholas, yes, I'll be your wife. Also, how can I say no when you're giving me my mother's ring? You'd have to take it back to the pawn store."

He shook his head at me. Regan and Alex stood up and started clapping.

"You know I got that recorded, right?" Alex said.

"Don't you dare post that," I said. "Now get over here and give us a hug."

The girls came running in for a family hug.

"I'm going to miss this when we go away to college," Regan said.

"We'll always be here, and our home will always be your home."

"I think I'm going to college to become a librarian," Regan said. "I never really read much as a child, but now I can't get enough. There's a book for everything! I feel like so many friends are waiting for me at the bookstore. Every book is an adventure."

"Are you sure she isn't my daughter?" I said to Nicholas.

They all laughed.

"Now, if you could just get your dad to pick up a book."

"I read the newspaper," he said.

"Oh honey, you just don't get it. Someday we'll get you to read books, we just have to figure out how to get you to finish one first."

"I'm feeling outnumbered already. I think we need to get a male puppy."

"I think that is exactly what we need," I said, surprising myself because now that I said it in front of the girls, I knew they would hold me to it.

"Really?" Alex and Regan said at the same time.

Teenage girls and puppy dogs equal a stampede.

Nicholas shepherded them toward the door. "Time to head to my dad's. He's really excited to show off his new motorized wheelchair."

I locked up the bookstore.

Nicholas placed his hand in mine and kissed the ring on my finger as the girls climbed into the back seat of his truck.

"Who ever thought we would end up together after everything we've been through?"

I nudged my shoulder into him playfully. "Who would have ever thought I would marry the man who gave me the Heimlich maneuver in the parking lot while I choked on a cream puff? I must have looked pretty sexy, huh?"

"I have to be honest, you had this tiny bit of whip cream on your nose, and it took everything for me not to lick your nose that day."

I hit his shoulder. "Oh, Nicholas. Why can I see you actually doing that? You are crazy, you know that."

He kissed me. "You ended up saving my life by clearing my conscience and the weight I've carried for so long."

He turned toward me again and gently ran his hand over the scar on my forehead with his thumb.

I rested my forehead against his and closed my eyes. "I just have one more favor to ask you," I said. "Will you teach me to drive my boat?"

"I thought you would never ask."

ACKNOWLEDGMENTS

First I have to thank my husband, Owen. You have been by my side, supported me, and believed in me from the very beginning of this journey. Thank you so much for your love and dedication.

My girls--Sidney and Alexis—Alexis, you are always there to read through my ideas with me and help me with my teenage character that was inspired by you. Sidney, you growing into an adult has been the hardest experience of my life, but I am so proud of you.

With thanks to my editor, Shirley Fedorak, you never disappoint. I couldn't do this without you. My photographer, April Patterson at Appletree, you are the best. Kirsten Bryant, thank you for making my covers so beautiful. They always truly capture Northern Minnesota.

The Weight of Change launch team, thank you so much for all your hard work and feedback. You are truly the best group of proofreaders ever.

I also want to thank the city of Side Lake for all your love and support throughout my writing journey. My hometown of Hibbing, and the Iron Range too. All of you inspire me to write and have supported me so much on my journey. Thank you.

If you enjoyed this book, please leave a review on Amazon here.

Visit www.jenniferwaltersauthor.com for more books by this author or to sign up for my monthly newsletter.

Made in the USA
Monee, IL
22 October 2021